RACING CERTAINTIES

Brough Scott

VICTOR GOLLANCZ
LONDON

By the same author

THE WORLD OF FLAT RACING
(with Gerry Cranham)

ON AND OFF THE RAILS

FRONT RUNNERS

Picture acknowledgements:
Ed Byrne, pp. 38, 62; Gerry Cranham, pp. 108, 125, 142;
Tony Edenden, p. 46; Ronald Frain, p. 8;
Robert Hallam, p. 12/13; David Hastings, p. 178;
George Herringshaw/Associated Sports Photography, p. 26;
John Houlihan/Guzelian, p. 156; Kingsdown Pictures, p. 82;
Racing Post, pp. 20, 23, 31, 67, 73, 88, 152, 160;
Alec Russell, p. 52; K. Saunders/Sport and General, p. 137;
Chris Smith, pp. 58, 97; *Daily Telegraph*, p. 164.

First published in Great Britain 1995
by Victor Gollancz
An imprint of the Cassell Group
Wellington House, 125 Strand, London WC2R 0BB

A catalogue record for this book is available from the British Library.
ISBN 0 575 06221 8

Designed and typeset by
Fishtail Design

FISH TAIL

Printed in Great Britain
by Butler & Tanner Ltd, Frome, Somerset

Contents

Introduction

Welcome to my world. A world strangely obsessed with trying to make one horse go faster than another. In the great scheme of things horse racing will seem a peripheral and probably meaningless pursuit. But to those within, horse racing is the great scheme of things. Make that leap and you are across the river and into the land where the herd never sleeps.

Make that leap and Desert Orchid becomes the great grey hero of the last ten years; Arazi becomes the superstar that flew too close to the sun; Lester Piggott is the old centaur raging against the dying of the light; Frankie Dettori the young wonder with talents to set the globe afire.

Do not decry the leap. In this world there is much glory, but it is often expensively and riskily bought. There can be untold wealth, but aching poverty too. There are great heroes but villains and victims aplenty. There can be miserable mornings and sorrowful nights, but at the heart there is a measurement of man and mammal that has been running for three centuries. Horse racing can still make the pulse race in a way other games would envy.

This book is a diary, not a detailed history. It is no more than a record of what we found in front of us at the time. For here is no hindsight. Here is how people, places, horses and riders looked when I got close to them. Six years around the trail. Six years of hopes and fears, triumphs and disasters, of sunny days and of sad. Sure, there were bigger matters out there in the 'real world'. But this was our cosmos. These, when I wrote them, were the images that had lodged in the forefront of what is laughingly described as my brain.

For above all racing is about colour and light, speed and striving. That is what makes it so thrilling when it goes well; what makes it sickening when fate smashes it to a halt. When young promise has turned to all-too-early despair. This is just one pair of eyes, but they are lucky to have looked upon all sorts of players on four legs and on two. The pieces were all written against (and often over) long-suffering deadlines for wonderfully supportive editors on the *Independent on Sunday*, the *Sunday Times* and now the *Sunday Telegraph*, and for my friends Michael Harris and Alan Byrne on the *Racing Post*. Some of the hassle of delivery makes me wince even now in recollection. But that very pressure does serve to take the smart-arse out of the equation. To detail only what mattered. To seek the truth as you saw it.

Every piece in its own way is a failure. For none of them has been included unless it was about something that moved me greatly at the time, and such feelings can never quite be recaptured. But they are my best shot. They are events and people I wanted to display a second time. It's the third such book that Gollancz has been generous enough to reap and bind and bail. Richard Wigmore and his team have my admiration as well as gratitude.

It's a small world but inside it's a very real one. Real because it is so wonderfully, hopelessly optimistic every day. New every morning in racing comes the dream. New every morning comes the bang at the stable door, the clink of the hoof on concrete. However unlikely, somehow, somewhere, we could be winners too. Come with me now. It's been quite a ride already.

HORSES

Never forget that it's the horse that does the running. Here are a handful who in their different and very special ways have made an impact on me. The first has to be the horse who won more hearts than all the rest.

The Desert Orchid phenomenon grew throughout the eighties to the ludicrous, feverish, anthropomorphic heights of Dessie-mania. But Dessie was still a racehorse and eventually the sands run out for all of them. With Desert Orchid it was never going to be a peaceful parting.

Orchid in shape for final test

22 December 1991

He's not as sweet as he looks. All those years, all those miles, all those fences, all those fans, those oohs and aahs and the old boy is still ready to rumble. It's probably the last hurrah but Desert Orchid isn't going gently into his good night.

Whitsbury Downs on Thursday morning, the most exposed part of wind-lashed, rain-scudded Wiltshire, the usual raw rehearsal spot for the most instantly recognized performer in British life. In a week's time the whole nation would be fussing over his attempt at a record fifth King George VI Chase at Kempton on Boxing Day. Out here it's simpler, harsher stuff. He wants to run. Run fast.

Run faster than Rodney Boult can control. Get that restraining bit between his teeth and smack a hole in the horizon. For the second time of the morning he thunders up over the brow of the hill towards us. The jabbing rhythm of the stride breaks into great surging plunges of extra speed. There's a glimpse of Rodney's face pink with strain and effort, a snatch of his voice reasoning for restraint. White horse still wild.

There's the truth. More than any other fact in this unique 34-victory, 70-race, £500,000, 10-season career, we must guard the underlying phenom-enon of Desert Orchid's vitality. Forget all the books, videos, tea towels and jigsaw puzzles. Dessie's actually a hard old bastard. He is, in that phrase hijacked by beer-bellied louts, a 'real man'.

Rather more than his audience on Thursday. There were some 25 of us hacks and snappers and camera crews in assorted ranges of inadequate clothing

Desert Orchid returns after yet another victory. But the strain is beginning to show

and inappropriate footwear dutifully trailing David Elsworth across the gallops. There were huddled, shivering, self-pitying conversations as if we were braving a polar walk. Then Desert Orchid first appeared through the rain. At the head of the string. In his element.

He brings a lot of baggage with him. Memories of delights, disasters, dizzy triumphs and national adulation as he progressed through from erratic tearaway youth to the white eminence over whom so many will cluck possessively this week. By now everybody knows most of the Desert Orchid story.

Knows how his first ever race ended in exhausted fallen wreckage when his runaway tactics finally capsized at Kempton's last hurdle way back in 1983. Knows how nobody imagined that such a natural trailblazer would ever last the three miles of the King George. Then we had that sensational 16–1 all-the-way annihilation in 1986 and he has been centre stage ever since.

Brilliant, brave but not invulnerable. The quirks became part of the attraction. He suffered from corns. He wasn't as good galloping round to the left. The world went mad when he beat that handicap and the wettest March day of the decade to win the Gold Cup at Cheltenham in 1990. Should he run in the Grand National? *Daily Mail* readers voted an overwhelming 'No'. Was he over the hill? 'Yes,' said trainer Elsworth, 'but remember that it was a very steep hill he was up.'

Now he was being led back down the lane which winds towards the stables. Rodney Boult scampers alongside, a wrinkled, brown jodhpured figure whose squirrel alertness belies his 55 years. The Indian file behind him includes the mauve and pink waterproofs of Janice Coyle, his perky stable girl we remember from so many paddock side dramas. Rodney of course is the ultimate race track hoodoo. Every time he has been there Desert Orchid has lost. He will be at home on Boxing Day.

But are they and we abusing the dream, trying to bask one year too long under our hero's spell? Hasn't he been well beaten in both his races this season? Steeplechasing is an unforgiving game. It forgives champions least of all.

Sheep scatter close to the hedge on the right. Desert Orchid's pricked white ears swivel across with interest. Rodney slaps his hard white neck in appreciation. 'I am still very confident that he is as good as last year,' he says in a voice that doesn't need to boast. He has been with Elsworth since they started out with slowcoaches two score seasons back. Down the years they have progressed into one of the most powerful yards in the country. Now they even have next year's Derby favourite amongst their hundred strong team.

'I must have walked down this road with him 2,000 times' Rodney continues, 'and he still shows such keenness, such interest. And in his gallops he has been pulling me all the way. We went seven furlongs last week and Oh So Risky couldn't get to me. He is meant to be a Champion Hurdle horse.'

We have reached the yard. Dessie is unsaddled and circles whilst the cameras snap. Age may have whitened him but the way that big raking frame dominates even at the walk is a tribute to the engine within.

David Elsworth looks on reflectively. 'If you jumped into your car and drove all day you still wouldn't have been as far as he has galloped over the years,' he said, with that untutored eloquence.

'But you have still got to do the preparation. If you begin to feel sorry for him and ease off, then you feel even sorrier for him when he's knackered on the racecourse. It was hard graft for him all the way at Huntingdon last time but he needed it. Obviously I will be glad when it's all over but he's ready now. I don't really believe he could win for a fifth time but I tell you he's not just making up the numbers.'

Meanwhile Dessie is into the less dignified duties of being a tabloid celebrity. His exercise and grooming may be over but his head is coaxed over the box door, Janice is stood on a stable bucket to make it *tête-à-tête*, out of snapper's pocket comes the Santa hat. Janice does her best at the smirking pixie bit and for a couple of minutes Dessie waits and wonders where the sugar lumps are.

Then he cuts it all out. With a sudden emphatic intolerance he whirls his big head back with a crash that bends the steel bars of the door frame. He storms off into the corner of his box. You remember the scars across its walls where he has stamped out over the years. He's a fighter. Win or lose, he is ready for one more crack in the ring.

He has given us so much. Simple, raw, brave, beautiful, sometimes brutal things. May he go out in glory.

Desert Orchid was typically dramatic to the very end, this final race bringing not triumph but disaster. A dreadful, crashing, somersaulting fall at the third last fence closed his career where and as it had begun all those years before.

It was the sort of fall that breaks a horse's neck. As he capsized there was an appalling, wincing moment when you felt that this could be the last image of all and we could have a fatality on our hands that even the die-hards would find hard to handle. But then he was up; a white horse galloping loose with mud on his bridle and the whole grandstand applauding him into retirement. No horse ever deserved it more.

Desert Orchid was a star who would take some replacing, yet in its most perversely optimistic way jump racing had already come up with a challenger for the crown. It was not to end happily, but what excitement was abroad as winter turned to spring and expectation grew about Carvill's Hill and Cheltenham.

Enter monster, Cheltenham-bound
1 March 1992

Some horizon, some speck. Carvill's Hill thunders up out of the Somerset fog. The biggest, most powerful, most hyped, and most maligned galloper of them all heads for his Cheltenham showdown. Will the monster make our day?

You cannot overstress the size of him. Almost six foot at the shoulder, more than 550 kilos on the weighbridge, the athlete that stretched up Martin Pipe's famous all-weather gallop on Tuesday morning has been spreading tales of wonder and of exasperation ever since he first appeared in Ireland as a huge, unfurnished five-year-old on Cup Final day in '86. But never quite like this. This time the dream could come true.

It's every racefan's fantasy. The big horse who attacks from the start reducing opponents to routed cavalry, who, being Irish, even evokes comparison with 'Himself'. At last another Arkle.

For Carvill's the coincidence was too exact. For his Irish days were masterminded by the same shrewd and gentle Dreaper family who nurtured steeplechasing's ultimate champion three decades ago. But the comparison wouldn't fit. This was power without nimbleness. For all the awesomeness of his talent Carvill's Hill was too often a wingless giant. Fourteen victories but usually en route to the injury box.

Last season he ran but twice, the second time ending in a first-fence crash at Gowran Park in January. Even his greatest supporters cried 'enough'. Unbelieving Britishers muttered 'paper tiger'.

So to the move. If ever there were a test of Anglo-Irish racing relations this was it. Carvill's Hill's joint owner moved him not just to another trainer, not merely to an English stable, but to Martin Pipe.

As if the little, limping, Taunton record-breaker hadn't done enough damage already to the accepted norms of training jumpers. Here was the absolute antithesis of the light-framed, ex-flat horses with which he made his name. Here was a heavyweight with incurable flaws to match his genius. If Martin could solve this he could walk the Bristol Channel without a boat.

Half the miracle has already been wrought. Carvill's has run three times in the last three months and has each time won by a street. He's a racehorse again but one of the central doubts remains. You can back him as Gold Cup favourite but can you make him jump?

Down the Irish years his efforts were too often disfigured by alarming aberrations at the obstacles. In 18 races he only actually hit the deck twice but neither spectators nor pilot ever seemed sure what would happen from one fence to the next.

Blame was shared equally between Carvill's supposedly faulty back and the luckless Ken Morgan who had the unenviable task of sitting atop it. This year with a Martin Pipe miracle cure on the vertebrae, and with Peter Scudamore putting discipline down the reins, all should have been plain sailing. Tell that to the Mounties.

The two races at Chepstow and the one at Leopardstown have each had moments you would not show to those of nervous disposition. Assorted awkwardness in those opening efforts in Wales might have been adjusting to the Scudamore regime. But then in Ireland two Sundays ago there was again a howler of inexcusable proportions.

At the third fence the seven-times champion jockey used legs and body to urge Carvill's firmly into the take-off stride. At full gallop the big horse ignored him. The Leopardstown fence took the sort of blow stranded cars get from express trains at level crossings. Somehow Carvill's stayed on his feet and Scudamore stuck in the saddle. It won't be so easy at the downhill fence in the Gold Cup or at Becher's Brook which is scheduled after Cheltenham.

Time for the wiseacres to re-emerge from the woodwork. This was the same old Carvill's with just a few running repairs on the back and a more

When dreams were mighty. Carvill's Hill on Martin Pipe's gallop before Cheltenham

confident pair of legs in the leathers. He had only been beating donkeys. Cheltenham and Aintree would find him out.

But better to gaze than to gossip and what we saw on Tuesday was quite an eyeful. When we found it. Pipe's little kingdom is not exactly into neon hoardings. Dense fog shrouded the West Country. We were only 40 miles from Dartmoor. It was the kind of morning to get the Hound of the Baskervilles out of hiding.

Our monster was almost as daunting. Or the first glimpse was. It was from the passenger seat of Martin Pipe's ageing Range Rover. We had roared away from the other horses in pursuit of a blurred shape in the mist. We got alongside and there was the star in rehearsal, carrying his exercise rider Eddie Buckley up the bank with an ease and a punch that made the old car cough with envy.

There's a rippling ease to the rhythm but it's the power that talks. We have all seen it from the grandstand but up close it's a living, spreading thing. The big ears are cocked forward. The great neck arched, the valves in the nostrils flicking as the air pumps in and out. After half a mile, Martin stops the car, and the continuing Carvill's is swallowed swiftly in the gloom.

All sorts of rubbish have been written and whispered about the Pipe phenomenon. Roger Cook even had an unsuccessful shot on TV last season. If you get into Pipe's slip-stream the reasons for his success are blindingly obvious. He has more detailed an enthusiasm, more wide-ranging a back-up and more closely monitored an exercise routine than any of his rivals.

But we talk of Carvill's, and as with all 'public property' there is a tendency to well-worn statement. Looking out from under the tweed cap he wears in office and open alike, Martin repeats the received litany of the season so far. Of how Carvill's came over from Ireland on 22 June. Of how he started 'with a clean sheet', had the horse fully checked at Bristol University. Of how physiotherapist Mary Bromiley helped with remedial exercises. Of how all his team had 'done a wonderful job'. Of the thrill of having such a champion.

There is belief in the air. There is tangible pride, there is admiring praise for those who have got him this far. There is a pointed wish to avoid any criticism of Carvill's earlier incarnation. But a check with the dates in vet Barry Park's diary reveals that this is not the whole story.

For it was not until 2 September that Barry journeyed down from Lambourn with an 8-inch needle to take what may well be the most crucial action in Carvill's life. He had to stand on a bucket to do it. He had to inject cortisone into the sacroiliac joint.

Get out your diagrams folks. The sacroiliac joint connects the spine to the pelvis. 'Martin is a real pro,' says Barry Park. 'He wasn't going to train the horse until he was sure what was wrong with him. When he had checked everything else out, he and Mary stood behind Carvill's and noticed that the near-side quarter was nearly two inches lower than the other. He had obviously done his sacroiliac in and taught himself a special way of going.'

Mary Bromiley is a persuasive lady. A rider and trainer herself along the way, she is now the set of hands that jockeys turn to when the ground has come up to hurt them. She was instrumental in helping Scudamore back to fitness after a bad fall last season. She knows all about sacro-iliac joints.

She was convinced that damage here was a common problem in the jumping horse. That with an anti-inflammatory injection like cortisone to ease it, remedial exercise could put things right. Against his better judgement she got Park to practise on one of her own.

But Carvill's was quite another thing. 'I had only ever done it twice,' said Barry Park last week. 'The horse looked as if he would eat me. He might well have done if it hadn't been for his fabulous girl, Sara Hancock. I had difficulty even putting the needle in. The flesh was like cardboard, lots of muscle tears and fibrose. You just had to angle it and try to remember your anatomy. I thought it was a waste of time. I thought we were five years too late.'

Mary Bromiley had other plans. With ultrasound and laser treatment she spread the drug around the area and then devised an exercise routine as exact as any rehabilitation unit. Carvill's was shod with a three and a half ounce heavier shoe on his near hind. Eddie Buckley was instructed to walk behind him with long reins, and for six weeks the big horse did his number to build muscle around the joint.

'The biggest fallacy,' says Mary in that direct, professorial way of hers, 'is that rest heals things. It doesn't. It's controlled activity that counts. Carvill's just didn't have the muscles there. There's a subtle conversation between joint, ligament and supporting muscles. If one of the trio is damaged the conversation ceases for a period of time and the muscles deteriorate.'

It's all a long way from the old days of giving big jumpers six weeks on the roads and then two months of two-mile canters. Pipe doesn't believe in the roads. For the first two-and-a-half months Carvill's was confined to the indoor school. Long days of trotting and turning, gradually conditioning and reducing the vast frame which turned the scale at 600 kilos on arrival.

No long canters either. The Pipe work bench is a six-furlong, 20-foot wide all-weather strip which runs straight up the collar of the bank along from the Nicholashayne turning. All the horses breeze up it, stop, hack back down, and breeze up again. No other trainer does this. Can't think why. Unique among his profession Martin Pipe has cracked interval training. Winners to date this season 136, nearest rival 72.

'The object is to get the horse fit,' he says as we peer into the gloom for Carvill's second coming. 'I think the distance is irrelevant.' Our heads turn as the Gold Cup favourite powers past. 'This horse has adapted well. He's coming to his peak at the right time. It's been a great challenge.'

We are out of the car now as Carvill's trots back, snorting and ready. Martin Pipe scurries over to him, quick as a limping fox. 'He's a big, arrogant horse, a super individual and he knows it. I suppose one's a bit frightened of him. I know I am.'

But awe-inspiring though this is, it's all on the level. What's going to happen when the fences loom up? Martin gives detail of the schooling indoors and out, but an even closer witness needs calling. Phone for Scudamore.

There is now no more lucid or thoughtful performer in sport. 'I think his sense of self-preservation is improving,' he says of the horse who will present him with the greatest test of his unique 12-season, 1,500-winner career. 'But you have to think for him. He's very, very big, and has an enormous stride. It's not easy for him. He's always going to make mistakes.'

Cool to the point of pessimistic, you might say, especially if you had backed Carvill's at 6–4. But then you remember the wonderfully positive way that Scudamore sent him at his fences. A tight hold of the rein some way off the obstacle and a strong body impulsion for take off.

Remember that the player Peter is sending airborne is five times the bodyweight of Dean Richards. Carvill's head alone would weigh some three stone. Balancing that and the rest as it comes down from five foot at 30mph takes real strength and balance as well as the nerve of an astronaut.

As you begin to ponder his dilemma when he points Carvill's for home at Cheltenham, the pace building up, the incline running away from him, you understand that there's no point in flannelling.

'He's getting better,' said Peter, giving pensive credit to his partner. 'In the latter part of the Leopardstown race he was getting a lot more confident. Once or twice he even came back on his hocks a bit. Those fences away from the stand are quite tricky and I thought he jumped them beautifully. He lobbed along in front, just wavered at them looking for his stride, then came up.'

There was noise in the background. One of the Scudamore boys was having his birthday party. Their father would return to it in a second but not before considering the unmentionable. No one likes thinking of falling, but on all known form it's only that which can stop Peter winning the Gold Cup and then the Grand National with Carvill's Hill.

For all his modern-day trappings Scudamore is a deeply traditional, religious young man. For all his successes, victory in either of jumping's two greatest races has always eluded him. It would in every sense be a crowning glory, but everything will depend on whether he can get Carvill's co-operation 22 times at Cheltenham, no fewer than 30 at Aintree.

'I am not saying he will or will not get round,' Peter says baldly about his chances of Gold Cup survival. 'What I am saying is that he has a good chance of doing it.'

Some rider, some neck.

There had been hope and effort and skill, and indeed cash enough to build an empire, not just win a horse race. But Cheltenham's story has often been an unforgiving one. The fates were not kind to Carvill's.

Anatomy of a favourite's downfall

15 March 1992

Twenty-eight was the fateful number. It was 13 seconds, 28 strides into Carvill's Hill's Gold Cup. But he should have taken off at 27. Horse and fence were not meant for each other.

It was an enormous blunder. The whole half-ton of him galloping slap into that first Cheltenham obstacle, 4ft 6in of thick, hard-packed birch. It was exactly what his allies feared, what his opponents had hoped for.

One of those had helped to cause it. When Scudamore had launched Carvill's out across the start line 200 yards from the first fence, Michael Bowlby on the impetuous Golden Freeze had set about his business. He was going to see how Carvill's liked having someone at him.

As Scudamore pushed his huge partner forward to try and gain the initial dominance which had made his three victories so awesome this season, Bowlby revved Golden Freeze alongside. The two horses were stretched nearly flat as they bore down on that first fence at over 30 miles an hour. It was racing's ultimate in early pressure. Carvill's didn't handle it.

Looking back we can see that all the mental and physical rehabilitation work, all the hopes and dreams of a new 'wonderhorse', were floored in this instant. Carvill's didn't fall but he was exposed as a 'glass jaw' heavy-weight, and the six-and-a-half minutes and 21 more fences of the Gold Cup journey will scar him for ever.

The expectation had been so great and the final hobbling humiliation was to be so complete that the search for scapegoats soon began. Could Scudamore have played it differently? Was Bowlby's blatant and well-predicted spoiling game on Golden Freeze an illegal ploy on behalf of his stable companion Toby Tobias?

With hindsight Scudamore would no doubt have lined up at the other end of the eight-runner field to Golden Freeze, rather than just one away as on Thursday. But there's psychology here. He knew that Bowlby was going to come looking for him. He was on the supposed champion. He needed to impose himself under this early barrage. He had to feel confident that Carvill's would come up for take-off under pressure. The horse didn't.

As to the tactics, the best analogy is the first high ball to a suspect full-back in a rugby international. Whether the tackle you get in breaks the rules or not, you are going to do your damndest to make it hurt. Then you see if he can take it. Mentally, as much as physically, Carvill's couldn't.

The Jockey Club is now considering an inquiry into the Golden Freeze strategy, which has drawn as much public outcry as professional indifference. The authorities will have to consider not only how to square the horse's effort with Rule 151, which says 'every horse shall run on its merits', but the implications of inactivity.

If Golden Freeze is legal what's to stop a big owner fielding a whole team of 'spoilers' in a race? Pacemakers have always been tolerated, although they probably contradict the letter of the rule. 'Spoilers' add a newer, more cynical dimension. Would they have done it to Desert Orchid?

Now there's the rub. For early in the famous grey's front-running career they almost certainly would have. Desert Orchid's morale did then seem vulnerable to an attack on his early dominance. But at his peak he would not have been fazed by Golden Freeze. He would have let him go, and when he did get upsides he would have socked it to him with some of those spring-heeled 'Dessie' specials.

What the Pitman team correctly diagnosed was a two-fold weakness. Not only that the lumbering Carvill's might make blunders under pressure but that those mistakes would dispirit him.

The third fence told us everything. Carvill's had thrown in a massive leap at the second, giving it about a foot of daylight, and as Scudamore pushed him up to attack Golden Freeze it seemed as if all the old long-striding aggression was back. But at the wings his heart wasn't in it. He jumped all right, but upright and timid and careful. The monster just looked meek.

All the way down the back straight it was the same story. Carvill's was responding to Scudamore's intense instructions but with much more caution than flair. He jumped the seventh, the second open ditch with a bit more belief and Scudamore, sensing a revival, began to press on.

Golden Freeze came with him. They both took the eighth impressively and, with the others quickly left 10 lengths adrift, the hope formed that the favourite might begin to batter the course and even his 'spoiler' into submission.

The ninth fixed it. The fence comes at you out of the turn and off the crown of the hill. Scudamore asked for a stride and Carvill's failed him. In a classic case of half-commitment the horse's front end came up but his quarters kept down. His back end clouted the fence with a shock that made the whole racecourse wince. Golden Freeze was five lengths clear. For Scudamore it had become a very bad day at the office.

They swept down towards us at the downhill fence. Golden Freeze bold in the lead, Carvill's shortening up and tentative in pursuit. Away towards the stands and then another sickening hind leg trail at the 12th. Another at the 16th, Golden Freeze had dropped out but the whole pack now closed in to torment him.

The dream of a 'superhorse' was long since buried but even now Carvill's and Scudamore had strength for a last assault. The jockey's whip cracked on his partner's shoulder, the massive limbs stretched, and the favourite thundered down the hill towards us.

The red jacket of Adam Kondrat on The Fellow was ominously still outside him, Cool Ground and Docklands Express were close in as contenders. But Carvill's might still test them.

Scudamore drove him at the fence. The hind legs again failed to operate, an ugly jolt going right through the poor horse's body. The game was up and a final ghastly bungle at the second-last brought Carvill's to a ruined, trotting apology for a racehorse at the line.

It was over. There had been a fantastic finish between Cool Ground and The Fellow. But greatness hadn't happened. Cheltenham takes no prisoners. There was sadness in the Gloucester air.

Poor Carvill's Hill never fully recovered from the injuries sustained in that Cheltenham battle. His potential had been unlimited but racing had been ruthless with his flaws. It is ever thus. On the flat or over jumps. Ask Arazi: 1992 was supposed to be his year too.

The little Pegasus lost in the crowd
6 April 1992

Chantilly on Tuesday. Monster fireworks promised for this Flat racing season, but the most awaited rocket is just a little horse pottering around in the middle of the string. Arazi at exercise, he's the unlit fuse.

Can this really be the runner who robbed the bank of hyperbole last winter? Can the diminutive chestnut mooching about among 80 larger, flashier stablemates actually be Arazi The Wonderhorse, whose annihilation of America's best juveniles in November's Breeders' Cup has been widely hailed as the greatest two-year-old achievement in thoroughbred history? What's the French for 'handsome is as handsome does'?

So vivid was the impression that chilly Kentucky afternoon that you imagined close inspection would reveal the wings of Pegasus sprouting from Arazi's withers, or at the very least the strutting swagger of the star performer. To visit him a week before his Saint-Cloud warm-up race in two days' time was in that sense a disappointment.

Here was no pacing tiger. Here was a tiny, short-necked three-year-old whose modest, bowed-head demeanour would always hide him in a crowd. Here in the dappled spring sunshine of the Gouvieux Forest was a self-effacing, John Major of a horse.

Such observations cut little ice with the trainer François Boutin. The tall, 55-year-old Norman has aged just as gracefully as we might have expected since he first burst on the international scene by saddling La Lagune to spreadeagle the Oaks field at Epsom in 1968. 'He has the looks of a boulevardier,' said Hugh McIlvanney's script for *The Year of Sir Ivor*, 'but he is a professional.'

Naturally, the figure is fuller now, and the whitened hair has receded, monklike, from the crown and temples. Yet the presence has only strengthened. François may hail from simple farming stock but watch him organizing his circling group of equine blue-bloods and there's no doubt you are in the presence of a master. Of all the trainers on the planet, none, for sheer style, can compare with M. Boutin.

The language helps of course. Like de Gaulle, Boutin doesn't often depart from his native lingo, and Arazi fans will relish the way words like *'fantastique'*

Hope in the forest. Arazi and work rider Raymond Lamonorca at Chantilly

and *'magnifique'* appear when the trainer talks of his champion of champions. Not for him any worries about the little colt's modest demeanour.

For Boutin the lack of fizz is very much a plus for Arazi. *'C'est sa force,'* he says before explaining how his charge has thrived during the winter, has progressed really well in recent weeks and is presently in *'très belle condition.'*

None the less, history demands we tread with caution. Twice in the last six months, with Generous in the Arc de Triomphe and Carvill's Hill in the Gold Cup, intended racecourse coronation has turned into unhappy rout.

True, Arazi's seven-race winning streak put him many lengths ahead of his contemporaries. But he wouldn't be the first precocious juvenile who found things much harder against later maturing rivals in his second season. And for all his sensational Breeders' Cup superiority didn't he end up in the operation box for knee surgery a week later?

It was fears of just such a problem which caused the narrow, rather straight-legged little colt to fail his reserve at the yearling sales. His speedy brilliance is unquestioned, but how will his slender, white-flashed limbs stand up to the hammer which his preparation and races will inflict? Especially as his first target after Tuesday is the Kentucky Derby, run on 1 May on that same hard-based Churchill Downs dirt-track for which he needed the pain-killer Butazolidin last November.

Even the move from forest promenade to more serious exercise did little to lift the foreboding. Arazi came whizzing up the long sand-canter easily enough, but he still looked remarkably small beneath the far from outsize bulk of his stable lad Raymond Lamonorca.

Perhaps it's a trick of the sunlight on the long white flash of his foreleg, but does the knee come up a bit more than it should as the little horse's stride reaches out for purchase? Drink deep on these caveats, for once he draws away from his untesting opponents on Tuesday we'll be sipping the heady wines of expectation.

Remember, Arazi is attempting the hitherto unthinkable. Not just a first ever European victory in the Kentucky Derby, but if Boutin can persuade the American Allen Paulson to cede to the wishes of his partner Sheikh Mohammed, a unique Churchill Downs to Epsom Derby double.

The trainer is having no truck with carping. François is no idle boaster and is all too well aware of how early in the season this 1 May showdown in Kentucky is coming. But he makes no pretence in his pride in this best of all the stars he has handled. 'There's nothing wrong with his knees,' he says, forsaking a more cautious tone in a pre-season video. 'In my opinion he never needed the operation in the first place.'

The much-trumpeted media worries of the switch from turf to dirt surface gets equally short shrift. '*C'est un cinéma des Américains*,' he says with the sort of magnificently dismissive shrug that would have made the old Général de G glow with pride. The problem for Boutin is not getting a grip on the surface, nor even getting dirt in the face, but the much sharper contours of the tracks. But Arazi has already passed that test at Churchill Downs. The trick, and it's no small one, is to get Arazi over in last year's shape.

Back in the clearing Freddie Head is running a seasoned eye over the Boutin team. Six-times French champion jockey, he partners most of the Boutin string in their races and shared Arazi's first two outings before his owner changed contracts.

'Yes, he's small,' Freddie says of the little chestnut, 'and there's not much neck in front of you. But he's comfortable to ride, has a good shoulder, he's thickened through the winter and anyway it's the engine that counts. He's a real, real champion.'

Fine words, yet as with others of France's quiverful of expected stars, it will soon be deeds that count. In the course of four hours last Tuesday the eye was filled with the four-year-old Pistolet Bleu, the three-year-old filly Hatoof, and most of all by Suave Dancer, last year's Arc hero in gleaming shape to defend his title.

But will the Arazi rocket fire? Two continents will hold their breath on Tuesday. Stand by for lift-off.

Arazi looked good enough at Saint-Cloud but little went right thereafter. The return trip to Kentucky was a sweaty, unhappy disaster. Royal Ascot was little better and a brief return to success at Longchamp in October was soon dashed by further failure across the Atlantic. Whether through unnecessary hospitalization or sheer precocity, the truth is that Arazi, unlike 'the wise thrush' in the Browning poem, 'never could recapture that first fine careless rapture'.

But at least he promised poetry for a while. That spring saw the end of a horse who had always been the real thing.

Swallow that made a summer

19 April 1992

They will never bury him. Nijinsky died on Wednesday. He now lies beneath three feet of Kentucky earth, but the memory still gallops free. The best I have ever seen.

Other things happened in that summer of 1970. Nixon sent troops into Cambodia, Edward Heath confounded the pollsters by winning the election, England got beaten by the heat and West Germany in Mexico. But to us it belonged to Nijinsky, his Derby, his Triple Crown.

To be exact it belonged to him and his people. To really evoke the magic you have also to mention the men who rode and trained him. You have to introduce Lester Piggott and Vincent O'Brien.

Nijinsky was the horse they were born to share. A giant of a beast, as light on his feet and taut in his temperament as his spring-heeled namesake, he seemed the complete runner that their combined riding and training talents were one day bound to spawn. This time, we thought, Lester and Vincent were bringing us the ultimate.

They had brought us so much already. In 1970 Piggott was 34, O'Brien 53, both at the absolute height of their powers and the only truly acknowledged geniuses in their respective professions.

Piggott had been centre stage since his first freakish victory at the age of 12. He had ridden his first Derby winner at 18, and after ruling the roost in association with Noel Murless up to the mid-60s, had found even that great trainer's horses not enough to satisfy him.

O'Brien had been a legend even longer. Between 1948 and 1955 the 'little doctor' from Tipperary won four Cheltenham Gold Cups and saddled horses to take both the Champion Hurdle and the Grand National three times in a row. It's an untouchable sequence. Switching to the Flat he had won the Arc de Triomphe

The nonpareils. Nijinsky and Lester Piggott after the 1970 Derby

with Ballymoss in '58, the Derby with Larkspur in '62. He was the foil supreme for Lester Piggott.

They were both great actors. O'Brien playing the shy, studious perfection-ist on whose soft-spoken words millionaires and punters alike would ponder. Piggott, even more sparing of speech and mercurially difficult to understand both on a horse and off it. As a double act Vincent and Lester brought mystery to match the excitement.

In 1968 they delivered. Sir Ivor won the 2,000 Guineas, The Derby and The Washington International. Piggott refined the big bay's finishing kick into an art form. He was as thrilling as anything ever before. But he was squarely beaten in both the Arc and the Eclipse. Great but not quite the ultimate.

Two years later we thought that they had found it. Of course everything they touched had an aura then. The news came through from Ireland of a huge horse with a beautiful name. Nijinsky, the new star from Tipperary, unbeaten, unextended at home, he was to come over for our Dewhurst and treat his rivals like ageing donkeys.

Now, as a three-year-old, he was to be Lester's ride in the Derby and all the Classics. This was Lester's prime. The nation would share the showdowns with him.

Of course it all tailed off at the very finish. Debilitated by a mid-season attack of ringworm and the effort of getting the mile and three-quarters of the St Leger distance, Nijinsky just failed in the Arc and signed off in sad, muck-sweat, nervous-breakdown defeat in the Champion Stakes at Newmarket. But that's not what we remember.

We remember the arrogant ease with which he beat our best milers in the 2,000 Guineas, the sensational destruction of Blakeney and the best older horses in the King George at Ascot. But above all we remember the Derby.

The French thought they had one to beat him, a big chestnut brute called Gyr, a son of the immortal Sea Bird whose trainer, Etienne Pollet, had postponed retirement for this final shot. There were doubts whether Nijinsky would stay a mile and a half or handle the helter-skelter of the Epsom track. Piggott had Nijinsky behind Gyr. Two furlongs out Gyr and his fellow Frenchman Stintino (trained by a young François Boutin) were in front and Lester was working without response.

In those days Piggott cast a sort of diabolic spell across a horse race, his whip the conjuring stick. Just once its tongue flicked fast and hard on to Nijinsky's quarters. 'I had switched him off too much,' Lester said quietly next morning, 'but once he woke up, it was easy.'

Much has happened since that glorious June, not all of it too comfortable. Nijinsky has had the best deal. Lauded as a superstud, he actually covered a mare on Monday, active, as they say, to the very end. O'Brien and Piggott are in the last glimmerings of their careers and the news of Nijinsky's end comes in the same month as Arazi bids to rob him of his place in the pantheon.

Little Arazi has already accomplished more than his giant predecessor had at a comparative stage, and his target of a Kentucky-Epsom Derby double is something even O'Brien never contemplated. If he pulls it off, he will deserve all the superlatives in the lexicon.

But in the meantime an arctic winds blows across the heath at Newmarket. A silver-haired grandfather, still lean and leathery from age-defying days in the saddle, looks back at the images of him and Nijinsky at their height.

The old man will not be drawn into exact comparisons. He just mutters the thought that Nijinsky was 'the most imposing.' But something about the way he watches the video pictures makes you feel that Lester knows what we know. That we'll never see their like again.

Throughout his life Nijinsky was at the top end of the international glamour tree. The richness of the racing beat is that if you follow it in these islands you will find that champions can come from very different parts of the thicket. And that visiting them is as much an insight into the people as the horses. It is certainly so with the era's outstanding hunter-chaser, Double Silk.

An everyday fairy story of farming folk

20 February 1994

A leap from the past. The Grand National favourite Double Silk jumps clear at Sandown and leaves the cynics trailing. Unlikely, unfashionable and unrepeatable, he and his team are sport as it used to be.

By the time the new Aintree starting gate tries to lay the ghost of last year's fiasco at around 3.15pm on 9 April, everybody will know the Double Silk story. The spring-heeled giant from Somerset who is owned and trained and ridden of a morning by Reg Wilkins, a 68-year-old retired dairy farmer; who is jockeyed by Ron Treloggen, another dairy farmer and himself no chicken at 38; the horse who was bought and still performs as just another hunter in the Mendips. They don't make them like that any more.

But to patronize is to miss the point. As Double Silk was led back into the Sandown winners' enclosure on Thursday we hacks were already slavering over the easy pickings of the tale. We noted Treloggen's rustic, upright style; Wilkins's quick, hunched little walk, the pointed, silver eyebrows beneath the flat green cap, the utter unpretentiousness of the answers: 'No, I won't run him in the Gold Cup. I was tempted but he might have a hard race and not win it.'

Maybe this was Farmer Giles and Nobby come to town, but they have come a long way and they have won in a hard school. See them on their own stage . . .

Treloggen has 300 acres and 140 cows on the edge of the Somerset Levels, just north of Street. On Friday morning he also had had three point-to-pointers to exercise, but first he looked out over sodden grasslands and countered the suggestion that he might have been daunted when Double Silk took him to the Cheltenham and Aintree big league last spring. 'Not at all,' he said. 'It was just going back to where I had got to 15 years ago.'

Treloggen is short, sharp and inquisitive as a terrier. He has very clear brown eyes, a narrow, pointed nose almost too delicate for such a rough old game. He goes through into the trophy-laden living room of the bungalow he shares with his wife and daughter and returns with scrapbooks detailing a riding career which now encompasses 29 winners from 209 rides under full National Hunt rules and a further 130 successes from 640 rides in the point-to-point field.

He started in local gymkhanas. ('That's where my style came from – stick on and stay there'.) His race riding began by catching loose horses at point-to-points and volunteering his services to their grateful owners. It worked at the eighth time of asking. The horse belonged to a bookie's son by the name of Martin Pipe.

Today's record-breaking Pipe training operation was then hardly in embryo stage, but Pipe was in hospital and there were rides to be had. The first

Double Silk and Ron Treloggen. West Country heroes as sparkling
as the cider

winner came on 3 April 1974 and, without actually setting fire to Somerset, the eager Treloggen became a small part of the West Country circuit.

By 1979 he was out of the Pipe set-up but was associated with a horse called Midday Welcome good enough to win at Sandown (Treloggen's last ride there until Thursday), finish second at Cheltenham and seventh (carrying 9 stone 7 pound) in the Irish Grand National.

But this was a farmer, not a jockey. Treloggen enjoys his summers spent on the land, horses forgotten and the racing action confined to the first half of the year. 'Point-to-pointing is what it is all about,' he said. 'The National is just the cream on the cake.'

It has to be said that if the race gets tight at Aintree, Treloggen's straight-legged, hunched-shouldered finishing style won't please the purists. But this is no one-horse wonder. This is the man who kidded the cranky Brunico to no fewer than 13 victories in the past two seasons, and whose self-confidence is obvious as Double Silk goes into and over a jump. He has been with the horse from the beginning.

So too has Wilkins. At his farm at Litton, 15 miles from Street, he had just finished feeding Double Silk and his companion Salway Zipper. They are huge horses housed in two vast boxes converted from a disused cowshed. That morning Wilkins had received a cheque from Weatherbys 'for the staff'. A winning twinkle shows beneath the eyebrows. 'I am the staff,' he said.

And proud of it. The boxes are deep-bedded in shredded paper ('Wood shavings are too dusty'), the tack room is dispensary clean, the flagstones are swept. Wilkins has lived for his farm and his horses all his life.

He remembers the days he went hunting on a thoroughbred: 'A horse called Battle Scent. I didn't want to ride anything else after that.' He recalls visits to Cheltenham and his one trip to the Grand National: 'It was 1948. Prince Regent just got beat carrying lumps of weight, I thought he was a hell of a horse.'

There were his own point-to-point efforts which ended with a stoop-making fall at Minehead. The pleasure of hunting and training his own. The final blessing of buying the raw and broken-winded five-year-old that was to be Double Silk.

But there is also grief. Wilkins is the third generation to farm in the Mendips, but there will not be a fourth. Twenty years ago his son John did not return for tea. It was Reg who found him. 'It had been a freak accident, the tractor turned over,' Wilkins said. 'There was not a mark on him but his liver had been ruptured. His watch was still going.'

He does not dwell on it, but it obviously adds a dimension to the enthusiasm with which he takes you back to his pride and joy. 'It was a wrench stopping the cows after so long,' he says, 'but there really wasn't any point in going on farming for ever. At this stage I should be enjoying myself.'

What followed Double Silk's hunter-price purchase in 1989 is beyond any book of fables bar the Grand National volume. That would fit perfectly. The patient old man and the bold young horse. The successful hobday breathing operation, the education in the hunting field – 'He jumped an iron gate on his first day' – the unsung two-race first season; the startling three successes in 1991 but the good sense to call a halt when immature legs became sore; the graduation to the very top of the hunter-chase field over the last two years which made Thursday's success his seventh in a row and left Double Silk's score 14 out of 20.

We are back at the box. Double Silk has been rolling and has paper on his mane. 'He rolls all the time,' Wilkins said reflectively. 'He can be a funny horse. He is perfect in a race but at home he will bite and kick and fuss when you are getting him ready.

'When he first started hunting he would rear like a circus horse. He's in good shape now and I think there's a bit of improvement in him. I love to get a horse fit.'

It is a moment of such perfect promise that you can hold it in the palm of the hand. Old sports, old country values may be doomed in our increasingly urban world. Even in Litton many of the cottages have barn conversions and satellite dishes, and the oak-beamed pub has a six-page menu. The past is changing, but will it change utterly? Trust Double Silk to stem the tide.

The magnet that is Aintree was drawing stars from very different quarters that March. For the race at Cheltenham before Double Silk had something of a victory romp to win his second Foxhunters had seen The Fellow become the first French-trained winner of the Gold Cup.

That epic victory, after two short-head defeats and a fourth in the three preceding years, is recorded later in the book. Suffice to say that in all the celebrations it was easy to forget just how tough The Fellow and his trainer François Doumen must have been beneath their surface glamour.

Now they were going for something tougher still. Like Double Silk and Reg Wilkins, they were heeding the siren sounds that only Aintree sings. Time to cross the Channel and check them out.

Heads turn to Aintree
5 April 1994

Forget the pricked ears and Gallic charm. The Fellow and François Doumen are as hard as nails and a lot cleverer to boot. They will need to be. Even in its new softer guise, the National is no picnic romp.

And that tent pitched on the stable lawn is no frivolous extra. As the likely favourite this Saturday, The Fellow will carry millions of pounds of punters' money. Doumen's Lamorlaye yard is a well-organized place, but as extra security his eldest son Xavier has taken to sleeping outside the champion's box. The French team may not be honoured at home – only the Paris Turf newspaper gave The Fellow's Gold Cup triumph more than a cursory mention – but they will not travel to Aintree unprepared.

They have a fair bit of history against them. Even though the 1909 hero Lutteur III was French owned and trained, he spent his final month in England. No truly French-based horse has won since Cortolvin in 1867, while no Gold Cup winner has doubled up at Aintree since the immortal Golden Miller in 1934. 'Just 23 days between the races,' Doumen said succinctly. 'So little time.'

But Garrison Savannah only just failed in the '91 National three weeks after inching out The Fellow at Cheltenham, and the evidence in the Chantilly Forest on Thursday morning would have warmed the hearts of Anglo-French supporters. If The Fellow was suffering from his efforts in the Cotswolds, he was finding an odd way of showing it.

He was leading a 30-strong Doumen posse as they trotted round a sanded collecting ring which is soon to be called Le Rond The Fellow. As protection, his legs sported orange bandages and his head a blue night cap against the morning chill, but no amount of swaddling could hide the extravagant well-being of his stretched neck and extended gait. He will have worked a mile and three-quarters up the unrelenting incline of the Piste des Lions yesterday morning, but the real graft was done a while ago. Winding up for the Gold Cup, The Fellow was going out not once, but three times a day.

The first exercise would have been as on Thursday; the early climb up the hill from Lamorlaye as the stable cockerels crow scoldingly at the rising sun, the long limbering-up process of trotting interspersed with that ultra-slow hack-canter the French rather inaccurately call the *galop de chasse*; finally a swinging, full-action but strain-free mile up between the trees and past the trainer's watching eye. In all, it is a two-hour promenade, longer than that of almost any English stable. But after breakfast The Fellow would do all bar the final session again. And at tea-time his devoted lad walks him out for another 45 minutes. Four and three-quarter hours under saddle. None of his rivals would have been through anything near it.

'It is logical,' Doumen said, 'but expensive. You need more staff, it costs more. When some of my owners complain about my fees I say it is easy. I will run a special string for you. The horses will just go out for 45 minutes and I will charge you less.'

At 53, Doumen is in the prime of his professional life. The son of a trainer (with whom he quarrelled enough to be sacked a couple of times), he is 17 seasons into a career which has seen top-class success on the Flat as well as fame over jumps. Yet the suaveness of his dress and the slickness of his presentation remind you that he was once in the clothing trade in South Africa.

If The Fellow was a lone star you could ignore the Doumen system. But although he has already amassed a world-record £860,000 (compare Desert Orchid's lifetime £654,000), The Fellow is not even the best horse, nor even perhaps the second best, in the stable. These honours belong to the two handsome geldings directly behind him on Thursday's outing, Ucello II, winner of last year's Grand Steeplechase de Paris (the French Grand National) and Ubu III, victor of the Grande Course de Haies (the French Champion Hurdle). All three carry the scarlet silks of that remarkable horse-lover and bridge fiend, the Marquesa de Moratalla.

Around the stables there doesn't appear to be a lot left to fluke. Every load of straw has the dust shaken out of it before being used as bedding. Every box has an ionizer to purify the air flow, every chain a rubber cover against unwitting teeth. The Fellow's box has a clip on the handle to stop him trying to pick the lock. 'He is cunning,' said Doumen, 'like many of his type.'

That type includes both Ubu and Ucello. They are Selle Français, a hardier breed from the pure thoroughbred, and one which Doumen has exploited from years of reconnaissance in the cattle lands of central France. Belief in outside talent has reaped rewards. It has with his jockey, too. Adam Kondrat came from Poland as a six-year-old and from Mick Bartholomew's Flat stable 12 years later when delayed puberty saw him put on 10 kilos and 10 centimetres in one season. But his talent transferred instantly to jump racing even if English sceptics were not converted until this year's Cheltenham.

His will be the most stylish, forward-leaning crouch at Aintree, but it will not be unrefined. In January he spent three weeks under Peter Scudamore's tutelage in Gloucestershire. He now talks with unexpected fluency: 'The Fellow has a lot of patience. He does not hurry his jump. He knows what he is doing. At Aintree, it is important to know what you are doing.'

The pilot doesn't look a soft touch either.

The Fellow travelled hopefully to that Grand National, but in the race a time would come when his many supporters would wish he had never arrived at all.

On the second circuit he failed to get high enough at the Canal Turn, turned over and as he rose got flattened again by a horse behind him. There was a dreadful fleeting frozen image on the TV monitors. The Fellow, the horse that had never fallen, sticking his neck up from the carnage and then being poleaxed flat by a thundering pursuer. The camera swung on. We thought we had seen the last of the Frenchman.

But at the stables afterwards he was walking back almost without a scratch and it was Double Silk who was the casualty. He too had never hit the ground before. He too had been flattened by a pursuer and for him there was the head-hanging pain that a bad shaking and broken ribs can bring. For him the dream was over.

Yet the dream is what sustains us over the jumps or on the flat. And no dream is wished for more fervently than the ultimate super-horse in the classic game. It will never happen, but we keep giving way to hope. In the autumn of '94 we were at it again.

We had been hooked by Celtic Swing.

Wonderhorse

30 October 1994

Could this really be it? Could the dark brown two-year-old scudding up a Sussex bank under Bob Mason, his 61-year-old stable lad, on Friday be the wonderhorse the racing game will always await? The unbeaten Celtic Swing looks good, but can he be that good? Haven't we all been here before?

Not up this particular road we haven't. Not here beneath Gibbet's Wood where, in other, harsher days the corpses swung for such heinous crimes as poaching pheasants.

Not here, galloping up to the little copse called Friday's Church, where the lepers used to limp in hope of redemption. In the feverishly optimistic world of

Celtic Swing and Bob Mason, his 'evergreen' stable lad. The autumn of '94, and too good to be true

racing a new 'Horse of the Century' is hailed about once every three years. Celtic Swing may prove merely to be the latest. But he comes from a very private collection.

At first glimpse this is entirely a family affair. We stand high on the Downs, looking across the valley to Arundel Castle, where Lady Anne Herries and her sister Mary spent their childhoods as daughters of the Duke of Norfolk. Down to the left of us the sun glints on the sprawl of Littlehampton and the calm waters of the Channel.

Lady Mary has just come back from a royal tour of India. Lady Anne has returned from Celtic Swing's triumphant march at Doncaster. The nearly black horse with the white blazed face coming past us and the dogs could be the pony that first took the red ribbon in the Hunter Trails. He would not be loved any less.

Racing, like all other sports, is big business. Celtic Swing's value is into seven figures and climbing. Such numbers speak of pressure and professionalism and people with heavy frowns that suggest it may all be gone tomorrow.

Here at Angmering Park there is a railed drive up through the stud, a gold and russet beech hedge, a grey flintstone French château and, out to greet you, Lady Anne's husband, himself one of the bravest, most skilful and disarmingly Corinthian figures British sport has ever produced, Sir Colin Cowdrey.

Cowdrey is in plus-fours and brown woollen stockings. He is going shooting, but not before we have all had breakfast and he has fussed over us as if we were MCC big cheeses and he just a young tyke from Tonbridge all those years ago.

Of course he purports to know nothing about racing, just as his wife would affect that her whole operation is just a super-enthusiastic hobby alongside her devotion to spaniels and positive obsession with hedgehog insignia (they are everywhere: cushions, pottery, doorstoppers, even a brass hedgehog tap on the hose). But Cowdrey was one of cricket's greatest victors, and even a quick skim through Lady Anne's record shows that she also is gifted with the winning streak.

Sure, it began as just a bit of fun. On 12 December 1970, she saddled her first winner, an old horse called Stagshaw in the selling hurdle at Catterick. 'She was a hunting lady in Yorkshire in those days,' Tommy Stack, Stagshaw's jockey, said last week.

'She had some good jumpers before she moved back south 15 years ago. But don't ever be deceived by all that amateur charm. Lady Anne's horses were always very fit. She know what she was doing. After all, she was the duchess's daughter.'

Mention of Lavinia, Duchess of Norfolk, not now in the rudest of health, will bring a wry smile to the faces of the professionals. For 50 years she was renowned as just about the cutest brain in the whole racing patch.

It was she who started up the stables at the back of Arundel Castle from which John Dunlop now saddles Classic winners.

It was her stud that produced Dunlop's St Leger hero, Moon Madness, whose ungainly half-brother, Sheriff's Star, put Lady Anne firmly on the Flat-racing map in 1988 and 1989.

This is the same stud that has finally reared a young superstar in Celtic Swing, but he carries, not the Duchess's sky-blue silks, but the maroon jacket of racing's most professional of all owners, the Cayman Islands-based businessman, Peter Savill.

For success attracts. Once Lady Anne had agreed to have 'the odd Flat racer' in 1986, once she had shown, with the broken-footed Sheriff's Star, that she could win big events like the Coronation Cup and the Grand Prix de St Cloud, the enquiries were bound to come. Whatever she was doing could she not do it for others? One of those was Savill.

Savill is a balding, bespectacled, softly spoken Scarborough-born Cambridge law graduate in his mid-forties who made his first tax-exiling fortune out of in-flight magazines. He has a brilliant brain and his hobby is racing.

For 15 years he has been playing racing as though it were a game of Monopoly, investing in low-rent animals, spreading his risks, keeping costs constantly under review. Gradually, he has upped his act. He now has 50 horses with 17 different trainers. Since last year one of those trainers has been Lady Anne at Angmering.

It was Maxine Cowdrey who made the introductions. Now married to Colin's son Graham and assistant to Lady Anne, Maxine has worked for both Savill and Michael Stoute, from whom she persuaded Savill to buy an unsung colt called River North, whose successes over the past two seasons mean that he will carry the Savill-Herries banner in the Breeders' Cup in Kentucky on Saturday. This spring Savill was looking for more.

So, on 18 March, Savill's jockey Kevin Darley was dispatched for a 'test drive', not on Celtic Swing, but on his more precocious stablemate Opaline. Darley was impressed by Opaline (fated to die after winning at Sandown) but devastated by the loose-limbed black horse that hacked up behind him. After another visit he advised buying the two of them. For less than £50,000, Savill got the bargain of the century.

This is where the story goes into a fantasy land from which owners, dreamers and those holding antepost vouchers for next year's Classics hope it will never return.

'From the moment he started cantering', said Bob Mason, whose racing experiences stretch right back to leading up the 1957 Gimcrack Stakes winner Pheidipides, 'I knew he was something special. He just seemed to float over the ground.'

'After we worked him with Jawal [a good handicapper], I knew he couldn't get beat first time at Ayr. I had £240 on him at 4–1. Everything I had.'

Such tales are the spice of racing bars down the ages, but it was what Celtic Swing has done this month, after a three-month layoff with sore shins, that has made normally sober judges drink deep of the superlatives.

First an eight-length track-record victory on fast ground at Ascot, then a 12-length annihilation of the Racing Post Trophy on a soft track at Doncaster last Saturday that brought spontaneous applause from the crowd and direct comparisons with such as Mill Reef and Vaguely Noble.

All this with a colt who is bred much more for the Derby mile-and-a-half than the Guineas mile, little wonder that Celtic Swing is already short-priced favourite for Savill's avowed intention of taking the Triple Crown. All this with a young horse still so immature that his stifle joint (just below the hock) often pops out in the mornings. All this with something as English as the ewes on the sheepgraze beside us.

But the record shows that this fantasy is desperately difficult to sustain. Celtic Swing is going to need very special qualities if he is to endure the physical and mental pressures that a top three-year-old's season will demand.

He had sweated up quite enough by the time he was loaded into the stalls at Doncaster, but connections insist that his temperament is bomb-proof.

His free-going style might set him up as a perfect target for the French 'finisher' Pennekamp, but Darley wonders if anything will be quick enough to get to him. He may, somehow, have deluded us all.

For the moment, what we have is a legitimate contender for greatness. Up close, Celtic Swing is a better specimen that the small and straight-legged Arazi, but not as massive as the brilliant but blood vessel-bursting Zafonic.

Standing in the box with him, you can put your palm on his withers at scarcely 16 hands. He has a sensible-looking head and is long-bodied without being awkward. Hand on heart, if you did not know anything about him, you would say he was just another horse.

But it is his presence on the move that has excited even cynical old laggards like me. The image remains of my first sight of him at Doncaster, walking calmly out of the paddock and then hacking off like a hunter.

Then the race itself, his rider asking him to lengthen – and, for a few wondrous moments in this ridiculously simple, absurdly impossible discipline, you thought you saw perfection on the hoof.

Dan O'Donovan, the head lad, lives in the lodge at the park gates. He and I go back a long way. We had a beer and talked of desperate days at Wye and Wincanton. O'Donovan looked tired. He had been up at 5am to feed the horses. He searched for an assessment of the two-year-old with the world at his still-immature feet.

'That Celtic Swing', he said, 'he's a freak, a bit like . . .'

O'Donovan paused and, not finding an example good enough in the Flat-racing lexicon, moved across to the jumping world to invoke the highest accolade any Irishman can attribute. 'He's a bit like Arkle.'

Celtic Swing did well next season; but not nearly well enough. He won the Greenham Stakes and the French Derby and was photo-finished out of the Two Thousand Guineas. Yet sadly he looks destined to be remembered for hype, not greatness. It was not his fault. His minor flaws could not match our dreams, and in the Irish Derby he gave way so completely that I publicly suggested he had fallen out of love with the game.

No matter that he was later diagnosed as having torn knee ligaments and retired for the season; the strain had taken him like all the others.

With so much other racing talk, it's easy to forget the pressure we put these four-legged athletes under. You wouldn't forget it at Cheltenham in '95.

That heady thrill of triumph
17 March 1995

Afterwards he stood head down with air coming in great heaving gulps through those sweat-soaked nostrils. All around him people were hugging each other in celebration. The crowds beamed down from the tiered steps of the surround to the unsaddling enclosure. But close to Master Oats you could see the effort that winning the Gold Cup had taken.

Of course it looks tough enough through the binoculars and even on TV. There was no mistaking the demands that 19 fences and three and a quarter miles of galloping would make of thoroughbreds on this still-sinking Cheltenham turf. No disguising the brutality as the race built towards its climax and the open ditch bit hard into Barton Bank.

No cloaking the destruction as Master Oats broke first Merry Gale and then Dubacilla on that impossibly long run from the second-last.

But all that can soon be drowned in the bubbling froth of applause that flows on and on. The winning party comes back into the enclosure and a roar goes up that the victors will keep with them to Doomsday. They remember all the effort and cold mornings and bleeding heartache this day has taken. All of us sense the heady thrill of triumph and, torn-up betting slips or not, we want to be part of it. Yet we are talking about the people.

There is an understandable but nonetheless unworthy switch of emphasis in the unsaddling enclosure which changes the winner's identity from four legs to two. While the jockey is still in the saddle the horse is centre focus, the rider at best a centaur figure. Once dismounted there are the obligatory group photos and then the reporters scrum close on trainer, jockey and owner. And the horse is led aside.

We on TV are the worst offenders. We need the 'quotes'. We try to wriggle microphone and cameras through the scrum to bottle naked elation and send it down the tube. So it was yesterday. The Cheltenham unsaddling enclosure, the best-designed of all the post-race amphitheatres, the whole arena still buzzing at the glory of this Gold Cup and the gently irrevocable remark from producer Andrew Franklin in my ear: 'We are fading your mike up.'

First victim was owner Paul Matthews, an almost intimidated figure despite his bearded, tie-askew build. 'I really haven't anything to say,' he gasped, clearly disorientated at the magnitude of the triumph that his long-term interest in racing and his small-time gamble into ownership had visited upon him. 'It's just unbelievable,' he added and you could believe it and wanted to leave him unmolested to enjoy it.

Across to Kim Bailey, who up until Alderbrook's Champion Hurdle win on Tuesday had waited 17 years to train a Festival winner. Kim has pursued a policy of openness with the media and it's good to see it pay off to his whole operation's benefit.

Now he was overwhelmed but not quite the tearful heap of two days before. He picked up the question and wanted to pay tribute to his owner, his horse and 'the staff who do all the work'.

A key member of that staff was coming round the horse's head. In three days and three different outfits Tracey Bailey has run away with the best-turned-out paddock person award at Cheltenham. Yesterday she was a revelation in pillar-box red.

But it's in early-morning anorak fatigues that she has scored the point that really matters. It was her hands and be-chapped leggings that calmed the jigging nervous breakdown that was Mr Frisk. It was she who has faced wind and weather to be always in the string. It was Tracey who wanted to give credit where it was due.

'Talk to Sean,' she said, 'he understands this horse like no other.' So we moved the microphone to Sean Ellis at Master Oats's head and we got as near as you can to an interview with an actual Gold Cup winner.

Sean came into racing in the West Country seven years ago. He moved to Bailey's and led in Master Oats in a small race at Uttoxeter 18 months ago. It had been a bloody beginning. The big horse burst a blood vessel and there was enough blood awash for a Macbeth production.

Master Oats was heaving enough now to make you fear he would burst again. But all those long mornings and afternoons that he and Sean had shared of 'stress-free' training had paid off. The big horse was equipped to go through the pain barrier. The man at the rein was proud of him. So were we all.

Jockeys

Jockeys are the talking part of the centaur, but what they do is often understood only by the horses. Race-riding is one of the most watched but least appreciated of the sporting arts. Nearly everyone has had a go at football or cricket or can drive a car. Not one in a thousand has ridden a racehorse at the gallop, so judgement can only be made on results, and sometimes wounded pockets. It's no bad way but it still means that those little centaur tops are worth examining.
    And Pat Eddery more than most.

Feeling good, and making history
24 June 1990

The mystery is in the freshness. Pat Eddery sits on the scales at the end of Friday at Royal Ascot. As his saddle and number cloth are checked you see the weariness seep over him, 38 years on this planet, 21 in the thunder-storm spotlight of the racing game. Five minutes later, as he comes out of the washroom and begins to talk, it's as if his hands are rubbing on a magic lamp.

    'I feel real good,' he says, the ungrammatical Irish voice surprisingly deep and strong for those of us used to his muttered replies in public. 'I am riding real well. Things are happening well. I am making the right decisions. Things, touch wood, are going just perfect.'

    The statistics confirm but do not explain it. By yesterday morning, Eddery had ridden 92 winners in the three-month-old Flat-racing season, 28 more than both Willie Carson and Steve Cauthen. His horses' earnings exceed £1,280,000 in Britain alone and what with Tirol's Irish 2,000 Guineas and Sanglamore's French Derby, his mounts are close to £2 million already.

    It is the fastest and richest start anyone can remember. At this time last year, Eddery had clocked 63 winners and just £900,000. When Sir Gordon Richards reached 200 winners in a season for the 12th and final time in 1952, his

100 came up by Goodwood at the end of July. Eddery could top the century next week and is on schedule to be the first 200 scorer since Sir Gordon's reign.

This purple patch has not happened overnight. Eddery's first century was back in 1973, the first of his seven championships in 1974. He has won every big

Pat Eddery – ten times champion

event bar the Boat Race. He is the most sought after of all the big race riders. Can it really be as simple as 'feeling real good at the moment'?

He is still in his breeches and boots, a blue towel over his compact, muscular torso. He sits on one of the plain wooden saddle-scrubbing tables of Ascot's extensive changing room and is unashamed of the simplicity.

'It's every-day riding,' he says, the eyes very blue, wide and direct. 'You go from day to day. You have a bad day yesterday, you forget it and think about tomorrow. Once the season starts it's seven days a week. With the contract [his six-figure retainer from Sanglamore and Quest For Fame's owner Khalid Abdulla] I never miss France on Sunday.'

As he talks a truth begins to emerge rather at odds with the perceived wisdom you normally read about Eddery. This has it that the be-all and end-all of the current champion is just god-given, shamrock-kissed talent. That this eldest of 12 children to former Irish champion Jimmy Eddery got lucky with first 'Frenchie' Nicholson as mentor and then Peter Walwyn as Derby winning trainer, and with his natural balance and intuitive understanding of the thorough-bred young Patrick simply sailed along from there.

Of course, all of the above is correct, but it misses out another essential part of Eddery's make up. A part which was rated even above that much-lauded natural talent by fellow jockey Dean McKeown as we drove to Gatwick later on Friday evening.

By relentless application McKeown has grafted his way to the top of the northern tree. He, of all today's riders, is entitled to recognize a worker. 'Determination,' he states plainly, eschewing the usual fancy things about Eddery's 'hands' and touch. 'Pat is absolutely amazing in the way he wants to win even at the littlest of meetings.'

Friday had been the end of the biggest of all meetings, 22 rides (and five winners) over the four days at Royal Ascot. There have been 340 rides since the season opened on 22 March. Three-hundred and forty public, competitive, high-speed, always dangerous situations in just three months. It's a relentless treadmill which should be enough to put some of the 'It's the pressure' whingers from other sports to shame.

But Eddery doesn't see it as that. 'It's much easier nowadays,' he says. 'I have had a driver since 1974 and now we have a plane that makes things even quicker.

'Sundays for France, we wouldn't leave 'till after 9.30. Two or three rides [this afternoon it is Tirol in the Grand Prix de Paris] and we're back by 6.30. Sunday is an easy day.'

That 'driver' has arrived in the sharp-suited, slightly crumple-faced shape of Eddery's brother-in-law, agent and general ADC, Terry 'The Book' Ellis. Terry, who still keeps a London accent straight from the *Minder* scripts, was a manager for an American firm selling reproduction antiques to the forces in Germany when he met Eddery's sister Olivia and then volunteered to do some driving when brother-in-law lost his licence by order of the magistrates.

Nowadays, Terry is one of the great originals on the international scene. His home, two miles from the Eddery stud near Aylsebury, is littered with the English, Irish and French form books which he scours for news of future winners for his team. It is Terry who calls the trainers, fixes the transport, books the tables. When he says, 'We have six rides today,' he has long earned the right to his share of the first person plural.

All this has freed Eddery for the job in hand, which cannot, by its nature, allow for the peaks and troughs of both physical and mental fitness which almost all other sports allow for. 'I am as fit at the start of the season as I am at the end,' he says. 'I am no heavier, no lighter as the months go by and in the winter I never let my weight go above eight stone seven. That's just by being sensible and keeping pretty busy at the farm and the stud.'

At this stage you should not run away with the impression that Eddery is some against-the-grain, strictly teetotal, fun-shunning Irishman. When the lights come on he can enjoy an evening with the best of them, and it was not so long ago that Terry knocked on a friend's door at Newmarket in the small hours claiming that he and Patrick needed re-inforcements for the brandy cupboard.

But this is an organized Irishman. At five foot four compared to Cauthen's five foot seven, the weight is not a 24-hour crusade of self-denial, but it still has to be worked at. 'This morning I would wake up at eight stone three,' he says. 'I have a cup of tea and toast and then spend an hour in the sauna to lose a pound and a half. Before the season starts I ride a lot of work for my main trainers, but once we are racing they leave me alone and I only go down to sit on the nice horses.'

Coincidentally or not, this regularity has drawn impressive dividends both on the physical and on the mental side. Eddery may have been lucky to have been born the right shape but he was trebly lucky to have also developed an astonishing degree of elasticity in his bones. Twenty-one years is a long time to be involved in the violent business of handling half-a-ton of thoroughbred at speed yet it is necessary to tempt fate by recording that in that time Eddery has never once had what could be classified as a serious injury.

'I have had plenty of falls,' he says matter-of-factly, 'and I have cracked a few ribs and broken a few thumbs but nothing very bad. The worst that happened was a fall at Leopardstown when a lot of horses galloped into me and I got badly bruised inside. But I was back riding in 14 days.'

'You have got to go out there and take your chance,' he continues, 'and not do anything stupid. Of course, some kids might do something stupid on bad ground and that but you know more than they know. You have just got to come to terms with it. Riding is dangerous and if you come down you are going to get hurt.'

Provided such spooks don't begin to prise loose in the psyche, there is no reason why good jockeys should not get better with age. Every race sees a fresh set of legs beneath them, their job is to know how to handle the gun and when to fire the bullets. Eddery never had much trouble with the fire-arms, although his present technique has only been refined in the last decade. And his coolness in the battle has been better than ever this season.

His two Derbies this month have been perfect examples; dropping Sanglamore out plumb last in the French Derby to protect his suspect stamina, and putting Quest For Fame at Tattenham Corner to exploit non-staying rivals at Epsom.

'You don't actually give Pat any orders,' said trainer Roger Charlton, who was going through the Derby experience for the first time. 'Pat doesn't like to say much in the paddock and as Prince Khalid is also very quiet there was really no conversation at all at either Derby. And when Quest For Fame came back at Epsom, all Pat said was "that was nice, wasn't it Rog?".'

It hasn't always been so easy, and on El Gran Senor in 1984 Eddery became almost as famous for losing the Derby as for the three times he has now won it. 'It doesn't bother me,' he says about this and other criticism. 'You are out there in the limelight every day and you are there to be shot at. You have bad runs. I have had a lot of them over the years. But you have just got to keep your mouth shut and wait for things to change. This game tames lions, it does.'

So it is that the most contentious public statement you can find attributed to Eddery dates back to a Classic trial at Ascot some 15 years ago when he dismounted from what later proved to be an ordinary animal called Leonardo Da Vinci and declared it 'the best horse I have ever sat on'.

'That taught me a lesson,' he says now with a laugh. But he is certainly coming off the wall a little over the stewards' rulings on the use of the whip which saw him serve a three-day suspension last weekend. 'A jockey is in a no-win situation,' he claims. 'This is surely the only sport where you get penalised for trying too hard. I have my methods, I never mark horses with the whip, but if they will go for it, I use it.'

The trouble is that the Eddery finishing method, even before he resorts to the whip, is one that would make his old mentor Nicholson wince. He was a great advocate of the classical, flat-backed smooth pumping rhythm best personified in the past by Jimmy Lindley and Joe Mercer. Eddery's style is an evolution of the Lester Piggott trick, lowering his backside right on to the saddle and bumping up and down in his efforts to galvanize a winning effort from the horse beneath.

'I have tried it' said Dean McKeown later, 'and I don't understand how a horse can go faster if someone is bumping his weight on their back.' The purists are wholly against it but Eddery is unrepentant. 'I know Frenchie liked the style of Jimmy and Joe,' he says. 'But I always thought Lester got more out of a horse than anyone else, and I have tried to get that way in a finish.'

Purist-pleasing or not, there is no doubt that Eddery's finish is damnably effective. When he drove Tolomeo up the inside to win the 1983 Arlington Million in Chicago, the ace American commentator Dave Johnson scoffed, 'Ride him cowboy', Johnson was at Ascot this week, but he's used to Eddery now and watched in wonderment as Batshoof wore down Relief Pitcher on Tuesday.

Cauthen had poached a lead on Relief Pitcher and Eddery and Batshoof still had three lengths to make up with 300 yards to run. He and Batshoof have formed a brilliant partnership whereby the colt does almost all his running without the jockey resorting to drastic methods. Right into the final furlong Eddery stayed his hand, and then clamped down to go for the whole whip-cracking bottom-bumping lot.

'When I rode Batshoof at the Curragh he was really brilliant, gave me a dream ride,' explains Eddery. 'But at Ascot he wasn't as good in himself, wasn't giving. He only stretched in the last 50 yards and that was enough.' Batshoof, you've guessed it, got up to win by a short head.

There is a challenging note in a fire in those extraordinarily wide blue eyes as the champion continues. 'Old-style is old-style,' he says, 'but this is different. This is 1990. We are doing faster times, horses are getting better. The jockeys, I feel, are getting better, and it's the way I ride and I am not going to change. I know that Frenchie would be ever so pleased. Right up to his death he was so proud of what I had done.'

We are on to top horses now, and it's almost like listening to a conductor listing famous performances of great symphonies. 'Dancing Brave and El Gran Senor, I suppose they have to be the two,' he admits. 'Brilliant horses at any distance. Fantastic animals, lovely temperament, good movers and they both had a terrific turn of foot. They were so classic. Real classic animals. They only come very rarely.

'And Pebbles,' he adds, recalling other glory days, 'she was incredible when she won the Breeders Cup in America because she didn't stay. It was only because it was such a tiny track and she got lucky up the inner that she won that day, but in the Champion Stakes before that she was fantastic. She slaughtered the colts, she beat all those Group 1 horses, on the bit.'

But as these top events mean so much and pay so well, why not, like star performers in other sports, reserve his powder for the major meetings. Why take five rides at Redcar? The answer flashes back, direct and revealing. 'Because I want to be champion,' says Eddery. 'That's the thing. To win the Derby is great, but I want to win the championship as much as anything else.'

'As for the 200,' he adds, 'I would love to achieve it. Things are going very well, I just have to keep on kicking. It's every winner that counts. They always have.'

We are back now to his original motivation, way back to his childhood in County Dublin. 'God knows what else I would have done.' he says. 'All of my life I have only dreamed of one thing and that is to be a top jockey. I couldn't wait to get out of school to get on a horse.'

Eddery is now extremely skilful and extremely rich. But his success has come from a lot more than avarice. Five years before Eddery, I also spent my formative riding years with Frenchie Nicholson at Cheltenham. Through all the things he taught (and he must have been some teacher to have got me through a hundred winners), the greatest of all was that the magical, boyish thrill of riding a winner could make any hardship worthwhile.

For Eddery, winners remain that magic lamp. And almost every day they still make his dreams come true.

Pat Eddery's championship reign continued until Michael Roberts wrested the
crown from him in '92. He won it back for a tenth title in '93 and then bowed to
the twelve-month barrage of the youthful Frankie Dettori in '94. But he remains
a marvel. A symbol of vitality, of what racing can bring when you ride the wave
successfully and come again and again into the shore.

There is another side to the riding game. A side that will always be. A side
that makes you wince as you watch. A side we should never forget.

No disguising the pain – or the relief

24 November 1991

A look through the hospital window on Monday, a neck-bandaged figure lying
very still after the latest operation. A young life laid waste 20 years ago. What
a price to pay!

Worcester racecourse had seemed an inviting place for jockey John
Woodman on 8 April, 1971. It was Maundy Thursday, the river in spate, the
banks full of daffodils, the old cathedral looking down in disapproval as the flags
went up for Eastertide.

John had just turned 25. He had a ride in the last, he had a contract for top
trainer Frank Cundell next season. He was, in the words of the great Stan Mellor,
'the up and coming guy'. And it was Mellor who was to cause his downfall.

Stan was due to ride a mare called Anthony's Best for Cundell in the
Novices Chase. But he had a fall in the previous race, and as he weighed out for
the next the officials didn't like what they saw. 'The clerk of the scales held up
his finger,' Mellor remembers. 'My eyes were going in different directions.
They wouldn't let me ride. So they got John Woodman. Poor chap.'

There were 16 runners. The first fence in the novice chase would always
be hairy. Too many people trying to be 'up in front out of trouble'. The wings
of the obstacle sucking you in much too quickly for comfort. The ground the
other side ready to reach up and bite you. Anthony's Best didn't concentrate, and
the jaws closed on her and Woodman.

Ron Barry was to ride the winner. He was the emerging star who would
break the championship record two years later. Macer Gifford rode the favourite.
He had just joined Barry in the lead when he fell three from home. Fourteen years
later his own candle was snuffed out by the long cruel attrition of motor neurone
disease. John Woodman is still with us. But you wouldn't have laid odds in the
ambulance.

If half a ton of horse somersaults on to 10st of rider, plenty has to give. The
miracle is that it doesn't happen more often. But for John Woodman it was a
direct hit. His neck was broken in five places, including the odontoid peg, that
most gruesome of titles 'the hangman's fracture'. Four vertebrae were crushed
and the breastbone was fractured. Worcester Casualty clinic had their hands full.

'It seemed they didn't know where to start,' says Stan Mellor. 'I went in to see him next day and they had put a plaster-cast all over. He looked like a letter-box, just his mouth, eyes and nose peering out.'

After five weeks Woodman was allowed home, still letter-box clad, to Chichester. His father Syd had been head lad to Ryan Price and now ran a small training stable in the shadow of Goodwood Racecourse. The letter-box lasted five months. At the end John was mobile but not exactly mended.

As the recuperation continued John set up a bloodstock agency from a wooden shed in the middle of the yard. His partner was a smart young man who looked as if he was going places. He was called Anthony Penfold. Today he's the stylish guru behind Generous and the other stars of the Fahd Salman empire.

'We ran cheap syndicates, had some nice winners,' says John. 'We had Sir Samuel who was second at Royal Ascot. But the headaches were always a problem and in the end I really couldn't help Anthony. He would never know if I would be well enough to turn up.'

Like so many survivors of serious accidents John was finding no respite in the after-life. The pain got worse and then three years ago the spinal column began to get so distorted that the use of his legs began to go. 'It had me beat,' he says candidly. 'Sometimes it would just hurt so much that I would lie in the corner and cry. They said that I would have to take to a wheel-chair.'

Enter Bill Smith, former fellow-rider, long-time family friend and, like me, privileged to be a Trustee of the Injured Jockeys Fund. Bill knew a colourful, cigar-smoking professor called Syd Watkins who for years has bolted the Grand Prix drivers back together. Watkins said that come the time, and given the money, he would have no option but to operate.

The Injured Jockeys Fund immediately pledged the cash. Ten days ago Professor Watkins and his assistant Mr Sparrow adjudged the time was right. No great Lazarus, 'pick-up-thy-bed-and-walk' miracle was promised. But the pain and the disability could be pushed back. Penny Woodman, and the two kids James and Rebecca, would have something more than a cripple around the house.

The operation involved removing two damaged discs in the neck and fusing the vertebrae with bone taken from the hip. The work would start by cutting a hole through the throat. When Mr Sparrow explained the excavations prior to theatre-day, John Woodman began to wonder, not for the first time, if it wouldn't have been easier if Anthony's Best hadn't finished the job.

There was a little grille window to his door at London Hospital. Through it on Monday you could see him lying asleep, his neck swathed in foam bandage. The years had thinned the hair and thickened the flesh from the willowy elegance of his jockey days. As he awoke he couldn't disguise the discomfort nor quell a sense of relief.

'Getting through the operation was important,' he said. 'I was really scared witless when they told me about it, but I was bound for a wheel-chair. Now I have a chance. I am one of the lucky ones. Think of Sharon Murgatroyd.'

Tomorrow morning there will be a meeting of the Injured Jockeys Fund in London, not just to discuss the Christmas Card sales on which we depend for so much of our income but to review 36 separate cases of which Sharon Murgatroyd, almost totally paralysed in a Newton Abbot fall this August, is only the latest and severest sufferer.

Sharon was taken to Bangor races last Monday. It was a special trip out from hospital to what is her nearest track. Stan Mellor was there as a trainer. He ran three horses. One was shot, the other two finished last. Back at the yard someone said, 'You must be very depressed.' The reply was direct and simple. 'No. I met Sharon. We are all lucky if we can get up in the morning.'

Now John Woodman will too.

The operation worked well for a time, but sadly much of the trouble has returned with a vengeance. Fate is not kind.

But just occasionally it can be forgiving. Occasionally it has to make exceptions. It gave up on Lester Piggott long ago. But by 1992 even Fate must have thought it had made exceptions enough.

Piggott's timeless Classic touch
4 May 1992

You could predict it but you still couldn't believe it. Lester Piggott won his 30th Classic at the silver-haired age of 56. Father Time should throw away his sickle in defeat.

Of course it was a horse that did the running. It always has been. This time it was a lean little chestnut colt called Rodrigo De Triano who carried the old man through the whirling thunder of this 2,000 Guineas field to take control 300 yards out and never flinch from his place in history.

The real Rodrigo De Triano was the look-out in the crow's nest who first spied land on Columbus's voyage westward 500 years ago. After yesterday's race the storybook symmetry of a horse bearing this name becoming associated with one of the most extraordinary landmarks in British or indeed global sport seemed to have an inevitability about it. It didn't beforehand.

The afternoon had begun in sunshine, but half an hour prior to the big race the heavens betrayed us. Black clouds rolled in and dumped a downpour that chilled you to the very marrow. In the paddock, Lester Piggott came past in Rodrigo's saddle. He was wearing the green and blue Sangster silks forever associated with the golden O'Brien days of yesteryear. The horse looked as pinched as a whippet in December. The jockey looked what he was, the ghost of ages past.

But not for the first time he had come back to haunt us and no demon ever earned such a welcome. The Newmarket crowd realized they were seeing something that should not be. With Piggott, sometimes tragically to a fault, all normal rules never did apply. Time may have ravaged the edges but it cannot put even a chip on the shining core of his talent for finessing the galloping thoroughbred better than any jockey ever foaled.

Lester Piggott wins the 1992 Two Thousand Guineas on Rodrigo de Triano. It was Lester's thirtieth classic

You can still deal the cards when your wrists have grown stiff and eyes have grown dim. So it was that Lester Piggott, in his 57th year, 38 seasons on from his first classic, the 1954 Derby on Never Say Die, and seven years since his 29th classic, the 1985 Two Thousand Guineas on Shadeed, could still come out and blend his mind and body into one-and-a-half minutes of something mightily close to perfection.

There have been times these last two seasons when many of us have thought that this unlikely comeback, this return from the unwanted exile of the ground, perceived the dying of the light. The old boy would have an unwilling, untalented or just plain unsuitable set of legs beneath him and all too soon his backside has been hoisted high out of the saddle in a despairing acceptance of the inevitable. It was brave but there could be sadness, even badness about the ending of it.

Not many 'live' horses were entrusted to him. The wins this season could be counted on one hand. But then came Rodrigo. His regular rider, Willie Carson, was claimed by Sheikh Hamdan for Muhtarram and Robert Sangster's young trainer, Peter Chapple-Hyam, did not hesitate. He voted for experience. A whole library of it.

Piggott was drawn No. 3, next to Steve Cauthen on the fragile-looking favourite, Alnasr Alwasheek, in No. 4 and two away from Carson in the No. 1 berth. But from the break, Piggott didn't want to be part of this inside group, where 80 seconds later the trouble would come. With one intuitive move of genius he tacked towards the middle to find a better place to play his hand.

Up in front the big, handsome Thourios was leading the inside group, the speedy River Falls towed the far-side posse and the heavy-topped Pursuit Of Love was moving best of all in the centre. Piggott was pursuing him.

With three furlongs to run Alnasr Alwasheek was only one of several strugglers getting in each other's way along the inside. Cauthen had a bit of trouble moving him through but there was no real bite in his gallop. No more joy for the French: Tertian and Steinbeck were going nowhere, Cardoun was making some progress, but not enough.

Up in front, eyes were having to accept the impossible. Yes, the old boy had outplayed them. The curled high body lowered itself into Rodrigo's saddle and asked his little partner to do what he was born for. The answer was the trump the world had wanted.

Rodrigo De Triano took Pursuit Of Love in half a dozen strides and so Lester was in front with only the Newmarket hill between him and yet more unthought-of immortality. For a few horrible moments you imagined that the ancient limbs might refuse him. Wasn't there a touch of rust about the way the whip came out, about the desperate wriggling drive behind the mane? Maybe, but it was always the results, not the style, that made the record books.

So home he drove, a length and a half clear of the outsider Lucky Lindy at the line, Pursuit Of Love another half back in third, the swaggering Epsom horse Silver Wisp a head away fourth and Willie Carson on the fast-finishing and now surely Derby-bound Muhtarram only another half a length further back in fifth.

With this victory Piggott keeps the old candle burning on. It's only a month to Epsom. As long as he's still around, the blood will quicken when someone asks 'I wonder what Lester rides?' Rodrigo De Triano is unlikely to last the Derby trip but on yesterday's evidence even the Almighty can't cast the same doubt about his rider.

Many things are, have been and will be wrong with the racing game. But it still spawned the most extraordinary, abiding, contrary sporting genius of them all. No, we won't see Lester's like again.

Apologies for ending that Lester piece with the same phrase as the Nijinsky obit. But it was true of both of them, and extraordinarily, but not unexpectedly, we got yet more drama from Lester before the year was out. First, an equally brilliant ride on Rodrigo to win the Champion Stakes in October followed just a fortnight later at Florida's Gulfstream Park by what seemed to be the fall to end it all.

More of that later. But first to a man who that same year carved his own little niche in history. A jockeys' title to the star from the Veldt.

From dairy farm to the cream of the flat

23 August 1992

He looked like an injured whippet. Small, sick, shrivelled and so stiff he couldn't pick a newspaper from the floor. Hardly perfect shape for his most crucial week of the season, but Michael Roberts had come a long way for this.

His 38-year journey from a dairy farm in the Cape Province to the top of our jockeys' table and on to the back of last week's sensational winner Lyric Fantasy now has an almost ordered look about it. An inevitability that the most gifted and successful rider in South African history should migrate to tackle and conquer the territory where this whole galloping nonsense began. But the orderliness is only hindsight. Many of the bumps remain.

Principally the unremitting ache of the two squashed vertebrae in Roberts' lower back which had threatened not only the York appointment with Lyric Fantasy but the healthy lead Roberts had established over Pat Eddery in the jockeys' championship. It had been a slow motion, sideways fall over the tail of a squabbly filly on the gallops a fortnight ago this Tuesday. At first it was the neck that seemed locked, but when physiotherapy eased that, the back pain became apparent. 'I promise you,' he says in the neat, nasal tones of the Veldtland, 'that if it wasn't for this title race and for Lyric Fantasy I would have taken three weeks off. But this is the chance of a lifetime.'

So it was in just four days that a set-lipped but rather wary-stepping Roberts returned at Newbury, and only five afternoons later there he was being hoisted on to the back of the pony-sized Lyric Fantasy and by now it was a case of mind over very little matter. When you are carrying an injury the one thing you don't need is to be dieting down to the bone. And when you are wasting, the one thing you must avoid is dose of flu. Now Roberts had all three problems at once. He looked like the embodiment of the man in the Stanley Holloway monologue, 'My Word You Do Look Queer'.

Although a natural lightweight at only 5ft 1in, he has muscled himself up to almost eight stone to cope with the extra driving he found British horses needed when he took up the challenge here in 1986. But Lyric Fantasy looked to be one of the fastest fillies for at least a generation. She was bidding to become the first of her age and sex ever to land the Nunthorpe Stakes, the most coveted and competitive sprint of the season. As a two-year-old she was set to carry only

7st 7lb. There never has been much flesh on Roberts's leathery, elfin face and now it was hollowed out like a museum exhibit. It's a good job it's the horse who does the running.

But it's a man who does the thinking and that has long been Roberts's strongest suit. Stiff or not he had walked the track before racing and noted a longer, potentially speed-sapping growth of grass ahead of his stands-side draw. Flu-ridden or no, he had studied the form closely enough to be sure that other horses, most notably Pat Eddery's mount Freddie Lloyd, were likely to have the legs of Lyric Fantasy in those speed-blazing opening furlongs. She would have to hurry but her little general must keep his cool. It has been ever thus. Teenagers who only weigh 4st don't get to cope with farm life, let alone become the first South African apprentice to rule the seniors, unless they have brains to match their brawn. 'It's a gift really,' Roberts says with a refreshing lack of modesty. 'I've always felt comfortable around animals. Felt I was able to communicate with them. I think it is very important. You've got to make them trust you. Down at the start I was pulling Lyric Fantasy's ears, talking to her, making her relax.'

He may be a millionaire, have a thousand-acre farm back in Natal and have kicked home horses to the tune of over £1.3m this season but the race is one not just of business but of vocation. His picture now hangs on the walls of the Jockeys' Academy at Summerveld on the rolling hills inland from Durban. Very soon after he arrived there in 1968 they knew they had something special. Seventeen seasons, 11 championships and several sideboards' worth of trophies later, the South African public knew it too. 'I had nothing left to prove,' Roberts said last week. 'I had a lot of support to switch to training but I knew I'd regret it if I didn't have another crack at England.'

Even now, six years in, a 20-winner lead in our jockeys' table, an ever-growing list of major prizes on his escutcheon, there is no hiding the hurt of that first abortive slow-horse summer of '78. True, he clocked up 25 winners, but for a man who was topping the century with Bradmanesque regularly at home it was a journeyman's total. And for those who had read the 'greatest living rider' cuttings which had preceded him, there was plenty of chance to gloat. 'It was degrading in a way,' Roberts says. 'I would sit in the weighing room sometimes, boiling over with frustration knowing I could do things better than the others. I felt like going up to people and saying "Just give me one ride on your horse and I'll show you what I can do". I think this is the hardest school in the world to break into. But once you are in it's the best.'

The second coming was not an instant sensation, but with the aspirant Alex Stewart and the seasoned Clive Brittain to back him, it was soon clear that this was a pilot who needed watching. 'Forty-two winners in 1986 was quite satisfactory,' Roberts says.

'But it was not until we beat Reference Point [the Derby winner] with Mtoto in the Eclipse the next year that things really took off. That Sunday the phone never stopped. It was like night and day.'

Soon the little figure, hunched slightly upright behind the mane, became a fixture in the big races of the European circuit, and centuries here became as standard as they had been in South Africa. But not a championship. Despite a keenness to oblige which mimicking critics put into the 'teacher's pet' category, Roberts couldn't get closer than third in the jockeys' title. For a man who had been raised as a phenomenon it was still not good enough. The astute and industrious Graham Rock was hired as agent, the ambition was hatched, and Rock, in an investment he will take to his grave as underplayed by a factor of 10, had £100 on Roberts for the title at 100–1.

'We didn't make that fast a start,' Rock says, adopting the first person plural which is the agent's hallmark, 'but things really began to buzz in May. Michael is incredibly thorough and never wavered all through the heavy two meetings-a-day schedule we've had over the last three months. We've had over 750 rides already. That's 200 more than Pat Eddery. With 155 on the board we have a 20-winner cushion but these last three months can still be very difficult because Pat will have many good horses to come.'

Roberts may not have wavered, but six weeks ago the plane carrying him did. One of the wheel struts snapped before take-off after an evening meeting at Chester. Two hedges were holed, a clump of trees was miraculously avoided before a mud-filled ditch claimed them and South Africa's foremost export had to remember those early swimming lessons on the beaches of the Atlantic. It was a mind-numbing episode by any standards, but was thankfully given a chuckling postscript when the little party, by now clad in hospital pyjamas, stopped at a late-night kebab joint *en route* to Newmarket and were reported by the owner under suspicion of escaping from an institution.

Roberts relates a story at the end of racing on Friday. The Sandown weighing room is emptying fast. Cauthen has already left. Eddery is pulling on that blue Oxford shirt and tailored slacks that are his uniform. Carson rubs a towel across that buttery, pigeon-chested torso. There's been another winner. The weekend schedule is less hectic, just a single ride at Deauville today, tomorrow off, one ride on Tuesday. He can begin to talk of the injury and the dieting in the past tense. But the riding remains in the present. 'She's always going well even, though the others can look to have her ruffled.'

We're back to Lyric Fantasy on Thursday and the 57 seconds' worth of decision-making under pressure which had been the highlight of his week. 'It's in the middle part of the race that her speed really showed. But I didn't want to use her too soon. When I finally asked her, she did it sweetly.'

The sentences are quick. The words exact, the affection, like the ambition, unashamedly naked. 'I really want to do this,' he said as he went to the car, 'I want to show I can make them run.'

*He showed them all right. He continued at such a relentless rate that by season's
end he had not only taken the title from Pat Eddery but had become the first
jockey to beat the 200-winner mark since Gordon Richards in 1952.*

*Being the champion becomes an all-consuming obsession. The early
morning demands of work riding followed by racing's country-wide daily
repetition, gives the aspiring champion the most exhausting schedule in sport.
One day we tried it with Richard Dunwoody.*

Refined to the point of perfection

22 November 1992

The figure aloof and apart in the storm, the face pale and hooded staring into the
rain ahead. Nine hours, 11 horses and two sauna baths later Richard Dunwoody
was to voice it. 'Concentration,' he said wiping the sweat from those flint-hard
eyes, 'is everything.'

Not much sign of sweat on Wednesday morning. The wind blowing hard
and wet over Mandown, six different horses to school for the trainer Nicky
Henderson and straightaway you notice that as educators go Dunwoody is a cool
one. Other jockeys will chaff and joke, give plenty of 'there's a good fella' slaps
along the neck, Richard is as silent as a centaur.

There can be an almost eerie quality about it. For this is not the frowning
concentration of the second rate, it's the detached absorption of an expert totally
wrapped up in his job. Watching him on Wednesday was to think, 'What an
expert, what a job.'

Although the remarkable Peter Scudamore has topped the numerical
winners list these past seven jumping seasons, Richard Dunwoody has out-
performed him in both number of rides and money won for three years now, and
by the end of yesterday led him 50–44 in winners and by £261,000 to £153,000
in prize money. That's a good return, but it's hard-earned.

The first horse to be ridden up the three schooling fences in the slightly
sheltered hollow was the talented chaser Sparkling Flame. He had run badly last
time and now was a-fidget and a-tizz. Dunwoody, in green waterproof jacket,
with matching leggings was there to put things right.

Twice they came thundering up over the fences, and that close you can
sense the force of mind over matter. Dunwoody's style has been refined and
refined since he appeared as an already beautifully streamlined prospect eight
seasons back. It's now a distinctive form of deep-balanced, forward-leaning
control which allows the horse beneath to operate with the minimum interfer-
ence from the man atop.

So as Sparkling Flame bore down on the fence beside us, there was no
primitive pumping of the arms and rousting of the heels for take-off. Look close
and you can sometimes detect slight sharp adjustments of the rein as the rider
organizes his horse's stride ready to flow up and over the obstacle. Racegoers

watch the finish, but jockeys talk about the stride. In jump racing it's nearly everything.

'Schooling' is their one chance of rehearsal. The racetrack will add the jostle and pace of competition, but out here you can test and tune the athlete on

Richard Dunwoody: compulsion in the saddle

which your money and your neck will depend some coming afternoon. Little wonder those long Dunwoody eyelids shutter down in concentration.

After Sparkling Flame came the high-fronted chestnut Billy Bathgate, whose apparent understanding of Wednesday's lessons did not last through Ascot on Friday when a mistake on take-off saw Dunwoody fired groundwards at the first open ditch.

Then a bold-jumping ex-Irish beast called Lisaleen Prince, his first lesson in 10 months, but no sign of his shamrock skills being forgotten. Three different chasers, three more rehearsals for the memory bank, but this was only the beginning. The rain was coming on strong now, but so were the hurdlers, a dozen or so of Henderson hopefuls braving the elements up on the top schooling ground above us. The only way to get there was by tractor.

Horseracing always borders on the absurd, and suddenly we were into one of those laugh-out-loud moments, trainer, jockey and journalist all piled into the covered tractor cab while the rains lashed outside. Dunwoody understood it, but confined himself to a smile. There was still much work to do.

Hurdles schooling never seems as risky a deal, the obstacles small and flimsy by comparison, the rhythm of the jump less crucial. But if Richard is to hold off the relentless Scudamore, every trick will need turning. And besides these are young horses still unfamiliar with the whole ethos of jumping. It only takes one false move to have a rider on the floor and half a ton of animal on top of him. On Wednesday we nearly got it.

It happened, as it usually does, at the very end of the session. Two other horses had been through their lessons with no more incident than one swerve right-handed. Now a narrow grey three-year-old was to have her first attempt at the hurdles after an intensive jumping course elsewhere. The weather was getting terrible, the lead horse went too slow, and the stubborn lady dug her toes in. No harm done this time. Dunwoody sat firm, Henderson re-routed the little posse to hop over some beginners' poles before coming back and finally completing the bigger hurdles without incident.

There had been no drama made out of the crisis but Dunwoody had needed to resort to plenty of goading to unravel the knot in the filly's mind. As she was ridden away afterwards and the three of us walked down the slope to the magnificent Seven Barrows spread Henderson took over from Peter Walwyn this summer, thoughts were of breakfast and for some of us a feeling that the day was half over. Richard had hardly started.

The Hendersons' kitchen is Aga-lined and dog-strewn, the classic trainer's mix in the Lambourn valley and far beyond. Dunwoody is later to eat a full bacon-and-egg breakfast, but first he hits the phone. Long, low and intense discussions of tomorrow's and other riding plans with his agent Robert Kington, who in the intricate relationships of the racing game is actually Peter Scudamore's brother-in-law.

As he talks, Dunwoody has the faraway look of a fighter pilot being briefed for a combat mission. So much combat, so many missions, some 800 race rides during the season, five of them that afternoon at Kempton. Francome used to laugh away the pressure, Dunwoody wraps it around him. 'Sometimes you talk to him and it's as if he is not there,' says the jockey's valet John Buckingham. 'I thought Scu was dedicated but this chap is something else.'

The track of course is the judgement ground, and this is to be one of the good days. Three winners, a third and a sixth. Scudamore has won the big race up at Haydock, but the championship lead has been extended even if the afternoon has had its moments.

Chief amongst these is the last-fence blunder of Calapaez when left clear in the third. The horse is tired, Richard shoos him into the obstacle to get one good long final leap, but Calapaez ignores the take-off call, gallops on to hit the obstacle, and he and his jockey land untidily on the other side.

Such mistakes are the spurs that drive the perfectionist Dunwoody into continuing to hone the skills he has been working at in his mind ever since he listened at his jockey father's knee in Northern Ireland. His unparalleled big-race successes – West Tip's Grand National in 1986, Charter Party's Gold Cup in '88, Kribensis's Champion Hurdle in 1990 – have only heightened that drive, not softened it.

Wednesday afternoon was a good example. Calapaez's victory was followed by Gambling Royal in the three-mile chase. This turned out to be an impressive warm-up for Saturday's Hennessy Gold Cup, horse and rider a powerful blend throughout the race bar one blemish four fences from home when Dunwoody sat still to allow Gambling Royal to 'fiddle' his way over, only for his horse to get too close and clout it.

But the best was kept to last. A novice chase in the gathering gloom, a well-balanced chestnut called Camelot Knight in against an odds-on but dangerously fearless favourite called Rocco. From a mile out the duel was joined. Four fences from home Richard allows Camelot Knight his head, and his partner repays him with a spring-heeled leap that disappoints his rival. Into the straight and he has him.

The fences come quickly at Kempton. Three in the run for home, three allies for Dunwoody, three dangers for Jamie Osborne on Rocco. Dunwoody presses on at the first. Rocco is too stretched for safety, hits it hard and the impact capsizes him.

Afterwards the riders sprawl in front of the weighing-room video, colours off, blue body protectors revealed to look all the world like flak-jackets, and the jockeys some police patrol reliving the action.

It was time to talk, and for all normal beings an excuse to switch off. For Dunwoody it's into the sauna. At 28, his 5ft 9in frame is the leanest imaginable amalgam of bone and muscle. You wonder why he should bother to boil off another pound to make 10st 2lb on what was to be an unsuccessful ride at Wincanton the next day, and the answer is revealing. 'I know I can get down to that weight and still be 100 per cent,' he says, the steam already taking its toll on his questioner. 'So why not?'

Richard Dunwoody abandoned what could have been a university education career to follow his calling and thus far in he is fascinated not by the pressures but by the possibilities. 'You can never get it absolutely right,' he says. 'Every day you keep on learning, but at this stage it's all in the mind.'

With the heat rising he has moved to the lower bench of the sauna. He admits that he was sweating too much in the early part of the season, but when pressed on achievements mentions not the Grand National or Desert Orchid's epic King George, but the five-timer he scored at Chepstow a fortnight ago. 'Desert Orchid was special, but the applause was for him. At Chepstow I felt I had done something.'

The door of the sauna opens and Jamie Osborne limps in, his right foot injured in Rocco's fall. Osborne, a dashing, more cavalier figure, joshes Dunwoody about 'getting me at it' and admits that he is happy to let his feelings hang out. 'Yes,' says Dunwoody. 'Some people accused me of looking glum after riding the first three winners at Chepstow, but I had two very good rides to come. I was concentrating on them.'

With awareness and rewards ever increasing it is no surprise that we are producing a new breed of enlightened but super-serious sportsman. Richard Dunwoody has none of the cussedness of a Boycott or a Mansell, but there is no doubt that he is a young man with an obsession loose in the psyche.

As he towels off, changes into suit and raincoat and then heads out into the Kempton night you remember the words of his long-time friend, the Jockeys' Association secretary Michael Caulfield: 'His dedication is amazing, but sometimes so much so that it is absolutely frightening.'

Tackled about this, about the possible self-defeating aspects of such a brutally self-denying regime, he thinks hard and says coolly, 'But if it gets success, it cannot be self-defeating.'

Richard Dunwoody is pitching at the most demanding title in sport. It's his predicament that the demands are still harshest from himself.

Dunwoody was eventually to win the title, which Peter Scudamore with his Martin Pipe support had so long denied him. It was a necessary adornment to one of the greatest riders in the game. But what a task these boys set themselves. By the spring it had finally caught up with Scudamore.

Scu: role model of commitment

11 April 1993

He looks younger already. Some twit on the radio had asked why he was retiring at 'only' 34. There are more than 5,000 rides in the answer. Peter Scudamore's 16 seasons and record 1,678 winners would have made a dodderer out of Peter Pan.

The miracle is how well he has lasted, for right from the start it was clear that here was a commitment quite daunting in its intensity. Mothers, rivals and camp followers alike, we were worried about him. The most common comment in those early years was: 'He must ease off or he'll kill 'is bloody self.'

All champions are dedicated. All young pretenders come in saying they will give it their best shot. But nobody ever had quite such a quiet sense of destiny as the young man at Worcester in December 1979. He had just ridden his 20th winner of the season, his 30th in just 16 months at the game. He spoke very levelly and there was not a hint of conceit. 'I don't want to compare myself with anyone else,' he said, the pale skin already stretched tight across the cheekbones. 'I want to be the best.'

To the mind, all other assets bow. True, Peter was a natural sportsman and his father Michael had won the Grand National on Oxo in 1954, but it was always that will to win which hit you.

Other hopefuls would flatter with their flair and polish. This one was serious. This one had determination deep into the toenails. Even if it was never a particularly pretty sight.

The unmatchable flow of Francome over a fence, the rhythm of Dunwoody in a finish, were not things you would associate with Scudamore. The style was effective rather than polished, but the memory left was of a compulsive presence behind the mane, an implacable stare inside those goggles.

The horses felt it too. Sometimes to a fault. He could be something of a whirling dervish with his whip at the beginning. It took several run-ins with the stewards before a compromise could be reached. Even this season there was one day at Taunton when the authorities, in their wisdom, penalized him and his now felt-padded whip for trying too hard. He understood the public concern but he was a hard man to argue with.

For he was interesting. He was an intelligent, God-fearing man who had thought his profession through. That was courage in itself. Many of us did not like to dwell on what might happen on the dark side of the moon. Peter was not afraid to field the question.

'It will never be very good,' he said about Carvill's Hill's jumping when the world waited for the ill-fated showdown at Cheltenham. 'I am not saying whether he will get round or whether he won't. All I am saying is that he has a good chance of it.'

But those who reason do not usually remain. The logic of the hurt, of the bad places down among the hooves, invades the psyche. The mind may make appointments but the nerve will not allow the match. Only right at the end did it get to Scudamore. So he quit.

What made him exceptional was that for all his success, for all his intelligence, his wider interest in his own and other sports, he retained the commitment of the driven man.

At times he would be so tired and wasted that you wondered why he pushed himself so much. Then you realized that the hardship, the brutal self-denial, had become essential to him. It was the whetstone on which the will kept sharp. He was a Christian. He knew the parable of the talents. He had been given opportunities and he had to make the best of them.

In later years he was even given Martin Pipe. They suited each other. The trainer, a self-taught bookie's son from Taunton prepared to challenge every principle in his search for winners, and the traditionally taught champion jockey with an open mind. They tore up the record books and rewrote the training manual. They stuck the silly jealous whispers back up the passages from whence they had come. If you wanted to believe bad about Pipe, you had to include Scudamore. You might as well describe The Mall as bent.

So we had all those memories of the Pipe-trained trail-blazers with Scudamore dictating things from the front. For a while it became possible to think that this was all they could do. But the excellence evolved, and the two finest moments for the partnership came with horses who attacked from off the pace. From a whole impossible fence behind in the case of Bonanza Boy at Kempton, the most implacable Scudamore ride of all. And cool and deadly through the Champion Hurdle pack last month in the Scudamore masterstroke that was Granville Again.

By then Peter had become a figure acknowledged throughout the land, honoured at Buckingham Palace, welcomed through the television screen for his blinding rectitude and common sense. But being a Boy Scout would never be enough of an explanation. The real fascination of Scudamore was that deep down he was the hardest of the hard.

It was never meant to be a game for pansies. You had to be ruthless or be wronged. Scudamore was normally very fair, but he took no prisoners. One day at Newbury he strayed across the line. He ran another jockey literally off the track rather than concede his position on the inner. Afterwards he took his punishment, but he never withdrew the threat. The words mean the same whether they are repeated hot or cold. 'I won't,' he said quietly, 'give way to anybody.'

But now he has. To the man with the scythe, and not before time. He went out with a flourish, with one final, sweetly ridden winner and as grateful and loving a pat as a horse ever got from its jockey. He will be missed, but how he deserves the new life up ahead.

He taught us something: that it is wrong to say the past alone has heroes; and that a brave man can still swing a tiger by the tail. He will be remembered as long as the game goes by.

So too will Willie Carson. For the quite astonishing vitality that not only drove him from the most unpromising beginnings to the commanding heights of the flat-racing team, but that kept him there in full flood right into his fifties. Whatever he's on, we ought to bottle it.

Carson bids for an Arc of triumph

3 October 1993

The rewards still beckon. Above the crowds, in the paddocks and even now, six weeks away from Willie Carson's 51st birthday, out there on the track. Today's ride on Armiger in the Arc could be the biggest pay day of them all.

Of course a lot more than lucre makes his treadmill turn, but never forget that Mr Carson is a Scotsman. At 13 he offered his mother the choice between his fifty two and a half pence newspaper round or the tips which came with it. 'She chose the wage packet,' he says. 'I smiled because the tips were bigger.'

Five hundred miles and four decades separate Mr Hogg's newsagent shop in Stirling from Tattersalls' gilded sales ring at Newmarket. But that Carson smile and his now trademark cackle as the gavel came down last week at 90,000 guineas for one of his Minster Stud yearlings was just the same. Then, and now, it meant that Willie Carson had cracked it.

Willie Carson. Into his fifties but still a major player

It has not been easy and neither is he. He has had to work too hard and risk too much to be tolerant of the frailties of others, or patient with his own.

The Cotswold manor house, the oak-railed paddocks and the state-of-the-art stud buildings have all been funded by his own work. By the extraordinary skills he has developed in the saddle, by the talent he found in his tininess.

He brought nothing with him. Unlike Piggott, Eddery and Dettori, all three of them sons of champion jockeys, Willie Carson had no racing connections. He only espoused the game because there are not many manual jobs for five-foot adults, seven and a half stones on the scale.

It was only through the newspaper round that he could fund the first riding lessons with Mrs McFarlane up at Dunblane. All he had to declare was an energy hot enough to brighten the national grid.

We all know the outline of the story that I helped him tell in his book, which comes out this month. The struggling apprenticeship in Middleham, the unpromising start, only 22 winners by the time he was 21, the car crash which nearly crippled him and his family, the battles with Piggott for the championship, the graduation to become the Queen's jockey, the near fatal fall in 1981, the accident to Dick Hern and the royal crisis it later spawned, the triumphs of Nashwan and Dayjur in the blue silks of Sheikh Hamdan. Yes, we know the story, what of the man?

He is more difficult than he looks. Sure, he can still turn on the wide-eyed Scottish charm for the TV cameras and his race analyses over the replays are an unmatched masterclass of their kind. But there is a chippiness about Willie that at times can give an uncomfortable edge.

It was apparent last week as he worked his way towards Friday's century of winners for the season, his 22nd in 23 years. (1984's score was restricted to 97 after he suffered a horrible fall in Milan.)

Monday's four rides at Bath produced a third and two seconds. Tuesday's six at Brighton provided one second and then four consecutive thirds before a colt called Wakt became the 99th of the year.

Six rides at Salisbury, followed by another six at Newmarket, failed to bring the 100 up. Summer Pageant was a filly a-sweat with worry. As she left the paddock and jig-jogged past our TV position you could see Willie's hand stroking soothingly at the base of the neck. A second later she came back. Upside down.

'She just flipped,' Willie said afterwards, 'just reared straight over. It's the worst accident you could have on the track.' The absence of emotion was just the same as it had been when the filly had got shakily to her feet in front of us. No shouting, no tremors, just this diminutive little general ordering his mount to be led out for a safer mounting spot. Of all the qualities in Carson, nothing warms you like the guts of him.

For he has been to where the bad times are. It was from another TV rostrum, at York in August 1981, that we waited in horrid silence as the ambulance brought Willie back up the course. Ambulances tending ordinary accidents speed hastily to hospital. This one crawled like a hearse. It nearly was one.

He admits the accident, which put him out of action for the rest of that season, changed him. 'I wasn't so happy-go-lucky,' he said. 'Life had been great fun before, everything was a joke, riding was a joke, I'd been determined to be a jockey, determined to win and be clever in my job. I don't think anything ever worried me. Until the accident.'

The headaches then became not only physical ones. He had just commissioned work on what has become a genuine dream house just east of Cirencester. He had unravelled both his first marriage and a subsequent relationship, and was about to embark on his present partnership with the devoted, if occasionally long-suffering, Elaine. He would need all his guts to get back in.

He did that and a lot more besides. He was champion for the fifth time in

1983, narrowly missed his century because of that Italian accident in 1984 and since then has always been at least fourth in the numerical rankings while actually topping the money-winning list in 1989, 1990 and 1991.

That most recent lucrative Indian summer came largely in the blue and white silks of Sheikh Hamdan al Maktoum, the real test of character came earlier. When Dick Hern was paralysed in a hunting crash, what had been the most powerful stable in the country was set on a downward spiral that would end with the severing of the royal lease at West Ilsley and the furore that would follow.

Willie says his oft-recorded pro-Hern piece but does admit that he obviously looks 'on only one side of the argument'. Unhappily and unavoidably, some of the old animosities will briefly re-emerge, but looking back it is clear that the real crisis came earlier when a wish to avoid comment on the beleaguered Hern led to a falling-out with the press, and a lack of consistent winners brought self-doubt high on the Carson agenda.

Of all the comments in the long hours of taping, one of the most vehement was about a small trainer replacing him with Pat Eddery. 'He said I wasn't strong enough,' Willie snorted. 'Troy, Henbit, and Nashwan were the three largest Derby winners this century. Me not strong enough!'

Yet phenomenon though he may be, you have to doubt how strong, at 50, those muscles can remain. While he has got the hundred up again and gathered more than £1.3m in British prize-money alone, Willie at present is only sixth in the jockey's table and admits that some of the joints are creaking now. One piece of logic says it is a young man's game. Another that it is the getting of wisdom that matters, that youthful energy is what is needed from the set of legs beneath you.

For the 1993-vintage Carson is a long way removed from the famous 'brute force and ignorance' assessment of the raw champion who won his first title in 1972.

Then, the wonder of Willie was his newly patented method of gathering more and more effort from his partners all the way to the line. He was a little compulsive figure clamped in behind the mane. If he was in against your horse, he was enemy No 1.

His cheery outgoing attitude, so different from the mysterious silence around the Piggott mask, disguises an inquisitive intelligence that is now apparent almost to a fault. Willie Carson knows the cost of things. He knows the score.

He knows there will not be many more opportunities to win today's five-million-franc Arc de Triomphe, the one big race which in 15 attempts has eluded him. He had not even sat on Armiger yet. That is no problem. 'He seems a straightforward horse,' Willie said of his chunky chestnut mount after a long conference with Henry Cecil and stable jockey Willie Ryan. 'He will love the ground, and his people are very keen on the way he's going.'

And if Armiger were to collect, might that not be a time to bow out while still at the top? As Carson comes to his aeroplane you notice the silver threads in the hair, but even after six rides you have to admit that this is certainly no jaded wreck. 'I think it's something I'll decide on the spur of the moment,' he said, 'but not just yet.'

He is always a ridiculously dapper little figure. White shirt, smart check hacking jacket, cord trousers and those deep blue eyes, clear and challenging still. You remember that he will be home with his feet up in 40 minutes, long before you grind towards the queues at the Dartford Tunnel. You recognize something obvious. That this is a heck of a good life for anybody to be playing.

Sure, it is a treadmill. If you have got your days as organized as Carson has, it is a treadmill any 50-year-old might envy. Still winning at a young man's game, still fulfilling a talent that has been a lifetime in the making. And, better still for a canny Scot, now making a success of the breeding business on the side.

'Yes,' he said from the co-pilot's seat, while the moustachioed Biggles figure of Alan 'Bilko' Biltcliffe did his final preparations. 'One yearling made 28,000 guineas last night, the other 90,000. Think of that.'

He snapped his fingers together like winning jockeys do. The Piper Saratoga taxied off and made for the western sky. Stormy weather was forecast. For Willie too? Maybe. But not yet.

An unhappy postscript to that story was the less than rapturous welcome received by the Carson autobiography I put together that autumn. Trying to avoid the usual 'ghosted' banalities, I left in more candour than readers could stomach, and also managed to make such a mess of proofreading that the first of many uncorrected errors appeared in the very first line.

I deserved most of the brickbats but didn't get them. For a brief while Willie had to endure such tabloid epithets as 'Racing's Mister Nasty'. Hurt though he was, he answered by buckling down and delivering once more on the racetrack. Another Derby winner with Erhaab in 1994.

Fresh talent is the lifeblood of any game. New shoots will spring up every season but it is only occasionally that you realize you are watching the emergence of a full new flower. That was the excitement of the autumn of '93.

Special magic of Adrian Maguire

17 October 1993

You don't need the tributes, you only have to look. Adrian Maguire is doing something special this jumping season. Go out there and watch.

What you see is magic down the reins. With a blend of technique, opportunity and self-belief, the 22-year-old Irishman is filling his mounts with a confidence that is a wonder to behold. You think I am exaggerating? Not a lot.

Adrian Maguire: muddy, maybe, but a shining talent in any weather

The statistics show that with 43 winners since the new term started at the end of July, Adrian Maguire has already built up a 17-success cushion over the champion, Richard Dunwoody. In the two years since he quit his native land and came over to England in the summer of 1991, he has already put a double century of winners and Cool Ground's Gold Cup to his name.

But these are early days, the good horses are only just emerging from their summer break. It's too long and risky a haul before the season closes next June to get into title-chasing talk. What matters, what is exciting, is what is happening now. It even happened at Worcester last Saturday.

There should be surprise in the statement. For Maguire it was a rare winnerless afternoon. For Worcester, with the welcome presence of BBC cameras re-routed from waterlogged Ascot and with the flood-swollen River Severn brimming to its banks, there were other things on the mind than the pixie-faced young pilot who ended both his last two rides in the ambulance room. But if you looked you could see enough. Oh yes, plenty enough.

You often see it better in the smaller arenas, on less heralded horses. The star shines out among the journeymen. It's a confidence you can touch. Even walking round the paddock you can sense it flowing from man to beast. Over 30 years I have seen it spill out from several very different champions. From Biddlecombe one remarkable five-winner day at Ludlow, from O'Neill with his extraordinary bubbling drive, from the peerless Francome, from the iron will that was Scudamore, from the present perfection of technique that is Dunwoody. Believe me, it's flooding from Maguire now.

The first race was a selling hurdle. Despite the mellifluous tones of Peter O'Sullevan celebrating 35 years of Grandstand in the commentary box, this couldn't pretend to be other than the lowest form of jumping contest and Maguire's ride, At Peace, one of the game's least talented performers. But the jockey might have been at Cheltenham for the Champion Hurdle. He had his goggles down over his eyes even before the stable lad loosed him to canter to the start. If you are on it, why not believe in it?

Once the race is under way you see the mechanics without which even the sunniest morale cannot prosper. The truth is that Maguire does it differently. He rides differently to any of the champions above, although because of his size and background there are several memories of Jonjo O'Neill. He rides like Adrian Maguire.

The central trick is in the body position. Most jump jockeys are either too big to fold away neatly behind the mane, or too small to generate the physical dominance which can be needed to lug some half-ton of steeplechaser round the track. At five feet five and one half inches and nine and a half stone in his socks, Maguire is the perfect package for the national hunt rider. The 18 hurdlers come sploshing past on the spongy Worcester turf. At the back of the field, balanced and breathing as easily as if this was just a hack to the great sunlit cathedral up on the bank, At Peace is at peace with himself.

Because of his size Maguire doesn't have to involve his body in any of the bent-around streamlining other rivals require. Because of his position above the saddle, he is able to balance his partner with a greater length of rein and therefore greater freedom with which to gallop. Because of his confidence they want to run and jump.

Not always fast or high enough, of course. Only Pegasus was perfect, and the wings on his fetlocks would never have passed a stewards' enquiry. There was no Pegasus last Saturday. The nearest thing was that super-popular 12-year-old Panto Prince, who jumped like a stag in the two-and-a-half mile steeplechase to record the 23rd success of a fine career. The trouble with Maguire and a grey horse called Mustaveaswig was that they had neither antlers nor wings to match.

But it didn't stop him asking. Turning into the straight for the final time the two horses were still together, with Panto Prince getting the better of things. They landed together over the third last and as they came towards us, Maguire crouched low into his horse, grabbed tight on the reins, used his whip once hard and left-handed, then let out a 'Geronimo' yell which recalled something a lot stronger than perfect mechanics at the root of it all.

From the very start, from teenage pony racing days, he has wanted winning like a wolf wants its meat. In fact he had begun as a nine-year-old. An older brother, Michael, had been a jockey and another, Vinny, would have been but for a fatal car accident in 1990. It was Michael who took Adrian off to 'the ponies'. Two hundred winners Adrian rode on those tiny, flag-fluttering circuits that abound from Wexford to Donegal. Ah yes and the Dingle Derby itself, the 'blue riband' of pony racing.

So while this little figure bearing down on us at the second last at Worcester is still comparatively new to the British racing fan, he is already well-seasoned in the winning game. He has even had his share of hurt and losing. At 15 he joined Con Horgan's stables in Berkshire only for homesickness to claim him back to Kilmessan. At 16 he prematurely turned professional only to change back to amateur to ride point-to-points for the strong-minded Michael Hourigan, at which discipline he broke all records by riding six winners one day at Dromahane in County Cork. 'Three of the winners were mine,' Hourigan remembered, 'but the others were real yokes. Adrian just carried them around.'

Mustaveaswig is no 'yoke' but he was floundering now. He and Panto Prince swept up to the fence, 'Panto' going the stronger, the grey at full and dangerous stretch. An old pilot on the ground pleads caution. Maguire leans in and looses more rein to his partner. Mustaveaswig comes up a long, long way from the obstacle, reaches right out to the other side and continues a vain battle to the line. 'Caution' has not yet been learned from the lexicon.

That has its dangers, as the next two races will witness. At that very same fence in the two-mile chase, a horse called Among Friends does not get the take-off message, takes the birch with his chest and somehow comes out the other side still galloping. But the impact has Maguire treading air, before gravity smacks him cruelly to earth. In the final race the exit is even quicker. A beautiful animal called Arctic Course slips up on landing over the first hurdle and our little hero lies biting the grass in agony of impact.

Back in the wooden changing room which sits likes a boating hut above the choking brown waters of the Severn, Maguire winces as he inspects the bruising where a stray hoof whacked his left foot. 'It's sore,' he says, 'but nothing's broken. I will be all right for Carlisle on Monday.' He goes off to wash, just a towel round a physique which is quite comfortably chunky compared with the honed-down bodies of larger-framed colleagues.

One of those, Graham Bradley, himself a skilled and stylish player who won his Gold Cup on Bregawn back in 1985, is not slow to pass judgement. 'Adrian Maguire', Graham says bluntly, 'is the most talented young rider that I have ever seen. I think he's as good as Jonjo now. Apart from his riding, he's got his life very organized. If he holds together, there is no limit to what he could achieve.'

Proof of that talent, and indeed of the organization, existed aplenty last week. Two winners at Carlisle on Monday, another at Sedgefield on Tuesday, and back south for a third at Taunton on Thursday. Three successes, 300 miles and counting from his home near Swindon made possible by Sabrina Winter, his supportive and hard-driving girlfriend, and Dave Roberts, his ever-questing agent, both of whom have been with him since he joined Toby Balding at Whitcombe two much shyer years ago.

'Sabrina and Dave take a lot of the pressure off me,' said Maguire, who has won a deserved reputation for treating all horses as if they were potential champions. 'I can just go out there and get on with the riding. There are some exciting "hosses" up ahead.'

Enthusiasm should not be confused with simplicity. 'You should have seen him this morning,' David Nicholson said on Thursday night. 'I put him on a hurdler who is a bit dodgy and said "See if he will jump". Adrian just went straight down one line of fences, ping, ping, ping. And straight back up the next.'

Nicholson was a very considerable jockey in his era, and last year provided Richard Dunwoody with a sheaf of big winners before his move to Martin Pipe on the retirement of Peter Scudamore. 'Watching him this morning was a joy,' Nicholson said lyrically of his new pilot. 'The way they jump for him is simply mouth-watering. My horses are just about ready. If I have a decent season, he will be champion jockey for certain.'

Maybe you don't need the tributes. But they sure make you want to look.

Adrian Maguire was the new star jump racing needed. He was the challenge that Richard Dunwoody had to face. Looking back now it is scarcely believable how much both men went through before the old wolf finally saw off his young contender at hay-making time. The final scores were 198–194. They had had

1,806 rides between them. Third on the list was Jamie Osborne with 'just' 105 winners from 497 rides. Maguire had not made it but he had pushed the champion to new heights. He had brought a fizz to the game.

Flat racing needs its stars too, and in Frankie Dettori it's come up with a real sparkler. Just as everyone was wondering if anyone could take over the mantle of Pat Eddery, or erase the ageless shadow of Lester Piggott, Frankie has taken over like an exhilarating breath of Italian fresh air.

But what in hindsight looks an inexorable rise to the top went through a hiatus in 1993. The next year was the one where young Frankie put everything behind him with a twelve-month tour de force. *No champion's season had ever been grabbed as early as this.*

Dettori's flying start in champion stakes

16 January 1994

He's a star back on course, back on any course, back at Lingfield on Tuesday. Frankie Dettori is staking out his claims for the Flat-race jockeys' title two months before most people thought it had begun.

Sure they started racing on the sand at Lingfield and Southwell four winters ago, but it was dismissed by purists as fourth-division betting fodder for unsung trainers and journeyman jocks. The big guns didn't return until the windblown grass of the Lincoln Handicap meeting in March. January was a time for Caribbean holidays and exotic 'busman's' in Eastern parts. That was Frankie last year. And to a fault.

For the first time we were worried about him. Not about his talent or his temperament, but of where he was going in life. He'd had class written all over him from the moment he started with Luca Cumani's Newmarket yard as the teenage son of Gianfranco Dettori, 10 times the Italian champion. And when the winners came he brought a flash of joking Neapolitan sunshine to an often pinch-faced racing world. He was champion apprentice in 1989, in the next season he topped 100 winners at 19, even younger than Lester Piggott had been 35 years before. Yes, the star was on its course. How then did we fear an eclipse less than 12 months ago?

There was a touch of provincial disapproval about it. Frankie didn't seem to want us any more. He was wintering in Hong Kong, he was talking freely about taking a contract out there but was avoiding discussions with Cumani back home. The grapevine insisted that Hong Kong had its reservations. Frankie sailed blithely on. Cumani had to hire another rider in understandable pique. There was much tut-tutting about 'burning of boats'.

Come April and it was bonfire night. With his future still uncertain, fewer than 10 winners on the board, Dettori was picked up by the police in Oxford Street and cautioned for drug possession. There was no charge. 'The substance involved was a small amount of cocaine,' the statement said. 'It wasn't me and the whole thing has been a big mix-up,' said Frankie who, to this day, clams shut at any mention of the incident. But the damage was done. Hong Kong was not even a mirage now.

The Jeremiahs shook their heads in doleful satisfaction, observant race

Frankie Dettori in full flow during his first championship year in '94

fans sat back and watched the action. If Dettori was half the star we thought him to be, he would make his own fireworks now. He was hungry and brilliant.

Ironically, the first real explosion had been the day before the Oxford Street unhappiness. Uncertain Frankie may still have been, but he had five rides and won on four of them, a 15,969–1 four-timer. However did we miss that? He won the John Porter Stakes on the 25–1 shot Linpac West. He took the Greenham Stakes for Prince Khalid on Inchinor. He won the big handicap for the Queen on Tissisat and the maiden race on Winged Victory for Paul Mellon, those last two horses trained by Ian Balding, who was already beginning to mutter things like 'best young jockey I have ever seen'.

The rides came but it wasn't until June that the winners started to flood. He began Derby week 23rd in the jockeys' table, 15 winners to Pat Eddery's 50. Over the next six months he out-performed the lot, was runner-up, 149–169, to

Pat in the championship, and was contracted to ride this year for John Gosden, Sheikh Mohammed's 170-horsepower trainer at Newmarket. At 23 Frankie has it all.

Prospects that is. Performance is what happens out on the track and this year there wasn't even a day to wait. Dettori returned from his Moroccan holiday to open up with the first two winners at Lingfield on New Year's Eve and repeated the trick next day. The jockeys' championship is now decided on an all-surface, all-year basis. The young Italian's strategy was clear enough. 'Pat is always very hard to beat,' he said. 'I must get nearly 30 winners in the bag before he starts up in March.' At the end of yesterday's Lingfield meeting the score was already in double figures.

Those are the words but it is the deeds that count. Lingfield's cosy little fish bar was not exactly overcrowded midday Tuesday, less than a dozen of us sampling sandwiches whose generosity remains one of racing's best-kept secrets. TV was showing a monsoon-swept re-run of Saturday's card. We munched and hardly looked. Until we saw Dettori.

In the great scale of things the Cowslip Auction Maiden Stakes, compared to the Derby, Prix de l'Arc de Triomphe, Breeders' Cup and other Dettori targets, rates about one to ten thousand, with £3,000 to the winner, and 13 runners, none of which will ever warrant more than half a hoofbeat in history. Yet this was a ride and a half, this was what earns champions a title.

She was a filly owned by the Queen but she either couldn't go or wouldn't go. On the blurred screen you saw the four-furlong marker come up and with it Dettori's arm in an unmistakable sign of desperation. Three times he used his whip and then grabbed the reins again to pump on his reluctant partner.

Somehow she kept in touch with the leader, but as they swung off the downhill final turn with a quarter of a mile to travel it had to be on sufferance. Dettori's whip was up again, in the left hand this time, but still he was two lengths adrift, still he couldn't win. He switched the whip and suddenly the leader didn't look quite so secure, the filly was travelling a little. He put the whip back down in that upright position and (absolute trademark this) ran the reins right through his hands as he transferred his grip on the rubber. The picture changed. The filly had the legs of the leader. She had it by nearly a length at the line. She was called Success Story.

Any of us who have ever tried to earn a crust in the saddle could only have one reaction. Wonderment. At both the technique and the fitness. I don't know what he got up to in Morocco (he claims he just walked on the beach and went to bed at 9pm every night) but this boy is as fit as a flea.

Close up confirmed it. Beneath the North African tan his face was as lean and taut as I remember it. 'Yes I am very fit,' he said, 'and I am going everywhere. Mind you, last Saturday I did the double stint, flew up from here to Wolverhampton for a full book and got beat on all six of them.'

Even if there remains quite a hint of the Mediterranean joker trying to get out, he is at present so tightly in check that, at Dettori senior's insistence, all requests for interviews are being declined. (This article, of course, is a report not an interview.) No matter, don't use your ears, use your eyes.

The Hood Selling Handicap would make even the Cowslip Maiden Stakes look classy. Fourteen runners on the short list for the worst horse in Britain. Frankie rides Kenyatta, who is favourite and is about to end a 22-race losing sequence thanks to another distinctive *tour de force* from the saddle. Dettori is different. He is the latest development. He blends the low forward crouch, toe in the iron, whip as radio aerial, American style learned on earlier winter trips, with the traditional English virtues of balance and body power as well as the understanding of what makes the thoroughbred run.

But he has something else, something you don't learn anywhere, something that you can recognize in any sport, something that sets him apart. It's the gift. It's what makes Frankie the jockey whom apprentices now ape, that bookies now fear. In their different ways they sense it's there.

Bruce Raymond was 50 last birthday. He is the wisest head in the weighing room and has been something of a Dutch uncle to Frankie since he stayed with the family in Milan 10 years ago. 'Just occasionally,' he said, 'a jockey comes along who has a bit extra. Gets a good position, takes the right decision, without seeming to think about it. Lester had it. Pat has it. Now Frankie's there too.'

Bruce paused, and his conclusion puts a zing into this hardly started season: 'That is what makes him so exciting.'

The record books will show that Frankie kept up this astonishing early barrage to ride 233 winners back to the handshakes before finally giving way to exhaustion in the December chill.

Yet the Dettori annus mirabilis *was also memorable for a reminder of quite how serious the risks can be. Come the second week in May and we had to stare death in the face.*

When racing becomes a lottery of life and death

8 May 1994

It may shock, but it shouldn't truly surprise. For it is a very dangerous game. We used to call Steve Wood 'Samson', but when the nightmare came on Friday, he never had a chance.

What we are talking about is the direct hit. In both Wood's case, in a five-furlong Flat race at Lingfield, and that of Murphy over hurdles at Haydock last Monday, it was not the fall itself that did the damage but the blow from another runner. It's the moment when a horse stops being something you shout at in a betting shop and becomes half a ton of heavyweight with a hammer in its hoof.

When you are down there with the rest thundering over, you need all the protection and all the luck you can get. Murphy was unlucky to be hit at all. His fall was at the final flight after almost two miles, and although the 35mph impact was enough to knock him unconscious and to break the pelvis of his mount, Arcot, the following horse was a couple of lengths behind and would have missed him ninety-nine times out of a hundred. The blow was nearly fatal, but it was on his helmet. That save his life.

No such luck for 'Samson'. The sprint course at Lingfield is on a downward slope. After a quarter of a mile of the Moorhen Handicap, the 16 runners would have been doing almost 50mph. When his horse, Kalar, stumbled and threw him off sideways, Wood bounced back towards the rails where Paul Eddery, on Purbeck Centenary, found him straight in his path. Still, the chances were a thousand to one. There hadn't been a Flat-racing fatality since Joe Blanks at Brighton in 1981. But the hoof caught Wood slap on the chest. Even tank armour would not have saved him.

You could complain that the original incident was caused by another horse, Slivovitz, coming so close that the two runners became entangled, but such minor crowding happens in every race every day. Even if you attempted to run sprints in lanes, you would still get the occasional broken legs and slipping saddles which are the normal reasons for ending up on the floor. It was one such accident – a double front-leg fracture for a filly called Silken Knot – which looked like closing Willie Carson's career with head and neck injuries in York in 1981.

All you can do is constantly review your safety procedures and equipment, and accept that you will still find trouble ahead. There was a bitter personal irony for me last week. Having visited Murphy in Walton hospital on Thursday evening, I was just finishing an article about his miraculous recovery when the tragic news of Wood's death came through.

On my desk was a proof of a thankfully unused *Racing Post* front page from Monday. It had the uncompromising headline, Declan Murphy Dies After Horror Fall.

Now it had become an update of Mark Twain's famous 'the report of my death was an exaggeration' cable to Associated Press a century ago. The feeling as I wrote on Friday was of how far we had come in safety terms. Notwithstanding the grief at Lingfield, that progress should not be forgotten.

For while Murphy looked a mess on Thursday, the wonder was that he was there at all. He had an oxygen mask, a white lint pad on the side of the head, three days' worth of beard on those almost delicately aquiline features, and eyelids as heavy and purple and closed as a royal cushion.

Somehow he got the left lid half-open, and there was a pause as his mind swam wearily to the surface and he said hello and spoke my name. Not bad for an obituary case.

Time was when he would have been dead for certain. When I started race-riding in 1961, we still had tight-fitting cork skull-caps with no chin harness.

The helmet today is light years ahead of that, and by coincidence a further-improved model was on display last week. In three decades, there have been changes to much more than headgear. All jockeys wear protective waistcoats. Every course is inspected to make plastic rails to the course and wings to the fences standard where possible. Ambulances and intensive care units like the one at Walton are into another century now.

All this comes from improvements in both knowledge and equipment. In the wake of last week's events, official bodies within and without the sport will anxiously examine everything once again. At the risk of upsetting one of racing's oldest traditions, it's time they faced the most obvious self-inflicted hazard in the game – dehydration.

There's no suggestion it had anything to do with the latest tragedies. Indeed, Wood was such a tiny chap that he could do 7st 7lb with a big saddle. Yet there is now plenty of medical as well as anecdotal evidence (I could tell you a few stories about the Jermyn Street Baths!) of the debilitating effects of the sudden dehydration you get in sauna baths, or worse with soleric tablets. And yet what do we do in racing? We put sauna baths on every major racetrack and still row along with gallant stories of jockeys sweating away for hours before going out to ride a winner.

The fact that many great riders have been habituées of the sauna – both Richard Dunwoody and Pat Eddery are every-day regulars – does not disprove the dangers of excess. Those superstars may well sparkle as bright as ever after boiling off an unwanted pound or two, but that just confirms that race-riding is above all a question of mind over matter. But look around this week and you will see plenty of dizzy-eyed young men standing with a gaunt look of triumph in the paddock. They have done the weight!

We have all been there. The poundage becomes an obsession. Victory is not the winning post but the needle on the scales. If you get it wrong you have already used all your energy up. The lightest I did was 60 kilos (9st 6lb) on some sweaty great brute in France at Auteuil. As we jumped the hurdle on the first turn, my head was fizzing and my ears popping. I vowed that in the unlikely event of my surviving the next four minutes, I would never ride as light again.

John Francome had a similar experience in his early days with Fred Winter, and always says that his apparent helplessness in what was a televised race put his career back many months. Thereafter, this greatest of all National Hunt jockeys was very aware of the dangers of dehydration. Typically, he had found out on his own.

All too often the young jockey imbibes all those old wasting tales of Fred Archer's purging mixture, of Lester Piggott's in-car sweat-suit, of Terry Biddlecombe in the Gloucester Baths steam room on ladies day, and does things to his body which would be ludicrous to any other athlete.

Imagine a footballer, or even a Grand Prix driver, going out to battle after spending the previous two hours in the sauna. Don't imagine a boxer. Dehydration among boxers has until recently been a scandalously unexplored fact.

In racing, it need be no more. At the same press conference where he unveiled the new helmet on Thursday, Dr Michael Turner, the Jockey Club medical consultant, revealed published figures that a five per cent dehydration causes a 25 per cent loss in strength. Racing is not all about strength, but those figures should make us pause before we next applaud the idea of someone knocking off six pounds in a hurry.

This is not to say that dieting and weight reduction won't always be part of a jockey's lot. It is to state that fitness should today be something of an applied science, not just the primitive effort of yesteryear.

This summer, Dr Turner, with the help of the Injured Jockeys Fund, will bring out a 64-page booklet called Ready to Ride, incorporating a nine-month monitoring exercise conducted last year. Afterwards jockeys can have all the usual excuses for lack of fitness, but ignorance should not be among them.

The truly important thing is to recognize danger but not be fearful of it. In their very different ways, Declan Murphy and Steve Wood knew that. It had brought Murphy fame and a lifestyle beyond the imaginings of most 27-year-olds. Wood was only a year younger, and if the fruits had been more modest, 129 winners still represented a towering achievement for the midget apprentice who started at Middleham 10 years ago.

There had been some luck in it, but he got there mostly through slogging, uncomplaining hard work. On Friday, the luck ran out.

Luck is a bad word to bandy around when it comes to jumping. For the rider needs to believe he can impose some order on an inevitably disordered universe. He needs to programme the power beneath him. He needs to see the stride. That trick in March '95 belonged most of all to Norman Williamson.

With the ungainly Master Oats he had done it in the Gold Cup but now he had to put it to the test. He had to get the big beast round Aintree.

Aintree set for third Norman conquest

2 April 1995

To see the stride, the most important phrase in jump racing, the greatest of Norman Williamson's gifts, is his biggest challenge on Master Oats next Saturday. The Gold Cup winner is indisputably the best horse in the Grand National field. But he is a long way from the brightest. The brains must come from the man on top.

There are plenty of them. Not academically proven of course, Norman left the Christian Brothers in Fermoy for permanent saddle studies soon after his 12th birthday.

But in the last month the world has come to see the graduate brilliance of the farmer's son from County Cork, who, at Aintree, could become the first jockey in history to complete the Gold Cup, Champion Hurdle, Grand National treble in the same season. He'll need every bit of brain to do it.

Norman Williamson and Master Oats: a jockey who always measures his fences; a horse who doesn't

For Master Oats capsized when favourite in last year's Grand National and while that remains the only actual fall in the big chestnut's 15-steeplechase, 10-victory career, nobody has yet nicknamed him 'Twinkle-Toes'. Examine the Gold Cup video and see why.

There were nineteen fences on the three and a quarter miles of the Cheltenham journey. Getting a pitch on the inside just behind the leaders, Master Oats and Williamson had an incident-free run for three-quarters of the opening circuit.

Then, first at the eighth fence and again at the ninth, the messages the 26-year-old Irishman was sending down the reins were lost in transmission. The birch parted but backers had their warning. The pilot didn't need reminding.

'He's very heavy-headed,' he said of his Grand National partner as we drove down the M4 for the unsung perils of Chepstow on Thursday. 'A sleepy horse really, you can't afford to relax on him for a minute. If you do, you find yourself on the deck. At Aintree he jumped very well until he got a bit crowded at the 13th. You've got to ride every fence like a brick wall.'

No cement yet at Cheltenham and at the 11th in the Gold Cup, thank the Lord for it. 'That time I totally blame myself,' says Norman.

'There were four horses around him and he did not see the fence. He's one of those animals who, if they cannot see, won't bother to jump.' Master Oats weighs nearly half-a-ton. At 30mph every pound of it whacked the obstacle but somehow he stayed upright. Drastic measures were not demanded.

With swift decision, Norman pulled round the leaders and attacked up the outside. The next fence was the water jump and with momentum gained he took it in full stride.

The next was an open ditch, the thick log of the guard rail growling at the lip. Master Oats could see it clearly but the stride was a short one. Norman's hand held steady, the big chestnut took it with as near as he gets to caution. Long hours of practice with show-jumping guru Yogi Breisner have had their dividends.

Another plain fence looms up. At every obstacle in a steeplechase a rider must read his take-off options. Will his partner's present stride pattern require a short or long leap to navigate? What adjustments are needed to stretch or check the flow? How much power, courage or intelligence does the runner beneath still have within him?

'On Master Oats,' says Williamson with no false bravado in his voice, 'a long way from every fence you have got to make your mind up whether you are going long or short, or leaving him alone. You have got to be positive.'

The 14th fence in the Gold Cup was on a long stride. Norman pushed on and the big horse arced over easily. Then the last open ditch. Cheltenham's most notorious receiving depot. Master Oats was a close third to Merry Gale and Barton Bank. The stride and the jump was with the flow. Barton Bank's wasn't.

So Master Oats was alongside the leader going for the 15th fence with the begoggled Williamson eyes staring out to read the rhythm. If the stride is short he focuses on the take-off board for ground line. If it is long, he aims for the birch top.

Not two or three but five full strides, that's a good 20 yards from the obstacle, he saw the pattern. He clamped low to his horse and with legs and arms pumped up and in and out and over. That's riding as it ought to be. It makes old heroes young again.

John Francome is only 42 but it was 10 years ago this month that he closed a career which had set new standards in the dangerous art of sending gallopers airborne.

'Norman sees a stride further away than anyone,' he had said earlier on

Thursday as he sipped coffee in the manor house he has built atop the hills of Lambourn.

'Norman knows what's happening and that it's not always the long one. That it can be just as quick to get over a fence by sitting still and not hitting it.'

In 15 seasons, John won seven jockeys' titles and over 1,100 races. In six years in Britain, Norman Williamson had, until yesterday morning, logged 332 winners and his present third place to Dunwoody and Maguire is the nearest he has been to a championship. But even before Williamson's brilliant Champion Hurdle and Gold Cup double on Alderbrook and Master Oats at Cheltenham, few failed to share Francome's assessment of our would-be treble maker. Even fewer after Thursday.

The Anvil Novices Handicap Chase at Chepstow was never going to be anything but perilous for the man who is to ride the National favourite. Norman's mount, Llacca Sam, looked keen enough and had won for him last time out. But that was the eight-year-old's only success under rules and had been achieved at alarming risk to the softer Stratford fences.

'Concentration is terribly important,' says Norman. 'There have been times when I have actually felt that with me concentrating and with a horse in my hands, I couldn't actually fall.'

As the tapes went up at Chepstow, Llacca Sam leapt forward intent on speed. At Stratford the approach of the first fence had brought a touch of caution. Not this time. 'He galloped straight through it,' said Norman afterwards. 'I thought "Oh my God". If he hadn't been that clever he would have come down.'

The second fence was the big open ditch right in front of us. Despite the blunder Williamson was once again the helmeted top half of the centaur in charge of the action.

From the ground this always looks an impossibly dangerous moment, a whole herd of thoroughbreds thundering up with four feet of birch to cross. Next week at Aintree, the fields and obstacles will be even bigger, but the relationship with mind and muscle will remain the key. See the stride and then control the flow.

Five strides off, Norman saw what he wanted. No tentative memories of the near disaster 10-seconds ago. He clamped down close to Llacca Sam's back and in an instant the novice became a spring-bok style expert.

For a full circuit, horse and man skipped round at the head of things with an exhibition of hand, eye and hoof-beat turning a gallop into a thing of beauty. It was to be Norman's 100th winner of the season. But a risk reminder was still to come.

It was at the same fence which had been a problem first time round. Five strides off, Norman spotted a stride pattern and went for it. At the fifth stride he failed to get lift-off. There was a flurry of leaves and birch as the fence shook; a jerk of arm and leg as the jockey took the impact through the saddle.

But the pair stayed united and they headed towards the open ditch in front of us. It was on a short stride. Norman's hand and boot stayed still as his horse hopped over. Normal service was resumed.

Afterwards there was a bit of joshing about this near-disaster.

'He's very intelligent you know,' said friend and fellow star Jamie Osborne with mocking fighter-pilot humour, 'but sometimes he will do things in a race that makes you think he's brain dead. He's certainly got the courage of his convictions. Mind you, next week he will need them.'

Races

The game's biggest disadvantage is that it involves so much talk and so little action. A race can last only five minutes, two minutes, even less than 60 seconds. But there is a plus side to this. When the tapes go up the focus is total, the recall strong and the gallop vivid.

Come with me through a score of the most exciting. We begin, as this era has to, with Desert Orchid.

Hard work gets Orchid home

3 February 1991

The legend is now stretching the reality and it is beginning to hurt. Desert Orchid won yet again at Sandown yesterday, great warm waves of applause swept over the Surrey hillside but the signs of age were unmistakable.

As Richard Dunwoody pulled the saddle and lead cloth off the great white wonder's back in the unsaddling enclosure, trainer David Elsworth put his arm across his shoulders and said, 'it showed a bit today'. Dunwoody looked across at the horse and said ruefully 'yes, it was hard work'.

Not too many had noticed. Dessie-Mania has taken such a hold that our hero gets cheered for just turning up. And if at the end he has won yet again, the adoring crowds don't care what it took. The legend has been made flesh. Dessie is still king.

Indeed he is. Yesterday Desert Orchid was conceding 15lb to second-placed Nick The Brief, 19lb to Kildimo, and so to beat them three-quarters of a length and one-and-a-half lengths confirmed his position at the top of the steeplechasing tree. But in the hour of glory the question kept coming back 'for how long?'

This is partly because, even this far in, seven seasons and 67 races behind him, much of Desert Orchid is still unbelievable. Was there ever a happier, heart-singing sight than Dessie leading the pack down the back straight at Sandown, fence after fence being flicked spring-heeled beneath him? The horse has defied belief but now, at 12, he has to defy the years.

For much of yesterday he made a right job of it. As a jockey Dunwoody has become very much the athletic extension of the horse that Simon Sherwood used to be and the pair led their rivals through a faultless circuit-and-a-half to the oohs and aahs of the crowd. Once or twice their leaps were daringly low and long but gone was the rusty caution of Dessie's defeat here in December.

Yet as they ran towards the Pond Fence, three from home, both Nick The Brief and Kildimo had closed up for serious discussion and it was suddenly clear that Desert Orchid and Dunwoody would need all the breath they had guarded.

They met that fence a fraction close and awkward. The three horses fanned into the straight. Dunwoody's stick came up in his left hand. Dessie would have to fight.

Running to the last Kildimo could not quite stay in the argument, but Nick The Brief was having his say. He is a big, dark and powerful bay. He does not have the liquid grace of Desert Orchid but he had a 15lb weight concession, and as young Robbie Supple pumped him up for take off it was he who looked the stronger.

The Sandown run-in is an uphill 250 yards which seem to stretch away from you. For half of it the younger horse seemed just in command of the champion beside him. But then, as the crowd's roar went up through the decibels, Dunwoody's stick cracked back in desperation, Desert Orchid stretched that old white neck long and low like a greyhound, and in 10 lung-busting strides the deed was done.

Afterwards the jockey spoke of the experience. 'It was hard all the way from the turn. I didn't think he would do it but on the run-in we were really hit by the roar of the crowd. It lifted me and I'm sure it helped him too.'

Elsworth confirmed that Desert Orchid will now go for the Cheltenham Gold Cup next month, but cautions that this will be the last appearance of the season and who knows after that? 'It's not getting any easier' he said, rubbing his hand worriedly across his mouth. 'So much is expected of the horse I am not enjoying watching him any more. He may still have the biggest fire, but it's not what it was.'

The long-term plan is for Desert Orchid to bow out in next December's King George at Kempton. So even if he does come up fresh next season we may never again see him led back a winner at Sandown. Those memories must not fade.

How good then that this latest addition was surrounded by the very best that Sandown can offer. Peter Scudamore snatching the Agfa Hurdle on Voyage Sans Retour after Fidway had stalled on the run-in. Best of all, beleaguered trainer Rod Simpson winning the big handicap with Rouyan under a great ride from Billy Morris, who may have even bigger challenges to come.

Morris is a Territorial reservist on call for the Gulf. He will not be found wanting. He too saw Desert Orchid.

'Dessie' was in the winter of his days but for us hacks it's the spring that gives us problems. In its wisdom the racing calendar places the Lincoln Handicap, the first big race on the flat, between the Cheltenham Festival and the Grand National. Baffled scribes try to work up enthusiasm for a huge field of horses who haven't run on the grass for at least six months and whose chances depend hugely on the draw, which doesn't take place until 24 hours before the race.

In recent years it has needed a 'silk purse from a sow's ear' method of reporting. No such worries in 1991. That was thanks to Alex Greaves.

Ice Cold Alex rises from the sand

24 March 1991

The lady scooped the lot of them. Lester was at Lingfield, but Pat Eddery, Willie Carson and the rest of the lads were at Doncaster for the Lincoln. They were just mounted spectators as Alex Greaves wrote her name in history.

For Greaves's victory on Amenable was the richest yet for a woman rider in these islands and but the latest achievement of the self-possessed 22-year-old who likes to refer to herself as 'just a jockey'. Some hope of that in these sex-obsessed days and if Greaves can continue to succeed way beyond anyone else of her gender she will be able to laugh happily all the way to the bank.

Race-riding in Britain has been open to women for more than a decade, but after the first giggling hurrahs the success rate has been very small considering the enormous impact of the fairer sex in other branches of the equestrian world. Even when Greaves shot to fame last year by heading the all-weather rankings in straight competition with male rivals, there was condescension in entitling her 'Queen of the Sand'.

Well, she has been Queen again this winter. She has ridden 26 winners to her nearest rival's 21, and since 17 of her scorers have been since 1 January, Greaves can fairly claim to be the year's leading Flat jockey. Not bad for someone who did not have her first professional ride until two years ago after originally setting out on a hotel management course.

Pardon the pun, but she certainly knows about waiting. 'Ice Cold Alex' has long been the cliché on the all-weather and Greaves's patience was quite remarkable again yesterday. At half-way in the Lincoln's mile-long journey she had settle Amenable plum last. Twenty-four others legging it for Doncaster Rovers' ground and Alex and Amenable cool and cosy at the back. It takes some doing.

What is more, she had been drawn 23 of 25. All pre-race predictions had claimed that a low number (far-side) draw would be essential and when the favourite Selaah (drawn four) led the field early on from Farm Street (10), few of us imagined the high-draw horses would feature.

To some extent this was nullified by all of them tacking across to join the far group, so avoiding the normal absurdity of entirely separate races developing on either side of the track. But most of all it was fixed by the power that Greaves clearly had stored beneath her as Amenable stalked his rivals. The second half of the race had a lovely unravelling which Greaves's connections will never tire of replaying. Selaah and Farm Walk downed tools sharply on the far side to be succeeded by Band On The Run and as Carson drove Lord Of Tusmore ahead of the near-side group you couldn't miss how still Greaves was on Amenable behind him.

Band On The Run cut for home as if the sausage machine was on his tail. St Ninian pulled close in pursuit but all the time the red and yellow silks on Amenable loomed ever more threatening out in the centre of the track.

Although the winning distance was only a length and a half, and although they did not hit the front until the final furlong, there was a glorious inevitability about this result. A contrast in styles too. Lanfranco Dettori, the most fashionable of all the young stars, attacked by Greaves, still eight winners short of clearing her apprentice allowance. She still tends to flap her legs rather out of rhythm but she gets horses to run and yesterday she was not above giving Amenable 10 hefty, mind-shaping belts with the whip.

For trainer David Barron this greatest success of his career had a wonderful symmetry about it. For it has been he who has single-handedly brought Greaves through with the simple message about his headgroom's daughter 'she is good enough for me'. Much more than that, Amenable is a perfect example of his skills. The horse who had broken down two years ago was now winning for the fifth time in a row, albeit for the first time on turf since May 1989.

'You have got to be patient with them,' he explained afterwards, adding that Amenable had benefited from having his tendons 'fired', a standard operation soon to be controversially banned by the veterinary profession.

It was a day when the first three past the post in the Lincoln were all trained in the supposedly disadvantaged realm north of the Trent. It was a day when only Eddery of the established stars rode a winner. It was a day that belonged most of all to Alex Greaves.

Lester Piggott? Oh yes, he scored twice on the all-weather surface at Lingfield. Graves could have told him. The sand has its uses.

Time was when bookmakers made a big thing of luring ante-post punters into the ludicrously difficult 'Spring Double', not just finding the Lincoln winner from its unlikely posse of unknowns and undesirables but coupling that with the Grand National winner. And we wonder why they are able to holiday in the Caribbean.

In recent years punters have seen the light. But while the Lincoln has struggled to hold the attention, the Grand National has grown ever-more popular. Thanks greatly to the unfailing magnificence of the BBCTV coverage, it has become the one race on which the whole nation holds a view. Indeed, matched only perhaps by the Open Golf, it remains the one great sporting event that never fails to match its billing. It's never dull when they have jumped the last at Aintree.

Seagram flies over the Savannah

7 April 1991

The longest run home in the world, the most endless 10 minutes in sport, the Gold Cup winner Garrison Savannah out clear but a little chestnut catching wind behind him. The Grand National went to a hound of a horse called Seagram.

How relentless, how tough he was. In this hour of hours he dug deep into a resilience bred in him at birth in New Zealand. He needed every ounce to pull back the brilliant Garrison Savannah when the hero of Cheltenham had laid out his aces with a magnificent race-claiming jump at the second last.

Garrison Savannah went four lengths, six lengths clear. Young Nigel Hawke cracked his whip three, four times on Seagram. The leader flew straight and unfalteringly over the last. The gap was still six lengths. On Garrison Savannah, Mark Pitman remembered his father's advice and kept cool. Jump-racing's Everest and the first National–Gold Cup double since 1934 was his for the grasping.

As always, the drama had taken some unravelling. A raw, raw day with wind buffeting 40 horses and riders ready to run for their lives. One of them, Ballyhane, was to pay for it with a heart attack after finishing 11th. A scuffling animal rights protest up from the start added an eight-minute delay. A whole nation on edge as the field thundered off for the first.

The morning's rain had brought a flood of money to make Bonanza Boy favourite, but from the moment the tapes went up Peter Scudamore was struggling. He eventually finished fifth. He would have won over five and a half miles, but he was never in the argument as Golden Freeze and the French horse, Oklaoma II, sailed off towards the first. The drop there capsized Docklands Express, breaking Anthony Tory's shoulder, the second fence claimed Run And Skip and as the great pack swept down towards Becher's it was clear that Garrison Savannah's stablemate, Golden Freeze, was to play a brilliant lead in the opening sequences.

Golden Freeze has often looked a runaway head-case but now with the eyes of the world on him he was bold and free but also respectful. He may have eventually run plum out of petrol to finish 17th and last of the finishers but for almost four miles he gave Michael Bowlby a ride to make the spirit soar. Bowlby returned the compliment. The fences flicked back effortlessly beneath them. It was not so easy for either of the eventual principals. Garrison Savannah took at least two jockey-shifting liberties, whilst further back Seagram had nearly lost his confidence at the effort of clearing the early obstacles. The crucial fence was the Chair at the end of the first circuit. All 5ft 2in of it towered before them but as Golden Freeze led his other stablemate, Team Challenge, over both Garrison Savannah and particularly Seagram gave their riders heart with the way they put the great mass of thorn behind them.

They have already been galloping five minutes but it's only now that the

Seagram and Nigel Hawke on the Aintree run-in in 1991

race takes real shape. Rinus, going up to join Golden Freeze, Garrison Savannah cruising behind them, outsiders like New Halen, Auntie Dot and Over The House close up, Seagram nearer, Mr Frisk already labouring.

Rinus got too low at the 19th, leaving Jenny Pitman's pair, Golden Freeze and Garrison Savannah, together. Michael Bowlby called across 'Let's steady it.' Mark Pitman didn't hear him but he didn't need any telling. 'I was going unbelievably well,' he said later. 'I was determined to save him.'

Garrison Savannah took it up round the Canal Turn. Golden Freeze kept company for three more fences but now it was Auntie Dot, Seagram and perhaps Over The Road who were more dangerous. Auntie Dot, a no-hoper, was the biggest threat of all.

Three to jump, and these last four were in the air together. Auntie Dot went almost as well as Garrison Savannah as they came across the cinders of the

Melling Road with just two fences and that pitiless run-in ahead of them. But it had been a long, long way already. The breath suddenly shortened on Auntie Dot. Now only the 11-year-old Seagram was still hounding. But Garrison Savannah was the class horse, he was conceding 9lb and that looked a feather as he put in that great leap at the second last.

Two stories called at us in the stands. Garrison Savannah to sweep home in triumph. Seagram to prove you can never keep a Kiwi down. Even half-way up that 494-yard run-in the class horse still had it. But the little hound had the scent. Up front the air became thin. Mark Pitman got to the elbow and history closed in to repeat itself.

Eighteen years before Richard Pitman had the giant Crisp utterly spent beneath him as Red Rum stormed up to grab him right on the line. Now it happened for his son, and even more abrubtly. One moment Garrison Savannah's stride was still biting the turf in rhythm, the next, the forelegs were wandering and Seagram was gobbling up the space between them.

Trainer David Barons has for some years been proclaiming the value of the New Zealand thoroughbred. Now the whole world has to acknowledge it, not least Ivan Straker, of the big race sponsors, who was offered the horse which had been enticingly given his company's name. The bold Straker was over-cautious for once. Thought that the gelding's carbon-implanted forelegs were too much of a risk. Now he has the publicity but not the winnings.

But in the saddle Nigel Hawke had never faltered. It was the 25-year-old Cornishman's first ride in the National but he believed in his horse and his faith was repaid. Hawke is a farmer's son from Liskeard. His father had 3,000 ewes to lamb this spring. Nigel was a late starter to the racing game.

It was to be his 62nd winner. It will always be his greatest. The moment when the horse he was driving answered the most important call of all – with 100 yards to run and the Gold Cup winner flagging. Seagram took him quickly and completely. 'Garrison Savannah was wonderful,' said Mark Pitman, 'but he was absolutely gutted.' The sight of victory exploded in Hawke's brain. He punched the air so hard that he almost went overboard.

The winner has to take it. Take the glory. Earn the story. Seagram and Nigel Hawke did that and more. But they needed their quarry. They needed the impossible hare. The National should never be ordinary.

Within a month of that great jumping moment, flat racing had seen Lester Piggott roll back the years to win his thirtieth classic on Rodrigo de Triano in the Two Thousand Guineas at the not just ripe but wrinkled old age of fifty-six. It was one of those occasions when you felt lucky to be alive at that hour. Privileged to be witness to something that could never happen again. Then we get to the Champion Stakes back at Newmarket in October and stap me if Lester and Rodrigo don't come back and do it again.

Like lots of things in Lester's unrepeatable residence on this mortal coil, it couldn't happen, it shouldn't, but it did.

Piggott and Rodrigo show Champion class

18 October 1992

The horse, small, plain and with bandages on his injured foreleg. The man, old, withered and, by any normal reckoning, way beyond his time. But the Champion Stakes was just the latest example that Rodrigo de Triano and Lester Piggott do not obey standards, they set them.

Like a great singer finding the song to suit, Piggott has long had the magical knack of picking up a partnership and making it his own. It's impossible to think of The Minstrel, Sir Ivor, Petite Etoile or Nijinsky without that tall, gaunt figure deadly behind the mane. That's true now of Rodrigo de Triano.

Indeed, it's highly arguable that this is actually the best horse that Piggott has ridden since Nijinsky swept all before him in the summer of 1970. Yesterday's narrow but decisive defeat of Lahib was the pair's fourth Group One success of the season and a victory even beyond its merit on the track.

For Rodrigo's preparation had been so badly interrupted by a recurring splint problem on his off foreleg that the trainer Peter Chapple-Hyam had to risk the unorthodox routine of galloping his dual Guineas winner a full mile on Friday morning. The little chestnut passed his fitness test, but the unaccustomed bandages in the paddock told of the tension.

At this stage, almost 57 years since he came muttering into existence and no fewer than 33 since he knifed Petite Etoile through to win his first Champion Stakes, it should hardly need saying that there were not too many nerves visible on the ghostly Piggott countenance. But even by his standards this was full-gallop impassiveness taken to extremes.

Even at this stage, maybe especially at this stage, nobody can ride a race like he did on Rodrigo. That's not a silly winners' adulation, its the simple, wondrous truth.

The trick is in the stillness. Of course Lester is not going to match some kid kick for kick, push for push. But that's not what Rodrigo wants. What happened yesterday was what happened at Newmarket, York and The Curragh. Lester jumped out of the stalls gently and eased him down at the back of the field as if the idea was to play the whipper-in.

It's one thing to set off like this, quite another to have the nerve to hold it. But now after Shuailaan and Zaahi had blasted off in front to ensure a final clocking within a second of the course record, the ice in Piggott's blood never even dripped as Carson drove Lahib into the lead and Rodrigo slid through behind him.

The cause was helped by Lahib hanging fire momentarily as he hit the front, but right into the final 300 yards Piggott let Rodrigo coast up in his own time. In any sport it's this 'bottle' that is the most treasured quality. Lester will have it until he dies.

Two hundred yards to run and he fired his gun. Not surprisingly there wasn't quite as much punch as expected. Willie Carson's left hand smacked a final effort out of Lahib. Lester had to push and flap and pull his own whip through for a left-handed flick. But he was always going to make it. By a neck on the line.

Environment Friend did well to be three lengths away in third, with Shuailaan a close fourth, but the delight afterwards was being able to look forward to at least one more Rodrigo turn. He and Lester go to the Breeders' Cup at Gulfstream Park in a fortnight's time. Trainer and jockey want to pitch against Arazi in the mile but Rodrigo's owner Robert Sangster may overrule them to go for the $3m Breeders' Cup Classic over one and a quarter miles of the Miami dirt.

Either way we have once again got far more than any race fan could hope for. Yesterday had many other things. The handsome Barathea in the Houghton Stakes putting himself in line for next year's Derby. The Irish gamble Vintage Crop running away with the Cesarewitch and being greeted by his trainer Dermot Weld's confident prediction that his real target should be next March's Champion Hurdle. But greatness does not share easy.

There are many problems with the funding of British racing. Not surprising since Britain Plc looks rudderlessly close to bankruptcy. But when many well-meaning people call for protests and owners' strikes they should surely concentrate not so much on the money but on the sport they want to preserve.

They and we should thank our lucky stars that we have just had a day like yesterday. What Rodrigo and Lester did took racing to a dimension way beyond local financing disputes. It was a sporting spectacle to match anything anywhere. That's what Britain still has. It's worth preserving.

Characters are a currency we should treasure. Down the years racing has always attracted its fair share of great if awkward individuals. Let's hope that our brave new modernized world is not going to be so squeaky-clean that nothing wildly individual can ever flourish.

How less a life if we never had a one-off like Harvey Smith in harness.

Kildimo is equal to the toughest test

22 November 1992

It was a V-sign to the weather and to all those faint hearts who said that this first autumn Aintree meeting in 20 years would not capture the public imagination. Kildimo, one of chasing's great eccentrics, relived his glorious if chequered youth thanks largely to the horse world's toughest card of all, Harvey Smith.

The rain was pelting down at Aintree, stair-rods over Liverpool, but the pride in Harvey's cheeks was as puffed as if he had returned yet another show-jumping *tour de force*. His wife Sue is Kildimo's trainer and his beloved Ilkley Moor has been part of the rehabilitation of the craggy-necked veteran who was the best novice of his year and one day at Wincanton got a decision over Desert Orchid.

Aintree has always welcomed eccentrics but has rarely needed them more than yesterday. The heavens mocked the poor old place, a group of middle-aged Brummies called the Jolly Bunch gave us their New Orleans repertoire regardless, and while Richard Dunwoody eased to his half century with a stylish double, one disbelieving Southerner asked 'where can I get some tea without someone nicking the sugar from the cup?'

Nine runners for the Crowther Homes sponsored Becher Chase, Becher's a lurking threat somewhere in the mist, an official parade an extra hassle to test jockeys' mettle to the quick, even getting to the start would be a feat. For Lorcan Wyer, finding himself being carted by the rejuvenated Kildimo, it was his hairiest moment. He was not the only one.

Johnny Bradburne makes Harvey and Kildimo seem a pair of sobersides by comparison. A 6ft chartered surveyor by profession, an amateur rider by compulsion, he was 47 yesterday and as Interim Lib gathered speed on the way to the start it looked like Johnny would be celebrating his birthday with an unscheduled dip in the canal as in 'Canal Turn.'

Soaked and slippery reins made the brakes pretty useless once the ropes went up but no matter. Interim Lib, upsides with The Antartex, gave his jockey a ride he can remember with honour if he lives another 50 years. Who knows that J. Bradburne won't still be creaking round in 2042?

One player who did not appreciate the new fixture was Seagram, hero round these fences of the Grand National itself in 1991. After a mistake at the first, Seagram clearly registered that one dose of Aintree glory was enough for any horse and his final removal of jockey Nigel Hawke at The Chair fence had looked a certainty all the way to take-off.

With so few runners compared to the National this race was always going to have an exhibition feel about it, in which case television viewers would forgive the bending of the rules which allowed Richard Dunwoody to replace Mark Perrett on The Antartex once his own ride Brown Windsor had been found lame in the morning. The grey made the running and, with Dunwoody the current master of the blended equestrian style, viewers were in for a treat.

Backers of the favourite Cool Ground had less fun. Close up on the inside he did not get high enough at the 13th and he and the rising star Adrian Maguire joined the legions who have rolled on the famous Aintree turf.

The next fence was Becher's Brook where the gallant Bradburne hustled Interim Lib up the rail to take off close to The Antartex in the centre with Kildimo moving powerfully on the outside, and the other greys Stay On Tracks and Four Trix also in the hunt.

The Antartex led over the Canal Turn but once they started the long slog home it was clear that Kildimo was strongest of all. He was in front five out and once there it was just a question of whether the past would come back to haunt him.

Time was when either the fences would get in the way of his great long-backed bulk or more than a suspicion of quitting would be given by the way he flicked his almost-Arab arched tail. Two out The Antartex closed. The doubters gave tongue. Another great jump at the last and all the way up the run-in Kildimo galloped as honest as a pilgrim. The rehabilitation was complete.

So too was his ticket for next April's Grand National. He will be 13 then but Harvey Smith is no spring chicken either. 'I have always dreamed of having a Grand National runner,' said the old wonder. 'And this could be it. He is a smashing jumper now. I have had him doing all sorts of show-jumping things and I rode him over 16 steeplechase fences on Tuesday.'

There's a deep scar down the left side of Harvey's face but you do not notice it when he is smiling. It was hard to find yesterday. A man, a horse, a course, a fine madness everywhere. They are made for each other.

If you make racing your beat there are hazards aplenty, most of them connected with the Scylla and Charybdis dangers of the Members' Bar and the betting ring. But for the weary hack there is also the less obvious but equally debilitating danger of becoming blasé about it all. Of losing the thrill that lured you there in the first place and about which your readers want to be told.

The best antidote is the big race in the big arena that grips you by the throat. Like Jodami's Gold Cup at Cheltenham. Now that was the real thing.

Heavyweight with all the shots

21 March 1993

There should be no room for might-have-beens. With 566 kilograms of Jodami around there is precious little room at all. At Cheltenham on Thursday the new champion was a massive old-fashioned heavy-weight of a contender, his Gold Cup as good a title fight as you will see any season.

Now was the time and here was the place to settle all the arguments. Everybody could hold an opinion and most people did. Would The Fellow at last take the crown back to France? Would Garrison Savannah and Cool Ground show their short-head victories in 1991 and 1992 were something more than two anti-Gallic flukes? Was Peter Scudamore's choice of Chatam the right pick of the Martin Pipe trio? Would little Docklands Express sparkle on the fast ground he loves? Would elephant-head Jodami now finally fulfil the promise of his mighty physique?

A great championship should trade heavy on expectation, and as the runners filed out you could suck it down by the jugful. Desert Orchid presided jauntily over the parade. The old white hero packed up racing two years ago. Last December half his guts were removed and we all got the obituaries out. We of little faith.

Mark Dwyer shows his delight as he and Jodami are led back after winning the 1993 Gold Cup

Dessie's 1989 Gold Cup was a desperate, rain-swept, mud-cloying slog, and the only question was whether 'himself' could triumph over adversity. This was another day, a spring afternoon with Cleeve Hill and the Cotswolds balmy in the sunshine. The Fellow was a question all right. But three and a quarter miles and 22 fences suggested he would not be the only one.

So it all came down to this. The 1993 Gold Cup field lines up, the pukka tones of the starter nag: 'Keep off the tapes.' The 16-strong posse is dispatched towards those first two fences and you know and they know that now there is no escape. On and away past us they thunder; goggles down, right tight, fences coming quick, and two laps, three miles still ahead.

Hindsight is a desperate liar, but even on that first circuit one contrast stood out. Close behind the leaders, Mark Dwyer rode Jodami with a long-reined stance so upright he might have been whistling in the park. At the back Adam Kondrat crouched low and streamlined on The Fellow like a collie herding his flock.

Three minutes and much oxygen later, they returned with some of the die already cast. For Cherrykino it was cast complete. A fatal fall at the second open ditch had taken him out, and in swerving around him The Fellow had been forced back to the end of the queue. As Rushing Wild and Sibton Abbey led the gallop past us, Dwyer was still upright and confident close up, Kondrat low and already pestering as he tried to take closer station.

Take it he did. Those who claim that The Fellow 'was never put in the race' are talking through either their pockets or bile-tinted glasses.

From the water jump to the last open ditch, six fences from home, The Fellow was within two lengths of Jodami right on the heels of the leaders. But he was already a vulnerable favourite. There was no attack in his jumping, no great threat in his pursuit. Dwyer, Richard Dunwoody on Rushing Wild and Mark Pitman on Garrison Savannah had plenty of engine beneath them. Kondrat, for all his stealthy stylishness, looked in need of an extra gear.

Then Garrison Savannah attempted a one-horse demolition job on the open ditch. Pitman did a no-stirrups rodeo act to stay aboard. The Fellow lost ground in the shemozzle and also got squeezed by the passing Run For Free.

They were now at the top of the hill, six furlongs and four fences from home, and Dunwoody set off down the slope like an Apache. He knew Rushing Wild would jump and stay all day, he could see he had Sibton Abbey beat beside him, but behind there would be others whose speed needed blunting.

Over the third last they came, where any mistake is a roller. The outsider Black Humour could not take the joke, and as Rushing Wild pressed into the bend before the long, staring run home it was clear that Jodami was the only dog to catch this hare. He was three lengths adrift but answering Dwyer's insistent elbows. Four lengths further back, Kondrat's whip cracked on The Fellow. At the post, nine long lengths behind Jodami, he would only make fourth.

But the focus was up front. Dwyer's left hand flicked up from the rein to snatch down his sweat-soaked goggles. He could see clearly now. Two fences and the noisiest hill in racing and, before that, Dunwoody still to catch.

Dunwoody had only got the ride on Rushing Wild that morning. So far, all his prized Cheltenham fancies had been found wanting. Jodami got to him at the second last, but there was still a fight to be had. The two horses came up together. On take-off you could not choose between them. On landing you could.

It was only a fraction but it was obvious. Rushing Wild's legs had buckled a touch, Jodami's not at all. The big horse from Yorkshire was suddenly the stronger. He may have come from the little family stable of Peter Beaumont, and up to this season had always been ridden by either Beaumont's daughter or son-in-law, but he had talent from the beginning. He had won 12 of his 20 races, and three years ago the stable had cleaned up at 33–1 on his opening shot. Now was the big time, and he was ready for it. So was his pilot.

As a 22-year-old, Mark Dwyer had won the 1985 Gold Cup on Forgive 'N Forget, and as long ago as his all-Ireland pony racing days he had learnt the need for coolness. He was just in front of us, legs and arms punching like pistons as Jodami's long mule ears flickered forward at the bedlam from the stands. Dunwoody was still level on the far side and yelling Rushing Wild into one final effort. Dwyer had him covered, but what of a late attack from the other quarter? Without losing momentum or conviction, the jockey's head swivelled and saw only grass.

It was there for the taking. With three huge strides, Jodami was at the last fence and over. Rushing Wild has earned a rematch for the way he kept up the challenge, but this was Jodami's hour. Everything he had been reared and trained and bred for.

Up in the drink-sozzled stands and to the TV-watching nation, it's exciting but it's still just a horse race. Down on the track, as Dwyer's stick came through to drive his huge but now idling partner all the way to the winning post, it was a little more. A form of immortality. There are no might-have-beens in that.

In jump racing disaster awaits at every fence. Whether we like it or not, the risk, the sometimes mortal risk, to riders and especially to horses, is part of the addiction. This is especially so at Aintree, where each year you find yourself unwittingly doing an equestrian version of Brian Hanrahan's immortal report from the Ark Royal during the Falklands War. 'I have counted them all out,' you say to yourself, knowing that you won't count them all in.

Watching the National always has this tension of potential disaster about it, but in 1993 we had a horror story with a difference. In hindsight it was one of the great comic turns in Britain's sporting history. No horses hurt, no bones broken. It was Balaclava without the body count. But at the time it was absolutely headless. And that goes for the reporters too. Oh dear, oh dear, oh dear.

Flag mix-up caused the race that never was

4 April 1993

You didn't know whether to laugh or cry. But it was simple just the same. It was a red recall flag that did not wave. It showed everything up. It showed a shambles that beggared description.

The rules are clear, whether it is the Grand National at Aintree or a selling hurdle at Market Rasen: if the starter is not happy with his dispatch, he waves his red flag and, at this signal, a man with another red flag 200 yards down the track steps into the runners' path waving madly that the game is not on. Yesterday, the first flag waved but not the second. The whole ludicrous, shameful, impossible chapter of accidents stemmed from that.

The Aintree starting gate has long had a pretty gimcrack look because of the very length of it. It is a double-stranded set of tapes like the ones you saw in the racing movies of yesteryear. Trying to get some 40 charged-up horses and jockeys to line up is no easy task. It was made no easier yesterday by a 10-minute delay caused by animal rights protesters, and rain and wind which made the 100-metre barrier swing and sag heavily.

The first false start was acutely embarrassing, but only because it was the Grand National. The second one was just as necessary. If a jockey has a tape round wound his neck, as Richard Dunwoody did on Wont Be Gone Long, the starter has got to stop things. Keith Brown, the starter, waved his arm but somehow Ken Evans, down the course, did not get the message and did not march in front of the oncoming cavalry charge.

It is worth stating that this man-to-man system has, until now, stood the test of time. A few years back, the Jockey Club experimented with electronic signals but reverted to human hand as more reliable. Almost 30 years ago, I rode in a big televised hurdle race at Taunton where the false start man bottled it after a couple of hopeful waves and we continued with a complete race which was then declared void.

But yesterday the system was cruelly exposed. Something better than a flag needs to be found. Keith Brown's did not properly unfurl. That may have confused Ken Evans, who surely should have had a colleague waving beside him.

Certainly, the wisdom of trying to line up some 40 Grand National horses like guardsmen needs re-examining. But in the end, everything comes down to a foolproof method of getting the message to the man with the recall flag. In these days of man-on-moon phone-ins, there should not be anything difficult in that.

All the unwinding shambles of the race that never was followed from this catastrophic opening blunder. Since it should be absolutely unthinkable that 30 jockeys, including some as experienced as Peter Scudamore and Carl Llewellyn, should continue when the false start has been signalled, it is not surprising that there was nothing to stop the humiliation of not just one meaningless circuit, but a whole Grand National course of make-believe.

I was down at The Chair fence. The official there was the experienced and reliable Charlie Moore, who only a week before had run the Lincoln meeting at Doncaster.

He walked up and down desperately trying to make sense of his walkie-talkie. Only when the horses were a fence away did he and his team get the message that they were meant to stop the rot. He rushed out with bollards and flags and tried to wave the runners to a halt.

To the horror of those of us close by, and to the bewilderment of hundreds of millions of TV viewers around the globe, the cavalry galloped straight through his handiwork. It seemed impossible but it wasn't. Jockeys have a clear set of instructions. A bollard in front of a fence indicates trouble the other side of it, but it normally means that you should still jump the obstacle to either side of the markers.

Andy Orkney was making the running on the grey, Howe Street. He is an optician in his other life. He saw clearly enough. 'I was sure we had to go in and jump,' he said. 'I imagined there were some protesters or something the other side. I just concentrated more.' To some effect, for there was not one faller at this, the most massive of all the Grand National fences.

True, the 'it's over' message then got through to the riders of such as Captain Dibble, Party Politics and Garrison Savannah, but it is hard to think quite how you could guarantee to pull up the whole field. Riding in the Grand National is one of the most tightly sealed capsules in sport. If you have just completed the first circuit, the one thing you are not looking for is little men running around telling you to stop.

So we got to that desperate, doomed finish. Adrian Maguire and Charlie Swan working furiously on Romany King and Cahervillahow while John White on Esha Ness swept past them, the Grand National, the sweetest cup of triumph, his for the taking; a cup that would spill in bitterness the moment it was touched.

Then the last stage of all. Sans race, sans plans, sans everything. Trainers and jockeys milled around as the offending barrier looked down in mockery. Maguire came up, his young eyes still ablaze. 'I had a great ride,' he said. 'I thought it had been a great race. But I saw no flag.'

Afterwards a frightfully high-powered committee of racing's great and good studied all elements of the fiasco and came up with a detailed report. But the simplest step had been taken within two days. The flag men round the country were equipped with fluorescent coats so that they at least were visible to the oncoming hordes. It wasn't difficult. They had done it in Ireland for ages. 'For want of a nail' wrote Benjamin Franklin a mere two centuries ago, 'the shoe was lost; for want of a shoe the horse was lost; for want of a horse the rider was lost.'

Old Benjamin is best remembered for helping to frame the American Constitution – 'We must indeed all hang together, or most assuredly we will all hang separately' – as well as penning the immortal lines about someone's pet squirrel:

'Here Skug lies snug, as a bug, in a rug.' What would the versatile Mr Franklin have said of what happened at Aintree 'for want of a coat'?

But back to real racing. Let's close with three marvellous moments from Cheltenham's Hall of Fame. Even if the first is unlikely to be anything but a hazy blur in its hero's eye.

Get thrown, get up and win – that's Murphy's lore

14 November 1993

Even Lazarus would have had second thoughts. Declan Murphy won the Mackeson Gold Cup on Bradbury Star within 40 minutes of taking the sort of fall that normally has you phoning for the undertaker.

Steeplechasing is used to mind over matter, but this was something else.

The fall was a typical Cheltenham crippler. Arcot, Murphy's horse, was getting the worst of things at the second-last hurdle, the obstacle grabbed at rather than jumped over. Arcot had momentum but no front balance and at 35mph there was half a ton of thoroughbred somersaulting on top of 10 stones of man.

The bad things get frozen in the memory. This was a bad thing all right. For, as Arcot's hindquarters came catapulting over, the near hind hoof appeared to clobber Murphy across the neck.

The race thundered away from them, but both horse and rider lay still. When binoculars returned to them after the finish nothing seemed to have changed except that both ambulance and knacker wagon were speeding to do their duty.

The first miracle was that the horse got up. Poor Arcot had looked to have 'pet food' written all over him. But here he was walking about with only mud on his bridle. Amazing, but nobody was going to ask him to race in the next.

The best Mackeson field in years was already in the paddock. Surely they would have to do without D. Murphy?

Even if Bradbury Star could understand human panic, it's unlikely it would have fazed him. He strolled around with that extraordinarily long springy stride of his and with his tongue stuck lazily out of the side of his mouth.

Behind him the Middleham horse Armagret was asweat with worry, the now Nicholson-trained Second Schedual an impressive example of the powerful jumping horse. But the lot of them were outshone by the gleaming black muscles of the Lake District favourite, General Pershing.

The jockeys were being called out. Murphy had never been unconscious (automatic seven-day suspension from riding) but when he had got back to the weighing room the doctors put him through the hoop. What was the name of this horse in the next race? When had he got to the track? What day was it? How was he driving home?

Murphy got the answers right. His damaged wrist seemed to work. Jump racing is not a cautious world. Doctors can only do so much.

For a jockey, Murphy has always been a tall, rather imperious figure. As he walked out now in Bradbury Star's royal blue and red silks, his lean and ascetic face had a particularly faraway look. He was focused all right. But how clear was the target?

The triumph will take some replaying. A good strong gallop was set all the way by Jamie Osborne on the blinkered Egypt Mill Prince. Brandeston departed at the first fence, but after that the 15 survivors locked into one of those battles that only Cheltenham can give.

Once the tapes have sprung clear there's a relentlessness about the two-and-a-half-mile Mackeson that can make the mere spectator catch his breath.

The fences loom up and are taken. The horses stretch onwards as the jockeys' hands begin to betray the strain beneath. Down the back stretch Egypt Mill Prince led from Guiburn's Nephew, Storm Alert, General Pershing and Second Schedual.

Bradbury Star was stalking them as usual. The big Irish fancy General Idea, was only briefly holding out hopes of a Melbourne Cup–Mackeson double for the Kildare stable of Dermot Weld.

Up to the top of the hill with three to jump, and Egypt Mill Prince led just four close pursuers: Storm Alert, General Pershing, Second Schedual and Bradbury Star. 'Declan has that horse off to a tee,' said Storm Alert's rider Simon McNeill afterwards. 'They looked to be going easily as we turned down the slope.'

But at Cheltenham it is never easy, and this time for more than the usual reasons. 'Suddenly I could see two Egypt Mill Princes in front of me,' Murphy said. 'It wasn't too bad until I was pulling up after the finish. I took a deep breath and everything fell in on me.' He could say it later. He still looked deadly now.

The third-last took Second Schedual. 'He overjumped and the downhill slope turned him over,' Adrian Maguire said. 'But we would only have been third.'

Egypt Mill Prince and Bradbury Star were leaving their pursuers adrift with just their one last duel to be decided. 'In truth I felt he had me beaten,' Osborne said, 'but I had to make him have a cut.'

So to the final fence of all. Two horses with the breath coming short but the rhythm still racing. There was no weakness in Murphy's now-ungoggled eyes nor in the low angle of his driving body. If Bradbury Star jumped this well he could take care of his rival. He could.

Seven lengths was the verdict. But with the roar of the crowd and the collar of that Cheltenham hill, not one stride could be complacent. Bradbury Star got over the winning line. Murphy put his hands down on the reins, and black clouds rolled in.

As he was led back you could see the bad thing on him. Murphy sat very upright in the saddle, the face set hard against the ordeal that the simple act of unsaddling would present. Trainer Josh Gifford took one look, turned to Murphy's brother Eamon and said: 'Get changed. He'll never ride ours in the next.'

He didn't, but the damage won't last long. What will remain is another entry into one of the finest books of heroism this or any other game can give.

Bradbury Star had brought us a long way from last week's Breeders' Cup in Santa Anita. Cheltenham's magic is very different. Long may it remain.

As the world now knows, later that season Declan Murphy was to go even closer to the limit. At Haydock in May he took a skull-shattering fall at the last hurdle, which in other times would have left him dead for certain. He was saved only by the speed and skill of paramedics and surgeons alike, and by his own remarkable spirit, so in evidence that Mackeson Day at Cheltenham.

He had been a dreadful sight when I saw him in hospital and still looked very flaky as he made the long journey back to recovery. But back he came and what a joy it was next March to be sharing a platform with him in, of all places, Fermoy, County Cork. It was a forum to preview the Cheltenham Festival. The evening was long and well lubricated, but with a very attentive audience. It was perfect proof, if proof were needed, that Declan's brain was back in working order.

But all that came long after the dramas of the Mackeson. The Haydock drama was not until May 1994 and before then Declan had been a distant spectator, back in ninth place on Halkopous, as Flakey Dove, the farm mare from Herefordshire, took the Champion Hurdle crown.

Plain Jane who simply would not be denied

16 March 1994

She would not be denied. The last hurdle and the long, screaming Cheltenham hill was still to be taken. Large Action was on the left and Oh So Risky was just pulling out to challenge on the right. Flakey Dove stuck her neck out. This truly was it.

Mark Dwyer had his goggles down, his eyes and mouth raw against the wind as he pumped and shouted the mare forward. She had Large Action held but now, surely, Oh So Risky's Flat-race class would tell. She met the last on a long stride and took it well.

Oh So Risky did the same, half a length off her, but as he landed there was just a hint of a waver. Flakey Dove was in front and hers is a hard old family to pass.

This is 'Plain Jane' with a vengeance. Lean and hard and a fair bit of hair around the heel. As the roar came fore that unflinching closing battle, the past flashbacked to her grandmother Red Dove's time. Lesser days at Ludlow, Hereford and Worcester but the same 'handsome is' qualities. Never any danger of getting the 'best-turned-out' award. Never any chance of any easy deal if you were in against her when the sticks were up and the money down.

Cheltenham's last furlong is a place of truth. It is where you and your runner push and shout and whack and drive. There is no waiting now. What you want is everything. Flakey Dove still had a length on Oh So Risky and every sinew of her and Dwyer's being signalled the 'no surrender sign.'

Mark is 30 now. Jodami's Gold Cup was last March, Forgive 'N Forget's another eight long springs ago; and before that there was the champion Flat-race apprenticeship, and even earlier days among the ponies at Dingle and the beaches of Donegal. There have been good horses along the way. He even won a Group race on the Irish 2,000 Guineas hero Dara Monarch. But Cheltenham has become the Mecca and for him the Champion Hurdle has never happened. The years have led to this.

In a way you had to feel sorry for Oh So Risky. In the wide scheme of things, among the 16,000 active thoroughbreds in these islands, he is a horse of rare and blinding talent, a runner with the speed to win a Group race in France on the Flat last season combined with the hurdling skills to take the Triumph Hurdle and run a good second in the Champion on this very course.

He's a brave horse too. For quite a bit of last season he was operating with a cyst in an extremely painful and personal place. But he's not Flakey Dove. He was not made for this moment, with the crowd baying and the Cheltenham hill making the air thin and the legs heavy. He battled all right, but a length is a long way when you have that Leominster mare in front of you and an Irish jockey in the red Welsh jersey working like a demon in a whirlwind.

The form-book could tell you one thing but your eye knew another. He wouldn't pass her if they ran all the way to Gloucester and beyond.

The race is not just for the swift. It is for the runner who digs deepest. And yesterday for the 'Plain Jane' who was never, ever, to be denied.

It's a sign of old age to say you remember someone's father. With Flakey Dove it was that grandmother I remember. She too was entirely ''ansome is wot 'ansome does'. She was much loved by the Price family but get her in a handicap hurdle at Worcester with the money down and they didn't muck about. Richard Price's father was thick-forearmed and agricultural by trade and didn't pretend to be otherwise in the saddle. But he lacked nothing in determination. Neither did his partner. No surprise that her granddaughter was just the same.

The Fellow's connections cut a very different jib. François Doumen and Adam Kondrat have all the style you expect of residents of Lamorlaye. But Cheltenham's challenge is there for all to try. And for The Fellow and Kondrat it was a famous fourth time of asking.

The day The Fellow proved a champion

20 March 1994

For most of the year it is just a stretch of grass. Then, for three days in March, it becomes the most pressurized patch of turf in the kingdom. The last fence has been jumped at Cheltenham, and there are 230 uphill yards to the winning post.

To Adam Kondrat and The Fellow on Thursday, they could have been Everest.

Great events have a poetry about them. For the last three years, Kondrat and The Fellow have faced this Gold Cup showdown. In 1990 and '91, it took the camera to declare them second. Last March, despite being the heaviest-

The Fellow and Adam Kondrat – success at Cheltenham at the fourth attempt

backed favourite since the race began, they could only manage a fourth to the giant Jodami.

Now, Jodami was beside them again. Failure could have finished Adam Kondrat. He is Polish-born and French-based, but he would have forever remained an England suspect if this one got away. Instead, it was he who made history.

For in the 70 years of The Gold Cup, no French-trained horse had won this most prestigious of all jumping races. No jockey from further afield than Ireland had ridden back between those two outriders in hunting pink. Not a few in England doubted if Kondrat was man enough. And didn't The Fellow now wear blinkers, the rogue's badge of the racetrack? Ah yes, but it was the blinkers, more than anything, that made the difference.

Wind the reel back a year, the field turning away from the stands with one final 10-fence circuit ahead of them. Jodami lobbed easily behind the leaders, his big mule's ears pricking forward as the jumps came up, Mark Dwyer cool and upright above the saddle. All about the pair was confidence. Look back down the field and Kondrat was already a worried man.

It was only a little thing, but it gave the game away. As Adam came past us then, he was to the casual eye his usual low-crouch, almost over-stylish, self. But twice his heel moved a couple of inches to dig The Fellow hard in the ribs. This was a jockey trying to get more steam without hoisting the panic flag. The hot favourite was running cold in 1993.

On Thursday, the roles were almost exactly reversed. Going out on that final circuit, The Fellow and Jodami were fifth and sixth behind the erratic Run For Free, and this time it was the French horse who was going more freely, the blinkers keeping his mind, as well as his vision, hard on the track ahead. Jodami was carrying the punters' money, and once or twice looked a fraction heavy-footed with the burden. Mark Dwyer was in a good position and he kept his cool. Yet, as he swung away from us, you saw his heel move. You knew then it was not going to be easy.

Down the back stretch, up and round the top bend, and then down the hill towards the great denouement of the Cheltenham homecoming, and it was reduced to a three-horse war. Two fences to jump and the so-aptly-named Young Hustler was making things hurt along the inside, The Fellow moving with menace in the centre, Jodami closing on the outside. The Fellow went best, but we had been there before.

For I remember so clearly the image of the leaders sweeping down and past us two years ago. The great Carvill's Hill dream was about to collapse, Adrian Maguire was already at work on Cool Ground, Docklands Express was being niggled by Mark Perrett and, in between them, Adam Kondrat on The Fellow looked to be absolutely cruising. He couldn't get beaten, but he did. Run out of it right on the line by Cool Ground. Such sights leave a scar on a punter's memory. Kondrat and The Fellow might still have had half a length on Jodami as they came to the last on Thursday, but they had a question mark too.

As you reach the final fence, the course narrows in front of you into an ascending, crowd-lined, cheer-laden funnel of green. Two days earlier, in the Champion Hurdle, Mark Dwyer on Flakey Dove who had been in front, shoving and shouting his mare forward as if the hounds of hell were behind him. Now he was the pursuer. On the inside, Young Hustler was still nearly level, but Carl Llewellyn's desperation showed that he wasn't the danger. That was in the centre. Adam Kondrat was driving and The Fellow was the one to beat.

'On Tuesday, there had been so much wind you hardly heard the crowd,' Mark Dwyer said. 'But on Thursday you could hear it all right. You look up that funnel and you hear the sound and you know it's going to be difficult. The Fellow had been going just that bit better all the way. Now I needed him to make a mistake.'

It didn't happen. Kondrat sent his horse at the last as neat and foot-perfect as at all the others. The Fellow may not be Arkle, but no Gold Cup winner ever put in so flawlessly clear a round of Prestbury's immortal circuit. Kondrat may not be Dunwoody or Maguire in the muscle stakes, but his crouched-forward impulsion was a model of poise and balance that any would have found hard to match.

The Fellow leapt that last fence and came on up towards us in one continuous movement of flowing muscle, his hooves punching the turf to the same rhythm as the clamped and urgent drivings from the man on top. Two long lengths off him, Jodami could not find his beat.

Sweeping up to the last fence, he was pulling in the advantage. Dwyer was pumping him with arms and legs and voice. Four strides off it, Jodami's long ears cocked forward in measurement, but the stride wouldn't come. A huge jump then would have put things nearly even. But he was too close. The leap was awkward. Dwyer landed with a slowing horse under him. He came past us grabbing the reins, trying to re-impose the tempo. But he had a mountain to climb.

He knew the terrain. He had been there in Gold Cup triumph with Forgive N' Forget as well as Jodami. On Tuesday, he and Flakey Dove had held Oh So Risky's challenge all the way to the post while the punters howled, and just 40 minutes before he had been first across the line in The Stayers' Hurdle on Avro Anson, only for his left-handed swerve to lose it in the stewards' room.

Now Jodami battled and the stands erupted into that particular roar that means the favourite is closing on the leader. But the leader wouldn't falter. Tight against the rails, The Fellow's blinkered head ran hard and straight all the way to the winning line. Kondrat's stick came up in encouragement. Five, six times the smack went out to keep up the pressure. The Fellow is still only nine, but this was his 43rd race and would take his winnings to over £800,000.

Suddenly the thoughts were only of victory. Kondrat was punching the air in triumph, in happiness, and not one whit in aggravation. After all the disbelief, it would have been understandable if he had produced one of those 'I told you so' gestures which Seb Coe resorted to so memorably at the Moscow Olympics. But as Adam came past us, something very extraordinary was happening. He kept turning across to the massed stands and punching the air and the applause came crashing back down in riverfuls of sporting salute.

When Adam comes over here, he takes off his gold earring in fear of our much-fabled English stuffiness. On Thursday, the compliments would have melted it right down to the Cheltenham grass.

Adam Kondrat had silenced his critics in style and his next visit, to ride The Fellow at Aintree, saw him win more friends again. The Fellow took a purler at the Canal Turn but afterwards, with horse safely boxed up, Adam came into the Press Room and regaled us with the sheer thrill of riding the Grand National fences.

Kondrat's delight was because he had faced the unique challenge that Aintree sets. In flat racing Epsom is the place that asks the questions others would rather avoid. There is a school of thought that thinks the questions are too much. There is usually a soft route. Except at Epsom. Here's a toast to it.

Classic first for delirious Dettori

5 June 1994

The rains came and so did reality. Epsom is not an easy course. Derby or Oaks, sunshine or sheeting showers, Erhaab or Balanchine, the greatest challenge is the track itself. That's what makes this the Classic test besides which all others pale.

Some faces do too. A few years back I was asked to attempt a bilingual promenade of the track with a young French trainer and jockey. They didn't say much as we made the first steep and right-handed climb, and by the time we reached the top of the hill, 140 feet above the start with Tattenham Corner descending helter-skelter away to the left, the words they wanted belonged to another age. 'C'est magnifique,' said the French observer at Balaclava, 'mais ce n'est pas la guerre.'

Epsom is magnificent all right. It's not ordinary racing, ordinary war. That's what's dramatic about it. That's what weeds out faint hearts on two legs and on four. That's what needs preserving.

For at Epsom, unlike almost all other Flat racing tracks, it's not just those last desperate whip-cracking, fist-flourishing strides that you remember. The images stick thick and fast. And this year they came right from the paddock itself.

Before Wednesday's Derby, Erhaab was a jig-jogging lump of bulging black muscle. He was like a boxer coming down towards the ring, so coiled within himself you thought any moment he might turn and beat up the crowd. The French colt Sunshack jig-jogged too. But there was a more evasive, wary quality about him. You worried if he were man enough for what lay ahead. He wasn't.

Sure, as Willie Carson said, it was rough out there. But what's new Willie? This isn't pony club. Everybody knew that outsiders would be a hazard, that's why top jockeys like Carson are paid millions to avoid them. That's why the ride of a lifetime Willie gave Erhaab was worth paying a fortune to see. But it wasn't that rough. The other Willie (Ryan), who has the rib fractures, accepts it. And those jockeys claiming that it was the most dangerous race since the last Palio, bareback round the cobbled streets of Sienna, have either got short memories or should be made to stand in for Dunwoody for a day.

It's exactly because this is the Flat racing jockey's ultimate test which makes it so exciting, which has made this week's two Classics even more thrilling than we dared to hope. It's only at Epsom that you could have that image of Mister Baileys out like an impossible hare from his pursuers at Tattenham

Corner. Only at Epsom where Carson's canny expertise and age-defying energy could catch his quarry in such unbelievable fashion. Only at Epsom where Dettori and Balanchine could fight their own Classic battle on the wrong side of the track.

The rain had come so you had to race on the stands' rails, at the top of the camber, where the turf has drained best. Even walking this strip you notice the severity of the slope inclining you to the left.

They were galloping now, pitched battle on three-year-old fillies for whom this mile and a half is as much as heart and lungs and legs can take. Young Frankie has many championships ahead of him. But he will always remember Epsom, always recall that rain-soaked afternoon when he set off with courage and finished with a balanced and a determination he will never better.

Those in charge of Epsom must, like the riders, be brave. Of course there will be moans from the locals about a Saturday, or even Sunday, Derby, about changes to last week's much-flawed, four-day format. But they are not playing with any old racecourse and, with the Derby, not with just another big day. With the course comes a responsibility to keep it as the ultimate test. It has never liked faint hearts. Its new owners must not fail us now.

Epsom has quite a way to get the doubters off its back. The 1995 move to a Friday Oaks and a Saturday Derby drew plenty of critics. Predictably quite a few of them were people who had suggested the switch in the first place.

But racing fashions move in cycles. There had been quite a move to rubbish our performances in the Breeders' Cup. But Luca Cumani has always been an internationalist. His Arlington Million success with Tolomeo in 1983 was one of the great breakthroughs on the transatlantic scene, and not just because I backed it at 25 to 1. Barathea was never going to be that price in the Breeders' Cup Mile. But he was still a banker.

Well, they always are in hindsight.

Barathea swoops

6 November 1994

It was the race he had waited all his life to win. Barathea, so often the nearly-horse of the European circuit, at last got the great victory his talents have so long promised, the Breeders' Cup Mile under Frankie Dettori in a race and a jockey that fitted him like a glove.

Barathea, the horse who ran second to the mighty Zafonic in last year's 2,000 Guineas, second this season in both the Sussex Stakes and the Queen Elizabeth II and who on his last trip to America was responsible for all sorts of mayhem when he failed to take the first turn and nearly flattened the field in the

Breeders' Cup Turf at Santa Anita. One year on, Barathea was a wiser and better horse.

This victory meant so much to Dettori, and it showed. Luca Cumani was his mentor. Barathea was the most brilliant prospect that Frankie deserted when he and Cumani split last season. This was back together with a vengeance. As Barathea passed the line, Frankie punched the air in jubilation. When he got to the winner's circle he leapt off high with arms outstretched like his hero, Angel Cordero.

The Cumani team were ecstatic. Stable team Keith Leddington and Ian Willows had screamed and screamed as the horse went across the line, and now they were dancing and kissing each other and Luca and Sara Cumani, and part-owner and breeder Gerald Leigh, were swept up in the air by Leddington as he ran across to his champion. Luca Cumani had a lean patch when the Aga Khan removed his horses, but he has always been a master of his profession. This race was his masterpiece.

'I have always believed this horse could be one of the great milers of the decade,' he said. 'He has won some good races, but he's been very unlucky several times. After last year's problems on the first turn in the Breeders' Cup, we were determined to try and overcome things.'

Nobody can exaggerate the pressure as the horses run to that first bend in the mile. It is less than 300 yards from the starting stalls. Fourteen runners are stretched across the track. Then, within another furlong, they have got to complete a full 180-degree turn at 40mph and counting. Barathea was drawn on the inside. It was essential that he got up to that bend in a good position if he was to handle the next crucial 200 yards. He did, but it was precious close.

'He didn't quite break as fast as I wanted him to,' said Dettori, still whooping in celebration afterwards. 'But he ran hard up to the bend, and there was a horse in front of me, and he remembered his lessons beautifully on the turn. Mr Cumani and the team have worked very hard on him and they deserve this.'

Indeed, back at Newmarket Luca Cumani had built an exact replica of this Churchill Downs bend and Barathea and Dettori had been fired around it. Now the field was straightening up. There had been predictable problems as the runners bunched. Ocean Crest looked lucky not to come down, but Barathea was poised in the perfect position, third along the rail behind the pace-setting Unfinished Symph and Dominant Prospect. What's more, he was moving sweeter than ever before.

All too often in Europe, the mid-race picture of Barathea is that of a runner not at ease with his rider, the reins stretched to breaking point, energy going to waste. Now the quicker pace of American racing, and the return of the gifted Italian hands of Dettori, produced an athlete in a moment of fulfilment.

Round the last turn they came. Barathea's great, raking stride still balanced beautifully. For his connections and for the hundreds of visiting Britons, who had backed him at 10–1, this was as good a sight as you could want to see.

Frankie put him at the leaders and the long bay colt stretched his neck and ran clear all the way to the line.

Lochsong and a few others apart, the visiting team did themselves proud on this long journey towards the Kentucky night. Distant View ran well to be fifth behind Barathea, Belle Genius and Erin Bird were good fourths in the Juvenile Fillies and the Distaff respectively. Best of all, Eltish ran the most splendid second to the American champion, two-year-old Timber Country, in the Juvenile.

The French came good in the Breeders' Cup Turf with three of the first four finishers, Tikkanen beating Hatoof and Intrepidity finishing fourth behind the American favourite, Paradise Creek, who palpably failed to stay.

It was that sort of superlative day, but nothing better than Barathea. Racing is by its nature a fleeting game. Barathea is now off to do the fathering business at the Rathbarry Stud in Ireland, but Dettori and Cumani look like being with us for many other great moments in the years ahead. Whatever happens they will be pushed to better this.

One of those times when you hold on to what you are seeing because you know it's just as good as it gets. 'When I was waving,' said Frankie, 'I was celebrating for everyone, for all the lads and for all of Europe too.'

There had been hopes of a rousing European finale in the Classic but we got the sort of drubbing which makes you want to pretend we'd never really hoped at all.

Cezanne was always struggling, Ezzoud got miles behind and only ran on a little in the closing stages, and although Grand Lodge looked impressive going to the final turn, he gave way quickly in the straight as Concern ran down Tabasco Cat on the post.

The French pair, Millkom and Dernier Empereur, fared no better. Dernier Empereur in particular had a frightful trip, being bounced around like a shuttlecock in midrace.

Barathea's Breeders' Cup was one of those wonderful days when everything seemed to fit. No apologies, therefore, for moving on to Alderbrook's Champion Hurdle. It was the race I had a decent financial interest in but was also quite a bit more than that. It was the centrepiece of our first day at the Cheltenham Festival on Channel Four. It was very important to us. But not as important as to those at the heart of it all.

Winners in the crying game

15 March 1995

It is the tears that tell it. Grown men come back to the winner's circle and blub like babies. They have spent a lifetime dreaming of this moment and, as it floods over them, the happiness is too much. Cheltenham takes you like no other place.

We all write and talk so much in anticipation that the whole thing has to be in serious danger of over-hype, of reality bringing us down to just another race day, and probably a losing one to boot. When it dawns you dare it to work the magic again. Yesterday's trick only took an instant.

You would have to be stony of heart even to survive the journey to the track. A pink sky above the Cotswolds, pheasants on stone walls, partridges scuttling on the roadways as you swing off from Stow and take the cross-country route through Upper Swell and Guiting Power to come the Winchcombe way to Cheltenham.

At the top of Cleeve Hill you see the great arena below you. It's 6.45 and sunshine is breaking through the mist. So much will have been settled by sunset.

On the track Montelado has already finished, Pat Flynn has told of the miracle he is trying to work after 728 days of absence. Jim Dreaper is out in the centre with Harcon, he looks at the squelchy surface and jokes 'best ground we have seen for months.' There are already 100-plus racefans gathered. We put a microphone to J.P. McManus. They crowd round every punter's idea of a hero like acolytes on the word of Buddha.

'Fortune And Fame,' says J.P. The encircling group turn to each other and nod at the wisdom.

Back on the members' lawn a deeply embarrassing pantomime was being enacted involving McCririck and Francome running in a mock race with the Big Breakfast's Keith Chegwin.

With first a jolt and then relief, I realize that I had promised to be there but now won't be able to make it. I skulk off to the Channel 4 caravans to collect schedules for the afternoon programme. The Big Breakfast has a very tasty-sized audience but the Champion Hurdle looks marginally more exciting.

A great race involves much, much more than just the participants. For the 14 runners yesterday, Cheltenham was going to be four minutes when an unturnable truth folded out in front of them.

But for all the rest of us it was an event that gripped like no other for ages. Bookmakers reported record activity in the shops. Boning up on facts and figures and TV links in the press room, you could believe it.

The weather was on the downward turn but the excitement was in the other direction. The TV opening shot was on the roof of the Tote building on the other side of the winning post.

Wired up with earpieces and microphones, it seemed further than you had imagined. The four ladders you needed to scale the roof more of a steeplejack's equipment. The adjoining big wheel and karaoke bars more fairground than Cheltenham Festival. But it's all part of the mix. It all leads to two miles, eight flights of hurdles and a champion returning to tearful coronation.

When we got under way all the talk of Anglo-Irish rivalry began to blow back in our faces.

It is one thing to make rather pompous remarks about the joy of the 'shamrock welcome' given to an Irish winner at Cheltenham, quite another to have to put up with both the first two races going that way and having to share commentary with Ted Walsh, for whom they invented the Blarney Stone. 'And now Danoli will make it three,' said Ted giving a painfully playful dig in the ribs, 'bejaysus I like to see you suffer.'

Right well was Danoli going. You could pick up Charlie Swan's white-and-blue jacket a lot more easily than the almost identical one on the white-nosebanded Alderbrook.

After filming at Kim Bailey's last week I doubled the bet I had made at Wincanton. Then on Thursday there had been that glorious attentive Irish symposium on the banks of the Blackwater in Fermoy. 'I can't have Alderbrook,' Charlie Swan had said. 'He won't handle it when the pressure is on.'

So great jockeys can get it wrong too. The beauty is in the returning. It's good enough if you are just a punter who has played it lucky. If you are Kim Bailey, the trainer whose whole life has led to this, little wonder that there are tears to shed. They are the proof of how much it matters.

Come the spring and how swiftly the racing spotlight moves. Within a month Cheltenham is long forgotten and all eyes are on the trials to the first colts' classic showdown in the Two Thousand Guineas. The 1995 build-up was the best we had had for ages. Celtic Swing had been officially rated the best two-year-old in twenty years and duly won his Greenham Stakes warm-up snugly enough. The French Dewhurst Stakes winner Pennekamp also won his trial satisfactorily and Newmarket, on a brilliantly sunny day, made a glorious stage.

These pieces were all written at the time. It was the truth as it was seen then. As the year progressed and Celtic Swing bypassed Epsom for French Derby success and then Irish Derby disaster, the received wisdom grew that he got beaten at Newmarket by the firm ground and by getting unbalanced in the Dip.

That's not how I saw it. I thought he ran a terrific race. He beat Bahri, whose subsequent St James's Palace success underlined him as a miler of the highest class, by an emphatic two lengths. My experience of racing is that you are better judging by results than by excuses. I thought Celtic Swing was beaten by, in Pennekamp, a better horse. Who cares? The truth is that it was a battle to savour, a contest we would not get again. Let's savour it now.

Ninety-five seconds of pure joy
7 May 1995

Ninety-five seconds it took and if the race was lost, it was lost in the first seconds of all. The stalls slammed open and Celtic Swing missed his kick. One mile later Pennekamp had it by just a head. On such fractions do Classics turn.

No decrying the winner, let's later give Pennekamp a champion's due, but you always have to remember the ruthless reality that is racing when the gates have whacked wide and the horses are out there to run. As these Guineas runners were loaded, it was easy to think Celtic Swing was just a minute and a half from coronation. In the saddle Kevin Darley knew it would never be that easy. In a second he had it hard.

Celtic Swing was in stall seven. The Yorkshire horse Chilly Billy came into stall six and tried to dive out the front. Celtic Swing looked across distracted, and when the bell rang his hindquarters didn't punch him out with the others. It was only a length but as he came out fractionally behind the others Pipe Major cannoned into him. Darley had to grab and balance his runner. These are the normal jump and scramble of race starts. But it was not the perfect Guineas start. Not when you are going to end beaten by just a head.

Way out to the right Pennekamp had started equally tardily but this was by design. Thierry Jarnet knew his best chance was to wait to attack Celtic Swing when the black horse had already gone for everything. He dropped in at the back of the pack and let the others do the racing.

The first furlong was a bit of a muddled affair. Silca Blanka and Zeb were already in front, but Tony Ives' straining arms showed Zeb was about to have the brakes failure which would change the course of the race. The horses ran close to the rail which gave longtime clocker Michael Tanner a chance to log every furlong. This first came up at a slow and muddled 14.40 seconds.

It gave Darley the chance to move up to a perfect pitch behind the leaders, but if there had been any squandering of effort it had already happened. From then on he had a clear field to play. He played it perfectly. But nemesis stalked behind. It was a bright bay colt with a coiled French champion tucked in above him.

Beforehand we had wondered if there would be pace enough to take the sting out of the finishers. As Tony Ives accepted the inevitable and let Zeb blaze up the Rowley Mile we got pace aplenty. Tanner started life as a schoolmaster and he now began to wonder at what the clock was telling him. Furlong after furlong reeled off under the 12-second norm. 11.12 secs, 11.23, 11.15, 11.36, 11.05 and 11.47 for that penultimate fraction. For the first time in Tanner's experience the middle of a Guineas was run at sub-12 second rate.

It should have suited Celtic. Certainly the doubtful stayer Diffident found his stamina wanting. But Darley is no poser. Two furlongs out he knew he needed to impose himself. Pushing and pumping and cracking he sent Celtic Swing ahead.

At that moment the dream still lived. It was never going to be devastating, Bahri was already too close and too competitive. But the unbeaten horse, whose breeding suggests the Derby distance is more to his liking, could take this and stay unbeaten. He could repel what was coming across from the right-hand quarter.

The calculations in Thierry Jarnet's head had to be exact. If he swept through and tackled Celtic Swing too soon the black horse might pull him back up the hill. The calculations had to be made in split seconds perched atop half a ton of thoroughbred racing at 40mph. Jarnet is a champion. Yesterday he showed why.

There was a beauty in the balanced and deadly way he spun Pennekamp down the hill to take the leader. Aboard Celtic Swing Darley had his stick up, arms thrusting as he made his still inexperienced partner run as he had never run before. But the advantage was with the pursuer. Pennekamp quickened past and then all Britain willed Celtic Swing's unavailing counter attack.

We came looking for greatness. In Pennekamp we might have found it. But the margins are so narrow Celtic Swing may yet find immortality too. The Derby re-match should be another treat.

The re-match never did, probably never will, happen. Celtic Swing went for and won the French Derby. Pennekamp was backed down to 11–8 favourite at Epsom, but a hairline fracture saw him fall to pieces on the turn just as completely as Celtic Swing was to in the Irish Derby with torn knee ligaments. The laws of attrition had reaped their vengeance yet again.

Without Celtic Swing this Derby had a slightly Hamlet-less feel, which probably had as much to do with the drop in betting turnover as with the much-discussed move to a Saturday. But on the day, as so often, the winning story was worthy of its stage. And certainly the winning rider too.

Swinburn believes his victory was heaven-sent
11 June 1995

For Walter Swinburn, in a very bittersweet sense, this Derby was heaven-sent. For even before Walter won on Lammtarra at Newbury last August, the chestnut colt's then trainer Alex Scott was telling friends that this would win the Derby in '95.

Walter was a friend. As the world knows Alex was tragically and violently killed in October. He was not there to see his prediction come right. Or was he?

'Everything went wrong after a couple of furlongs,' said Walter afterwards, 'so as we came down the hill and up the straight I was saying to myself "help me Alex, help me". I know he was helping me from above.'

As he came up on to the interview podium, still bathed in sweat and wreathed in smiles, it was easy to forget what a seasoned performer Swinburn has already become. This was his 15th Derby ride, his third victory following those of Shergar and Sharastani in '81 and '86.

Some people may persist with the 'Choir Boy' nickname from those

Walter Swinburn enjoys Derby triumph with Lammtarra in 1995

Shergar days. But for the once-raced Lammtarra it was experience that was required. Experience and a class rider's inspiration that he got.

For however much we bang on beforehand about Epsom's uniquely challenging helter-skelter of a track, the real thing is much tougher than the talk. It is the most demanding racetrack in the world. Yesterday, with a set of staying horses bent on drawing the finishing kick out of Pennekamp and Spectrum, it was demanding even more than usual. For a time you could have been certain it had asked too much of Lammtarra.

In view of his partner's inexperience, Swinburn planned to attack up the first sharp incline – the courses rises 135 feet in its first serpentine half mile – to ensure a position close to the leaders and out of the skirmishing that inevitably occurs in the mid and back of the pack.

For 300 yards the plan worked but as the line of the race came back towards the left-hand rail, his racing room was cut off and he and Lammtarra were abruptly shunted back to that netherland from which Derby winners rarely come.

Watching 'live', that skirmish attracted only the briefest of attention. It was the sort of thing you expected to happen to Lammtarra and the eyes were much more for French champion Thierry Jarnet's progress on the favourite.

After one early bump he had got Pennekamp into perfect position poised just behind the leaders. As the field began the decent – 40 feet in the three furlongs to Tattenham Corner, another 55 feet in the three furlongs thereafter – this was a Derby going to the obvious plan.

Not for long it wasn't. The first indication was Pennekamp's forelegs coming up a bit high and out of rhythm as he began the downward journey.

Moments later doubt became shattering reality as the field straightened up for home and Pennekamp was suddenly hanging out wide, and Jarnet changed from poised champion to just another struggling jock with a beaten horse beneath him. We would have to look elsewhere for the winner. But how many of us looked back far enough for Lammtarra?

'I know I was a some way behind,' said Walter, 'but I got a completely trouble-free run down along the rail behind Munwar and I still had a lot of hope in the horse.'

Our eyes were already locked into the emerging battle up front. Fahal battled, Presenting flattered, Tamure came with what looked a winning run under Frankie Dettori. Lammtarra had made up enough ground to make his race respectable. Respectable? Walter was about to make it sensational.

'He was keeping on so well,' said his rider afterwards, 'that I kept remembering how much he had found in that race last year. Three furlongs out I was sure I could get close. A furlong out, even though I was four lengths down, I knew I would win.'

Swinburn will never go through the daily grind to be champion jockey. With 25 winners to date he is fully 60 adrift of Dettori in the table. But in the big events he bows the knee to no one. He wasn't bowing now.

At 5ft 6in he is quite tall for a flat race jockey but at moments of crisis he uses every inch of toe to hand to elbow to galvanize the horse beneath him. He

is a great one to re-reel his reins, to switch his whip hand in the relentless quest
to stretch for the line.

At Epsom, even on the most experienced of horses, this final furlong with
its one-in-12 camber down towards the rail can be desperately difficult to ride.
At 33 Swinburn has many more Derbies ahead of him but he may never better
this one.

'The horse kept finding for me,' he said looking at the replay, 'then he hit
this terrific gear just like he did at Newbury and really took off.' It's a lot easier
to say than do.

The Epsom track had taken its usual toll. Both Spectrum and Pennekamp
were walking gingerly homewards while their riders had the bitter taste of
broken dreams.

For Swinburn it was so very different. The chestnut colt whose chance he
had had to accept on the evidence of home gallops alone had stormed through
and taken a full second and a half out of Mahmoud's long-standing Derby record.
In many ways it was a perfect day. And yet . . .

It was with grace and feeling that Walter spoke of Alex Scott. It cannot
have been easy with the breath still short after your efforts in the saddle and with
your words being tannoyed to hundreds of thousands around the track, not to
mention unseen millions of viewers watching on television.

But this was grace under pressure in its truest sense.

There are times when Swinburn's relaxed urbanity can make him seem a
man to whom even this hassled life has come easy. After all, his father Wally was
a champion jockey and Shergar's Derby came in teenage years.

But underneath the charm there is steel as well as style. It showed on
Lammtarra yesterday.

*Lammtarra went on to complete a famous double in the King George VI and
Queen Elizabeth Diamond Stakes at Ascot. No great surprise in that, except that
it was Dettori not Swinburn in the irons. Connections stuck to the line that as
they had a claim on Dettori they had just chosen to exercise it. But in view of
Swinburn's success on the colt, the best comment is probably to echo Yves Saint-
Martin's words when he showed up to ride Rheingold at York only to find
himself replaced by Lester Piggott at the last moment.*

'C'est bizarre,' Yves said.

People

If you travel the racing parish the people who impress you most are not necessarily those in the central spotlight of fame. In fact it's often the absolute reverse. It was certainly true of Mr Dillon.

Mick Dillon

20 June 1991

Let us now praise famous men. No doubt there were plenty at Ascot but the only time this one has ever worn a top hat was when he played Lord Lickspittle in *The Charge of the Light Brigade*. He's called Michael Dillon and he doesn't work for Ladbrokes.

Mick Dillon has been jump jockey, stunt man (not necessarily the same thing), film extra, and is now the oldest operating stalls handler. He was 65 on Saturday but was working at Ascot every day. He loaded up Lester before The Maestro won the King Edward VII on Saddlers' Hall. Their combined ages were 122. It keeps you young.

In Mick's case only until Lingfield on 29 June. For reasons of insurance and creaking arthritis, Dillon will hang up his helmet and something new will have to be found for one of the most cheerful spirits in the game. At a time when racing is into paroxysms of self-doubt, it's worth wandering down to the stalls and remembering how a real survivor works.

Young Mick first rode out at Epsom when his father was head lad to Bobby Dick in 1936; the stables are now a police academy. He did 5st 11lb on the Flat at Nottingham in 1941. He joined the Air Force with Fred Winter but was never any threat to him in a jumping career which drifted on to '61. 'I was a very poor pilot,' he says with that strong South London laugh, 'just a few winners. Very moderate.'

Not moderate in life, though. Starting with a Norman Wisdom film called

Just My Luck, Mick got an Equity card and began other games. An Oscar never threatened, but if a director needed somebody to play an authentic equestrian scene, as likely as not it would be Mick who would be togged up for action. The dialogue rarely stretched further than 'whoa there my beauty', but you knew that they knew that he knew what he was doing.

If you go down to the video library you can find him in all sorts of things from *Tom Jones* to *The Belstone Fox*. More surprisingly, doubling for an ailing Buster Keaton in *A Funny Thing Happened On The Way To The Forum*, and more painfully as an Italian motor mechanic in *Chitty Chitty Bang Bang*. His car capsized in a stunt down the side of Box Hill. 'Broke my skull,' recalls Mick. 'Off for three months, nasty.'

But for the past 15 years it has been the starting stalls, and in particular Peter Hickling's wonderfully well run southern team, which has been Dillon's permanent casting. A splendid lady called Dorothy Brandon is now organizing a presentation to mark Mick's going.

If she wasn't of a certain age and so obviously respectable, you would call Dorothy a starting stalls groupie, organizing picnics at Goodwood, talking about 'my boys', sending cards at Christmas. But while we can all get a bit dewy-eyed about these things there is still something magnificently old-school English about Mrs Brandon's insistence that it's the unsung loaders who deserve our attention.

At Sandown on Saturday the other end of the races belonged to Darryll Holland. He had been 19 on Friday. The winners are coming thick and fast. He has got the winning feeling and it shows. He was happy to tell us so for the TV interview.

At this stage the very top of the mountain is possible for the carpenter's son from Manchester. But it is a long, long haul, and Monday's news that Darryll was taken faint from wasting was a reminder of just one of the hazards which lie ahead.

Whatever happens, he should vow never to lose the good humour of the men who link arms behind his horses' backsides today. It's a grand life while it's lasting but one wrong move can threaten it.

Ten years ago this April Mick Dillon led a sprinter of Bob Turnell's called Winsor Boy into the stalls at Epsom. 'Lester was on it,' said Mick, 'he was second last to go in. The thing that Greville was riding came in, then backed out again. Then, *whoosh*, Lester's horse had gone down underneath, with him on it. His skull was pinned, I thought he was a goner.'

You will remember that it was just one week later that a temple-swathed, pain-killed Piggott won the 1,000 Guineas on Fairy Footsteps and all but expired in the weighing room afterwards. The 'Legend of Lester's Ear' was added to all the rest.

A decade on, the Long Man's saga goes into ever more extraordinary chapters. At Lingfield next Saturday evening another, rather less trumpeted, story will be over. No top hats maybe but Mick Dillon and his mates deserve a Miltonic re-write: 'They also serve who only stand and shove.'

Mick still comes out to the races on high days and holidays but the old bones are remembering some of the stunts he got up to. For all his tough times Mick in his own way should be classed as a winner. Sadly, you can't say the same about poor Glynn Wilkinson.

Glynn Wilkinson

17 October 1991

Let's get bad luck into perspective. To Cardiff on Saturday to watch Wales routed by the Aussies, a nation mourns. To Staines on Monday to see Glynn Wilkinson. No, you don't remember him. Does anybody care?

Wilkinson was a wagon-driver's son from Teesside who was apprenticed to Sam Hall in the late '70s. Energetic and naturally enthusiastic, he had ridden 24 jumping winners when his knee was smashed in a schooling accident at Middleham in 1983. Fate had decided to play dirty and ever since has kept toying with poor Glynn like some monstrously sadistic cat.

On Monday night he was an unhappy sight. He's 34 but despite thick glasses, thinning hair and a stomach that's beginning to push against the waist band, he has a quiet, deferring manner that makes him seem younger than his years.

He was sitting very upright at a table in his mother's terraced house just round the back of Englefield Green cemetery. You tend to sit a bit stiffly when you have a double fracture of the skull. It was his daughter Beverley Jane's second birthday. He hasn't seen her for three months. But that's only part of the story.

The first battle was to try to ride again and it took him three long years to lose it. Time after time he would visit the Rehabilitation Centre at Camden. He was the star pupil, the most optimistic in the class. We would watch him doing all sorts of amazing calisthenics with the knee. But in the end the flesh was too weak.

Unlike some wounded heroes, he wasn't big on self-pity. He got on to a training course for the brewing trade. He passed his exams in Shrewsbury and got a job at the Wensleydale Heifer, in West Witton, and then at the Blue Dolphin Holiday Camp at Filey.

From the outside he had graduated successfully from the racing game; he had learnt a trade and was about to marry one of his colleagues. But the knee wasn't made for barrel-lifting and the wedding was to bring neither party happiness.

For physical and family reasons he turned down a position in the South and started work at the Hytex rubber factory in Rotherham. Gareth and Beverley Jane had appeared but home affairs were not flourishing. As a fresh start he began selling milk in Teesside but after three months of enforced separation, the marriage was clearly over.

We are into the start of this year and a stay with his sister at Egham got him a job but ended in hospital with pneumonia. The cat's paw had grabbed anew but once again released him. Whilst in care the doctors had another look at his knee and with modern microsurgery were able to clear much of the old debris out. A month ago at the St Leger meeting Glynn looked better than he had in years.

He was due to visit his children next day. He had a job at the Schweppes plant in Ashford, he had just survived a car smash three days before. 'I think my luck is on the turn,' he said. So it was. Back again.

Next morning the family visit was disallowed in acrimony. Next week he was rushed to intensive care, the car crash (he had fallen asleep at the wheel after late-night overtime) had split his skull and blood had seeped out of the brain. Now there will be no work before Christmas. 'We were terribly worried,' said his mother on Monday.

But she is not the only one. At a time when racing's external image is besmirched by an unprecedented amount of internal wrangling, we ought to be very proud of what we have been able to do for Glynn Wilkinson.

For it was the Injured Jockeys Fund who supported him through Camden and through his brewery trade course. It is the I.J.F. and its heroic northern almoner Hilary Kerr who are involved with Glynn's latest help. And the I.J.F. only exists because of racing's goodwill. Over 500 cases have gone through our books, from paraplegics to multiple sclerosis to simple victims of misfortune. Last year's Christmas card and calendar made £120,000 but we paid out over £300,000. Let no one get charity fatigue.

Especially not today when Newmarket sees the unveiling of its newest visible evidence of what's possible when charities, local council and racing community work together – the Racing Welfare flats at Phantom and Moreton. Twenty-four old people's apartments are now in the pipeline.

It will never be easy. You remember the aching disbelief as the Wilkinson tale unfolded. 'I just can't get over my luck,' said Glynn, his eyes watering only slightly. 'But at least it can only get better.' It will do. If we bother enough.

It did get better. Not wonderful, but at least Glynn has found a way of keeping body and soul together. May his luck stay on the turn.

Now to luck from another quarter. In the spring of '91 my Racing Post *colleague Michael Harris thought up a wizard wheeze. We would combine the resources of the Tote's computer base with* Racing Post's *reader access to produce a giant 'Ten to Follow' competition for the coming Flat season.*

It has since increased more than five times in size, but the first winner was a publicist's dream. Of course to an Irish way of thinking.

Tim O'Mahony

14 November 1991

Oh the lakes, the lakes of Killarney. And the mountains, and the castle, and the people, and the Kerry Postman himself. And to think that we were there less than two short hours. A fine madness this is.

All right, it was in a good cause: to present Tim O'Mahony with his £34,000 winner's cheque from the Ten to Follow pool. But by the time we had scrambled across to Cork in the morning, driven over the Derrynasaggart Mountains of Killarney, rushed back for the 5pm flight to Heathrow and then got stuck on the M25 *en route* to Doncaster, there had to be serious doubts as to what was under one's own bonnet.

Like many an absurdity, it had begun life as a 'good idea at the time'. More exactly, it traced back to a touch of *Racing Post* over-excitement at the success of the Ten to Follow. Images of pools winners collecting their millions and a kiss from Cilla Black at some flash London eaterie led to a similar invitation to the star of Abbeydorney Post Office, just five miles in from that jewel of Irish beaches, Banna Strand.

Well, it was a slightly similar invitation.

Economic circumstances would mean me rather than Cilla to do the kissing, and lunch at Raynes Park's Il Camino rather than the Café Royal, but we wanted to have Tim O'Mahony over and push out the best boat available. The first snag occurred with the opening call to County Kerry. The other postman was on holiday last week. No London visit was possible. The mountain would have to go to Mohammed. The troubled road had begun.

The search for the 'photo opportunity' has a long and not always honour-able history in newspapers. One noted lensman didn't use to mess about. He would have a large shoulder bag with him and, confronted with the need to compose a striking picture for the back of the sports pages, would grab the targetted soccer player, unzip the case, pull out the cowboy outfit, and presto, next morning's photo would be headlined 'Hot Shot'. At Heathrow on Friday our Edward Whitaker arrived carrying a large bag. Be prepared.

The logistics of the operation meant that time was at a premium. The morning flight doesn't land in Cork until 11.30pm, there was no chance of making it up to Tralee and back, so O'Mahony drove south to Killarney. Coming in over Cork harbour with the sun dappling the green meadows inshore, the photo chances looked good. If the weather held. It didn't.

Neither at first did the luck. A traffic jam blocked our exit from Cork and by 12.30 black clouds had unleashed a downpour – we had only just made Macroom, and, with the two sheep lorries in the queue up ahead, the prospects looked bleak. 'Perhaps we could do an indoor shot,' said Whitaker hopefully, 'Tim in a bar peering through pints of Guinness.' A journey to the most beautiful location in Western Europe and we don't go outside. Not only the weather was gloomy.

Then came the rainbow, the sky clearing to the north. We bumped down into Killarney. A blue window was opening for our photo, but other clouds were gathering. Tim, his brother Noel, sister-in-law Brigid, and Aunt Eileen were already ensconced in the lounge of the Great Southern. No time for ceremony.

The handshakes were still warm as we turned off into Ross Road and headed for the lake. The racecourse is on the left, enlivened by Lester's visit this summer and graced by an irrepressible clerk of the course called Finbarr Slattery. Ross Castle should be at the end of the avenue. What a prop for the O'Mahony portrait.

On through a beech wood and into a clearing, the sky still blue but Whitaker swore just the same. The castle was covered in scaffolding. New backdrops now.

This is where photographers have to earn their corn. Edward Whitaker may look a casual youth but he has had to work alongside the likes of Eddie Byrne and Gerry Cranham. This means that you make the 'Oh dear, you mean Generous wasn't the horse on the near side' mistake only once. We decamped beside the lake. Whitaker was all business. He unzipped his bag.

For a dreadful moment I thought he was going to produce an outfit and dress up the hapless O'Mahony like Postman Pat. Fortunately it was only cameras. The clouds were closing. It was bitter cold. Tim O'Mahony is a lovely, intelligent man but even his best friend wouldn't call him an extrovert. It can be surprisingly hard to say 'cheese'.

After five minutes and what seemed like 50 rolls of film, the deed was done. We repaired to the Three Lakes Hotel. In a civilized world the shutters would have gone up for the afternoon. As the drink flowed we could have relived O'Mahony's remarkable season, heard of how he and Aunt Eileen danced round the table when Environment Friend won the Eclipse at 28–1, picked their brains about their 17 entries for the jumping Ten to Follow, and staggered home about Tuesday.

Instead we had hardly loosened the tongues before it was finish off the fish pie, drain the Guinness, and scarper back over the mountains for the airport. To avoid Cork traffic we tried a short cut through Kilpatrick and Cross Barry. There was a cattle truck in the way, children were going home from school; we were looking at our watches and wondering about flight times.

In Cross Barry, Mr W.H. Davies doesn't need to be required reading. He's the guy who wrote the all too accurate lines: 'What is this life if, full of care, we have no time to stand and stare?' Well, at least the photos were good.

*Ireland, ah Ireland; so many of your citizens have their priorities right. Mind
you, there are some of them who get into the sort of work mode that a pack-horse
wouldn't envy. But then Eddie Byrne has never asked for sympathy from
anybody. He is what he is. He does what he does. Let's thank the Lord for it.*

Eddie Byrne

16 January 1992

For our delight. Three words but a lifetime's work. A small bustling man with
a little silver beard and extraordinary eyes that twinkle like a leprechaun's.
Photographer Ed Byrne on the Saturday night plane from Dublin. The world
wasn't such a bad place after all.

It was certainly a holier one. 'You haven't met Father Colin,' says Ed,
introducing his companion whose dog-collar seems to be missing but whose talk
of racing you only get from an Irish member of the cloth. 'Marvellous man,'
confides Ed. 'Organizes the youth club, football teams, everything.'

The stewardess attempts to glower forbiddingly as lensman Byrne tries to
stuff his vast camera bag under the seat. She can't keep it up. Nobody can. You
can't glower at a leprechaun.

Ed Byrne begins to relate his day. It had started back home in East Ham,
long before dawn crept up from Barking. The car had been frozen but the plane
had been caught and so too, as ever, the crucial moment at Leopardstown.

The last hurdle in the Ladbroke. Whips up, the money down. Jungle Knife
and Adrian Maguire somersaulting as How's The Boss sweeps by. John
Mortimer, Rumpole's creator and Lady Chatterley's defender, once called
photographers 'overpaid button pushers'. Let him lay up with Eddie Byrne.

He sure wouldn't stay fat on it. Whilst we thirsty hacks hitched a ride on
the Ladbroke coach, Ed was winging off up the Kilgobbin Road to look over
another idea. 'You should have seen them,' he said later. 'Shire horse yearlings,
already 16 hands as wild as march hares.'

Which description looked as if it would soon fit some of us coach dwellers
so patiently assembled by the ubiquitous Mike Dillon. The night before the
driver couldn't start it. He had appeared to think that 'ignition' was something
to do with your appendix. Fun was on the horizon.

Not for us this time. Off through the dark, over the boat-bobbing Liffey to
make the quick way to the airport and face that hopelessly good-humoured
Garda waving his treasure detector at the luggage. Weariness comes seeping in.
Then Byrne appears, strap over the shoulder, back bent against the load. Who's
weary now?

He's London Transport's greatest loss. It's more than 20 years since he left
his native Dublin to say 'hold very tight please' on a Number 72. Get him to tell
you the story of his one attempt at taking the wheel which ended with Driver
Byrne being 'run away with' down Regent Street.

Destiny would out. Edward's backstreet childhood had hardly been the Slade School of Art but always, even fooling about the gypsy ponies, he had this unrequited passion for horses. Now, looking into those Dover Street galleries as the buses changed shift, a light bulb of an idea began to gleam. A Box Brownie was purchased. Top steeplechaser Pendil was the star. An unforgettable picture was snapped at Kempton. A prize was won. A dream under way.

Listening to him as the 737 hammered homewards was to wonder at our luck. To have a chronicler of our game who so perfectly combines the expert's hand with the child's eye. To have someone whom no amount of acclaim or success seems to lessen this labour of love.

He is given to making sudden unconnected remarks about horses as if they were pupils in the school we all attended. 'Cuddy Dale winning over hurdles,' he says of that day's opening victor at Ascot. 'Fancy that. Wonderful galloper. When he comes past, you can really see him stretch.'

There were oohs and ahhs. What a chaser Mutare might make. How great a champion Carvill's Hill could prove to be. How soon would we get the moment of truth with Arazi? The eyes flashed with anticipation. In them you could see the little scuffling, camera-toting figure that hovers by fences and finish lines from Churchill Downs to Cheltenham. There's a fire and a purity there. The man's a poet at two hundredths of a second.

A fighter too. Out in America he had gone to photograph Sunday Silence. 'What can we do to help?' said Charlie Whittingham. Back in England he had lensed some horses working after racing at Newbury. 'Can you tell me which one was that?' asks Ed. 'Mind your own business,' says trainer. He should be careful. This leprechaun has teeth.

Heathrow is regained. Father Colin goes off for the sabbath. Some of us head home for the telly. Ed sets his head east for two hours in the dark room.

It's been a long day. It's a cold, raw January night. The camera bag seems to have grown on the journey. But the man doesn't sound heavy laden. You can almost warm your hands on the willingness. 'I am still so keen,' he says, the accent very Dublin in the emphasis. 'I am just mad for it.' Happiness in a single frame.

In 1992 British racing tried to spread its happiness to Sunday. The serried ranks of the non-conformist conscience and a few concerned trade unionists had done their worst, but come July, Doncaster was the scene of a typical British compromise. Yes, they would allow racing on Sunday but, no they would not permit any betting on course or allow betting shops around the country to open. What about if you had a credit account and just rang up the bookmaker's seven-day-a-week number and had your bet on as usual? Ah, well, that's different.

So we all got to Donny. We needed to be in good hands at this hour. And we were.

Father Donal

30 July 1992

At last a star on Sunday. Seventy-one years since he first opened eyes on the ancient town of Listowel in County Kerry, Father Donal Bambury did the thing he was born to. At noon precisely he called racing to prayer. We were in the hands of a master.

A voice rang out which had seen life but had seen race tracks too. A man for whom Killarney is the favourite place in the world but who has tended the flock in the Doncaster area these past 40 years. A worker on the Sabbath, not an apologist for it.

You could even hear him in the gents' loo. Pre-TV stomach never had much chance as Father Donal's voice boomed across the cubicles. Clerk of the course John Sanderson read the lesson and then Father Donal led the singing of 'Abide With Me'.

Out in the fresh, rather than 'air-freshener' air, a mixed bunch of onlookers were swelling the chorus. They were mostly couples with children and complimentary carrier bags weighed down with free issue brochures. They might be moving from the Shetland Pony Grand National to the Scud Missile display but they paused to listen to the word. From that moment you knew that both Doncaster and Father Donal were winning big.

Other hassles about on- and off- course betting have to be resolved in their time, but seeing those families and listening to Father Donal, you knew the 'stay away to keep Sunday special' argument was dead. This was Sunday. These were families. And even to this hardened old racecourse hack, the atmosphere at Doncaster was special indeed. No jokes, it had a blessing on it.

Shame on the faint-hearts who would not come. When we last checked Doncaster was in England, yet the request to the Church of England to take part in the service was declined on the grounds that it was 'controversial'. Father Donal is the Roman Catholic parish priest at St Alban's in nearby Denaby. He always goes to Doncaster racecourse and altar boys in local quizzes are as likely to get questions about Lincoln winners as about the last pope.

'We pray that God will bless this occasion.' Father D. looked up in gentle, silver-haired rebuke at the rain clouds bunching overhead. 'We pray,' he continued, 'that whatever follows from this will be a source of blessing and healthy entertainment for many years to come, for generations still unborn.' Heathen or otherwise, you had to be moved by the feet-in-the- paddock sincerity of it all. Was it a wonder that the clouds rolled back, not a drop of rain did fall?

In an increasingly godless Britain it might even be common prudence for the men of the cloth to go to where the customers are, to revert to other days when betting and indeed galloping vicars were commonplace.

Back in the 1950s, way before fox-hunting was viewed as some form of political statement, a day with the North Cotswold was doubly insured as both

Canon Hodgson and Doctor Houghton regularly rode as 'unspeakables in pursuit of the uneatable'.

Both of them were not totally unacquainted with eccentricity. When running late, Doctor Houghton was apt to turn up for surgery and on one memorable occasion even to the school play, in full mud-caked, scarlet-coated hunting regalia. Harold Hodgson was a slightly more self-effacing man but he sat a horse like the former Canadian cavalry rough-rider he had once been. We used to call him Bronco Hal.

His memory was a bit variable. One day he couldn't find his wife after a shopping trip. He had stranded her in Cheltenham. During the Suez crisis he took to driving a pony and trap. Fine, until he tacked up the wrong pony who promptly kicked the trap to pieces.

But the big problem came when he let a new parishioner ride his old hunter mare Ruth. The parishioner was of some age but had been a horsey, even a racing man in his youth. He and Ruth looked a bonny pair as they jogged off along the gated footpath past the cricket pitch.

They found Ruth first in the next field. The parishioner was lying unconscious by the second gate. It was a week before he was well enough to tell the tale.

The galloping vicar had omitted one small detail about his normal perambulations. When he got to the footpath gates, he didn't open them, he jumped them.

As Ruth flew through the air unbidden, the poor old parishioner had sailed off sideways like a bale off a lorry. When he came round, his head was sore, his mind muzzy but the horse still there. He remounted and trotted to the next gate, Ruth skipped over, off he went and concussion ensued.

Bronco Hal was too kind not to be upset, but too well liked to be held heavily responsible. No doubt many of us will suffer other sorts of concussions on future racing sabbaths. Let's not lay anything but thanks at Father Donal's door.

When I wrote that, I was unaware of being in Father Donal's debt for something even greater. Twenty years before, I had been a bit mangled in a fall in a novice chase at Doncaster and had ended up with a broken arm and kicked-in larynx in the local orthopaedic ward. In those days this institution was a far cry from the smart establishment of the present day. It had been snowing and by the time my trolley reached the ward it had an extra white blanket of a colder kind.

The ward was a grandiose Nissen hut with a pot-bellied stove for heating. The other patients were mostly miners with mind-chilling stories which started 'There was this rumble int' pit'. On the first night the bed beside me was wheeled out, never to return. I wasn't feeling too brilliant and a priest came to keep my spirits up. It was Father Donal. I was one of the lucky ones and was up and about soon enough. Father Donal is now a Monsignor. Rome got it right.

So, too, did Jim Joel. And this was an odd but a lovely one. It was a wake.
But a wake, you will understand, of the very smartest kind.

Jim Joel

10 September 1992

The party after you have gone; it has to be the most difficult trick of all. Jim Joel got it right last week at Claridges. But then he would. They don't make them like him any more.

Of course it should be easy to be kind and generous if life has dealt you silver spoons with diamond handles, but think of all those viper-faces that prove otherwise. How many other multi-millionaires would have the inscription consecrated on Jim Joel's headstone at Willesden Cemetery on Tuesday 'meek above all men'?

Not a Howard Hughes recluse or Paul Getty misery guts, you understand. Jim Joel had a winningly unique approach to life. He wanted to do things in style but at the same time not make a fuss about it. Claridges last week was him to a tee.

A 'buffet lunch' the invitation said. Images of forking a few snips of salmon from the plate, raising a glass to the old boy's memory and buzzing back to the office. Not so fast.

After Jim's racing manager Peter Doyle had paid his opening tribute, the great doors of the banqueting room where pulled back, and there were a dozen beautifully laid tables and facing us, running the full length of the hall, a white cloth'd spread of every conceivable gourmet's delight. It was as near to the ordinary Rotary Club buffet as Hampton Court is to a motorway stop.

But it was self-service. Jim would have liked that. One winter morning a few years back we went to see him at his stud at Childwick Bury near Luton. There was snow outside, old masters on the walls and very soon there were crystal glasses on a silver tray.

Alec the butler poured the first time. But all too soon the golden bubbles had gone and then, despite our protests, Mr Joel pulled himself gallantly to his 90-year-old feet and tottered across to give us a refill. He looked like some tiny, frail old crow weighed down by the sparkling burden we gluttons never deserved. We misjudged him but not his generosity. He never split a drop.

Six monarchs he had seen and as so often the earliest memories had become the most vivid. Back through the years they went. The famous World War One tale of his father sending him the Middle Park Stakes second as a cavalry charger. Stories of seeing the King lead in his Derby winner of 1909, of the legendary tenor Caruso singing at his parents' housewarming party in Grosvenor Square, even of Buffalo Bill.

Yes, Buffalo Bill. 'Colonel Cody,' Jim recalled. 'My father must have brought him down in his special carriage on the Luton train. I remember looking out of my bedroom window and watching him throw sticks in the air and shooting them with his revolver. Amazing man.'

But at Claridges last week the memories were a little closer to home. Julie Cecil talking of the morning Jim's Derby winner Royal Palace didn't shine in his pre-St Leger gallop and Jim insisted on telling the Press Association himself. And then one of his fellow guests at Johannesburg airport in April 1987 who wanted to back Joel's Maori Venture when the Grand National came flickering up on the TV screen.

'He's got as much chance of jumping round those fences as I have,' chuckled Jim, 'what price do you want?' Ten dollars was invested at 100–1 and a cheque for $1,000 was despatched almost before the plane had landed in London.

Andy Turnell, Maori Venture's trainer, was there on Tuesday. So, too, Josh Gifford and Henry Cecil and jockeys Steve Cauthen and Richard Dunwoody, looking lean and purposeful amongst the slacker chins of the other guests. A small man in awe of his East End-to-South Africa diamond mine father, Jim Joel had always related to jockeys and to all the racing team. 'I like to get all the chaps involved,' he used to say in those clipped Edwardian tones, 'then the horses belong to them.'

No party is complete without its moment of discord to put the general goodwill into relief. In this one we got a beauty.

At the end of lunch the distinguished Peter Willett, long-time friend and trustee of Mr Joel's Charity Fund, stood up to give what became a typically lucid address. But not before some uncomfortable opening moments with a defective microphone and some raucous complaints from a notoriously outspoken lady whom Jim somehow always tolerated down the years.

Willett finally wrapped things up and came back through the applause to the table. He shrugged off the interruptions. 'Jim wouldn't have minded,' said Willett. 'You see, he loved consistency. Even at this party the old girl ran true to form.'

Jim Joel had served his full term and more. We all acknowledged his contribution over the years. The feeling is a bit different when someone much younger goes. God moves in a mysterious way.

Dawn Grant

29 October 1992

Sun and sand but a sinking heart. The big jet will lift off for the palm tree delights of Miami this morning but the bell will still toll. The bell of St Wilfred's in Bishop Auckland. The Breeders' Cup beckons but Dawn Grant has gone.

The Breeders' Cup is the biggest thing to hit horse racing in 50 years. Dawn Grant lived for just 33. Gulfstream Park this Saturday will be an event which will match up to its World Series billing. St Wilfred's funeral service this morning will be a rather smaller but not lesser affair.

Don't let's be mawkish about this. Death comes to us all, and for Dawn it was a blessed relief after years of agony with cancer. But when a lovely candle is snuffed out, you often wonder if the game is worth it all. Especially in Miami.

The Cuban taxi drivers will be waiting. They will take us to the racetrack and the knots of fans already following the four-legged millionaires. They will also offer other addresses you wouldn't find on the road to Hexham, Sedgefield, Kelso and the other North Country jump tracks where Chris Grant rules in the saddle. Not for nothing did they call the series Miami Vice.

Don't let's be prudish either. Original sin isn't confined to Florida and it was up in Chris and Dawn's territory that someone first coined the phrase 'where there's muck there's brass'. But this weekend Gulfstream park will have brass unlimited. Let's hope the manure heaps aren't overflowing too.

There were plenty of sceptics when the Breeders' Cup launched its seven-race World Championship spectacular beneath a blazing if smog-filled Californian sky at Hollywood Park, Los Angeles on 10 November 1984. In racing terms all but the hardened anti-drug campaigners have been won over. It's in the wider field of public consciousness that the war has to be won.

The battle field is television. The aim has been to establish Breeders' Cup Day into one of the major landmarks on the sporting horizon. It's been tough going.

Quite apart from the ratings, which have slid down from 5.1 (20 million) that first year to a low of 2.7 at Belmont in 1990 before climbing back to 3.0 (12 million) in '91, there hasn't been great progress on the awareness front. Ask shoppers in the candy store about the Breeders' Cup and they'll probably think it's some form of baby competition. You wouldn't get the same sort of ignorance about the Grand National over here.

It's an historic problem. Besides the Kentucky Derby, the Triple Crown races and some superstar like Spectacular Bid, American networks shy away from horseracing coverage and even the newspapers confine themselves to just cards and form for their local track. The Breeders' Cup was to change all that. NBC swept in with a four-hour all-singing, all-dancing bonanza. They even hired me.

One of a cast of thousands you understand. No racing programme ever screened can have had quite so many planning meetings, comedy acts, special film inserts and noble attempts at breaking the mould, not all of which were totally successful.

Chief among these was the use of Fred Astaire's wife Robyn Smith as interviewer on horseback. Everyone knew Robyn, and Robyn, as an ex-jockey, knew horses, but there was a central snag. When she galloped up alongside each breathless, mud-bespattered victor she was invariably stumped for anything to say. Mind you the sound effects were good.

NBC have had to cut the costs since then, not to mention the Scott employment. They will still do a hell of a show as specialist viewers at Haydock Park and at the Cafe Royal will see on Saturday night. But they have to face the annoying fact that public and journalistic acceptance is easier overseas than at home.

A week ago the Breeders' Cup organizers held a press conference at Ascot and something unheard of happened.

The first two rows of seats were full of eager hacks a full half hour before we were due to begin. Cynics will claim this further proof of guzzling self interest but the questions on the transatlantic hook-up betrayed an enthusiasm that only a world championship can engender.

And to think this was about Flat racing in November. And the Ascot meeting that day was jumping.

Which brings us full circle. It was at Ascot that Chris Grant on Blazing Walker scored two of his finest victories of the 1990–91 season. Dawn wasn't well enough to be with him but a couple of years earlier had accompanied her husband south to the Horserace Writers' Awards in London.

She was on our table. She was already stricken but from her shone a light that none of us there has ever forgotten. No amount of sadness, no number of Breeders' Cup bylines should dim that light today.

The reaction to that death and the churchyard overflow at St Wilfred's was a reminder that racing can retain some of its community feel. And for years that community has been lucky in one thing, above all. The unstinting support of its royal patron.

The Queen Mum
10 May 1993

The best journey was the shortest. We have been all over the shop in the last week. To Chester, to Taunton to see the Aussies, and of course on Dick Turpin's road to York. But the winner was only a 20-mile trip. Up to London to see the Queen.

Well the Queen Mother actually. But when it comes to happy royal occasions you could put this against the lot. It was a small lunch to celebrate 20 years of Queen Elizabeth's patronage of the Injured Jockeys Fund. The sun shone, the great names came and, for a few brief hours, you could believe all's well in Blighty.

That's not soppy royal fawning, it's the clear memory of all those who were at the Goring Hotel last Friday. And they were quite a collection. Paddy Farrell and Jimmy Harris in wheelchairs. David Mould. Bill Rees and Richard Dennard, those heroes of the Cazalet era. Bill Smith who rode the Walwyn horses. Peter Scudamore, the newest IJF trustee. Then three other champions:

The royal patron

John Francome, Jack Dowdeswell (from way back in '51) and the legend that is still Fred Winter.

Fred is not too mobile and words are difficult. But he laughs a lot and hears what you tell him. Francome had played chauffeur to him and had not even charged for petrol. Do you want any more proof of a special occasion?

The Goring is smart and discreet, just off Palace Gate. There were only a couple of London bobbies and a few curious bystanders when the royal car swept in. John Oaksey did one of his best bows and the miracle began.

No one else in the country illuminates a room the way the Queen Mother can. We all have relatives in their 70s and 80s who find more than a few steps too much effort. But here is a lady as old as the century yet still as spry, inquisitive and charming as she has been for as long as any of our memories go.

On Friday she had the hat, the veil, the smile, the outstretched hand. She makes it a simple trick. It's been the same whether it was London in the Blitz, tours of the Commonwealth, high State receptions or small private lunches. It's just being there.

She was among friends. There was no effort in the small talk. Mould and Dennard were ragging each other about the old days at Fairlawne. Edward Cazalet had then been the trainer's son, a stylish bespectacled amateur taking law exams. Now he is a distinguished High Court judge. But on Friday he was there as an IJF trustee and, as a man, has never lost his affection for the jumping game. He could marvel at our patron too.

So could Jack Berry. But in this case, as in several others that afternoon, the feeling was probably mutual. Down the years the Queen Mother must have had to put up with more than any ordinary mortal's shares of pseuds, frauds and charlatans. She would recognize the real thing. Especially in a red shirt with energy and commitment bubbling out like a fountain. Yes it was Jack Berry who was put at her left hand when lunch was finally served in the Garden Room.

For it was Jack who this winter led a special holiday to Tenerife of Injured Jockeys Fund beneficiaries. His own son Sam was cruelly damaged a few years ago at Sedgefield. Jack knew of this purpose-built resort and, for a couple of weeks, a team which included Paddy Farrell, Jimmy Harris and Jack Dowdeswell enjoyed a much-needed tonic.

Unfortunately the Queen Mother is not in the habit of owning fast two-year-olds but give it time. 'What a lady,' said Jack at York yesterday, 'and she was incredibly easy to talk to.' Of course there have been years and years of practice but there is still a sort of genius about the way the charm works. The guests diplomatically switched places. Oaksey gave a splendid speech in tribute. The royal acknowledgement was disarmingly kind.

The riders remembered other days. David Mould hadn't changed. The hair is thinning and silver now but you can still see the impeccable amateur-hating pilot who, after one mid-race altercation with John Oaksey, came storming into the weighing room and said 'all you ever had was a few effing brains and now even them have been knocked out of you'.

Close your eyes and the years roll back.

But outside quite a crowd had gathered by the limousine. There was a line-up for goodbyes, and a then a little wave before the car pulled off. It's a bad old world but at that moment it was impossible to hold a cruel thought in the head. There is a special gift the lady leaves. It's called inspiration.

Later in the year that inspiration spread to a slightly less swish party at Doncaster racecourse. It was a reunion for those who had been on the Injured Jockeys Fund holiday to Mar-y-Sol, the special centre in Tenerife that trainer Jack Berry discovered for his own son Sam. To Doncaster they came from far and wide. Not exactly household names most of them. But, in a week of more glamorous events, not short of qualities that make men special.

François Boutin and Lee Davis

10 September 1993

Let me give you heroes, two of them, François Boutin and Lee Davies. You will know Boutin, France's most charismatic trainer who keeps in the big time despite a relentless battle with cancer. But you don't know Lee. You should do.

He was at Doncaster on Friday. He had journeyed up from Swansea to tell us the latest on his already eventful life. At 22 he is now a rugby silver medallist with Cardiff Pirates. Not bad for a lad who on 19 October 1990 was still set on becoming a jockey and already had two winners to his name. Not bad for a boy who will never walk again. Lee Davies is a tetraplegic.

That means that apart from some limited use of hands and elbows, Lee is paralysed from the neck down. When they pulled him out of his mate's car on that Lambourn night you wouldn't have given odds of him even making the hospital, let alone ever leaving it. But the human spirit is an extraordinary thing. Lee Davies is full of it.

There is a mischievous look in those bright Welsh eyes as he astounds you with his latest triumphs over adversity. 'I was going to drive up,' he said, slyly casual at the effect he caused. 'But someone ran in to my car. I hope to have it ready for Newmarket.'

Did we hear him right? Is this young man who, a generation ago, would have been a no-expectation bed case, actually telling us he will be driving himself on the 200-mile trek from Swansea to Suffolk? 'Oh yes,' he says, tossing his pigtail in amusement. 'I was up there a couple of months ago to see Sharron Murgatroyd. I have got a specially fitted Escort. It works a treat.'

Then, carefully disengaging his crooked hand from the lovingly cradled glass of Laurent-Perrier, he proceeded to demonstrate how he has mastered the Queen's highway as simply as a computer game. The right fingers work the brakes, the right thumb the accelerator, the right elbow fixes the indicators, leaving the left fingers and wrist to handle the steering.

'We just made one mistake when I started,' Lee added blithely. 'I got all the controls working and went for a drive with my brother but on the first bend I fell clean off my seat. I need strapping upright you see.'

Self-pity is not in his lexicon, self-help is. Like Lee's living arrangements. He wasn't opting for any institutional deal. What he did was to badger the mesmerized local housing department into providing him a council flat from where an answering machine will assure you that 'Mr Davies will call you back'.

So to sport. Lee started with wheelchair bowls but that was clearly too steady a game for one with the valleys in his voice. Wheelchair rugby it had to be. A silver medallist at Stoke Mandeville, he is now off to Switzerland on a promotional tour. Never mind the rugby, Lee Davies is a promotion for life itself.

So too is François Boutin. For three decades the tall, silver-haired Norman has been the personification of cool, elegant professionalism. At Longchamp on Sunday he was at the top again. Star winners in Hernando and Coup de Genie, more than 17 million francs in prize-money for the season, the same tilted head for the press questions but just one difference. This year he wears a hat.

Needless to say he looked magnificent beneath it. Chemotherapy might have plucked every hair from the skull but it had not dimmed the mastery in the eye as François first watched Coup de Genie suggest she was the outstanding two-year-old in Europe and then saw French Derby winner Hernando cruise home in his Arc de Triomphe trial. As ever, Boutin looked regal. He was Yul Brynner with a trilby. He was the King and I.

We all know what the battle with cancer brings. François Boutin has been through more than his share already, but Sunday showed that winners don't only get counted in the record books. It was a bleak, sad, autumn afternoon at Longchamp, the stands unhappily empty for so wonderful a spot, for such quality among the card. But seeing Boutin made the heart sing. Every day a victory.

Except perhaps for the Channel 4 team. McCririck and I had stumbled, red-eyed, from the St Leger at Doncaster. In our unworthy way we were complaining about everything from the airplane seats to the washing, or lack of it, of our Parisian taxi driver.

When we finally reached Longchamp we started moaning again. We couldn't get across the road. Flocks and flocks of all-aged pedallers were skimming past in their best Tour de France biking kit. Perhaps the TV listings had not been wrong after all. They had seen 'Arc de Triomphe' and thought handlebars, not horses. 'Top cycling action,' they had said.

How dare we be grumblers when the likes of Boutin and Davies battle on. We hang down our heads like Tom Dooley. But this week's two heroes, they never cry.

Peter Scudamore was never much of a cry-baby either. Mind you, he might have been entitled to in the midst of the stunt he got involved with in October 1993. It was a hark back to the past. They must have been tough in them days.

Scu and the Squire

14 October 1993

At last sport is alive again. No, not big-time, prime-time, scream and shout, fake to the audience sport. But sport as it once was. Sport as in Scudamore last Sunday.

Of course the first thing to say about Peter Scudamore's breaking of the 162-year-old record of 8 hours 42 minutes for 200 consecutive miles on horseback is that it confirmed Britain's place as world champions at eccentricity.

Nowhere else in the world would get all mapped up to recreate the same four-mile Newmarket Heath circuit that the dashing and dangerous Squire George Osbaldeston used in November 1831. But then maybe nowhere else could realize what a challenge this held. And certainly nowhere else could get Scudamore.

Mind you, even *he* hadn't realized what he was letting himself in for. He was doing it for charity. Bookmakers William Hill were pledging £20,000 for the Animal Health Trust. Forty-eight assorted horses had been shipped in for the 50-lap event.

'I keep being told it will be difficult,' said Peter at Worcester races on Saturday. 'But it's only riding. Nine hours in the saddle is just a very long day's hunting. If the horses are OK I should be all right, and I should be a bit fresher than the old Squire was. He had hunted his hounds for five hours the day before and then rode 60 miles from Northampton that evening to dine and sleep at Newmarket. He must have been quite a card.'

You can say that again. Looking at Scudamore on Saturday, relaxed from race riding pressures but still marvellously lean and fit in his retirement, was to remember the incredible endurance of his 15-season and record 1,678-winner career. But when he set off at 7.10am on Sunday morning in what amounted to an almost non-stop gallop from London to York, he was taking on somebody from a quite unrepeatable mould.

Eton and Oxford might have been the Squire's education, but sport in all its dubious aspects was where his kingdom lay. He once downed 100 pheasants in 100 consecutive shots. He fought a duel with Lord George Bentinck at 6am at Wormwood Scrubs and terrified the peer by putting a bullet through his topper. (Imagine Scudamore doing that to Lord Hartington!)

A lady called Miss Buxton admired someone else's orchid at a ball, so he rode 25 miles to a conservatory to get a better one and so ensure his wicked way. Wagers were his thing and unlike Scudamore, he was at Newmarket with the money down. A hundred pounds at 10–1 – at today's rate that would be almost £200,000 in winning return. Quite soon on Sunday morning Scu was to realize the measure of the man.

On the first lap he was 41 seconds slower than the Squire's nine minutes dead for the four-mile circuit, on the second almost two minutes off his rival's time, on the third he went another 58 seconds behind. 'I had set off singing to myself,' said Peter in that self-deprecating way of his, 'I thought of things to say to the press afterwards, of how good a way this was to spend a Sunday. I soon realized just how seriously the Squire must have taken it.'

It was fine last Sunday as opposed to the monsoon conditions of 1831 but the Squire's specially trained horses kept thundering round in under 10 minutes. Scu's were less consistent but he began to claw some time back. By a quarter past nine he had completed 12 laps, 48 miles (the equivalent of London to Newport Pagnell) and the deficit was down to just one and a half minutes. By 11 o'clock he had done 92 miles (Watford Gap) and he was level. But then disaster struck.

First, on the 26th lap, his horse pulled up lame half a mile out and another had to be borrowed to finish. Then two laps later an unobliging mare called Gismo took a terrible 12 minutes before an exhausted Scudamore could complete an anger-filled circuit. At 120 miles he was almost 10 minutes adrift. If he had got to Exit 26 on the M1 opposite Nottingham, the Squire, complete with restorative mouthfuls of brandy and water, was already tally-hoing away from Exit 27.

'It was getting very difficult,' said Scu, 'it was hard work making some of the horses go. My leg was rubbing against the leather and I was worried that it would damage it so much that I wouldn't finish.' It began to look bad. Having often made changeovers in under 20 seconds, he now extended one to almost two minutes. The day was taking its toll. But it had in history too.

The Squire had taken six and a half minutes to eat half a partridge for lunch and then on his next round got thrown when a horse called Ikey Solomons stumbled. It cost a 12-minute lap. Scu still had a chance.

It's a glorious story how he made it. Only four minutes behind at 140 miles, and at 160, that's Doncaster now, he was just seconds ahead. 'But the muscles in my thigh kept going into spasm,' said Scu, who had brought Joan Collins along for just such mischance (no, not that Joan Collins – this one's a physio). 'It was only for the sport but I so wanted to do it.'

And so he did. Eight hours 37 minutes 51 seconds, just four minutes ahead. No duels, no money for himself, not even a plug for his excellent new autobiography. Squire or no Squire, who says that sport is dead?

While some of us bow-legged fraternity will always see racing as equine athletics first and foremost, no one should disguise the fact that the vast majority of the game's followers do so because they want the buzz-giving involvement of having a bet.

No harm in that, within reason. No harm at all, if it adds the odd happy pay-off for daily attempts at the galloping crosswords on the silver screen. Especially no harm if I wind up having to help sip the prizes.

Joan Graves

25 August 1994

There are good jobs, bad jobs, and then there is pouring champagne (and drinking it) for ladies who have just won £10,000 in the Tote-*Racing Post* Ten to Follow competition. Step forward Mrs Joan Graves, a school cook from South Benfleet.

Joan was into her story long before I got to filling the second glass yesterday morning. Her husband Peter, a tanker driver with Mobil Oil, and her younger son Darren sat in as a smiling audience for a show they still find hard to credit. As punters' yarns go, this one takes some beating. Abandon hope all who a flutter hate.

To say that Mrs Graves is a punter is to point out that the pontiff is of the Roman faith. 'I am an East Ender,' she says firmly, 'Dad was a dockie. I remember ringing him to check my bets before I got into my wedding dress and also when I went into labour with my first child. He was quite upset then. Thought there must have been complications.' What on earth would he have made of last Friday?

Joan knew that five of her six horses in the Placepot had come in, so she called round to the bookies to see how the last one had got on. She is not a mad gambler, up to £10 on Saturdays, and likes forecasts, trios and things like the Ten to Follow, which offer plenty of fun for little staked.

Her biggest-ever win had been £1,000 on the Placepot last year and since she and her family (a mere 20 of them) were staying last week in a holiday camp near Lowestoft, every little could help for drinks at the sing-song with which they usually ended the evenings.

But the sixth horse in the Placepot had lost. Joan muttered the reproaches that every punter knows and, seeing a Racing Post in the corner, thought she had better check up on what had happened to Lochsong at York the day before.

'Even though I didn't put her in any of my Ten to Follow lines I have always followed Lochsong,' said Joan. 'Peter and I were at Yarmouth races on the Thursday. We heard she had lost but up till Friday evening I hadn't read anything about what happened. So I opened the paper. I read about Lochsong running away. I read about Blue Siren winning and being disqualified but had forgotten that the new winner Piccolo was in what I thought had been my weakest Ten to Follow line at the start of the season. And then I saw it.'

Although still trim in her late 40s, you guess it would take rather more than a feather to put Mrs Graves on the deck. But a small item on page 2, column 1 of the *Racing Post* flattened her as surely as a wayward load dropping in dockland all those years ago.

It read stiffly: 'Mrs J. Graves from South Benfleet has won the York Ebor Ten to Follow Competition.'

'Eureka,' Archimedes had cried when he leapt out of the bath and ran starkers down the street in Syracuse in the third century BC. But he had only discovered some crummy mathematical principle with which to torture generations of schoolboys down the centuries. Joan Graves had done something much bigger. She had landed 10,000 smackers for a fiver outlay. Every punter's dream.

Her older son was so excited that he drove her off on the wrong side of the road. The celebrations began when she got back to the holiday camp and summoned a family meeting. 'They were that worried,' said Joan triumphantly, 'they thought there had been a bereavement. I said no. Tonight's on me.'

So it was, yet in the way of these things, it soon seemed to be facing a problem. Yarmouth races had not been a wholesale success and the Graves float was down to £94.50. This had seemed a tidy sum at the start of the evening but funds had quickly run short.

Before she had even half-finished telling of the five lists she had done for the Ten To Follow at the start of the season (entry for the three-day York competition is an automatic bonus), thirsty relatives looked in need of replenishment. No matter that they were already negotiating for shares of the £10,000, that Peter is aiming for a new set of golf clubs, and a trip to New York to see her daughter has plenty of takers. Something needed fixing for the next round.

When you are hot you are hot. Peter Graves had £4 left. He strode across the hall to the fruit machine. Within minutes £3 had been swallowed up as the oranges and lemons spun dumbly beneath his nose. One pound left. Peter gave it to 12-year-old Darren. You can imagine the rest.

There is that sort of gargle a fruit machine gives before it starts to cough the lot. It's the only vomit that has ever had anything the least beautiful about it. It was beautiful now. Again and again the coins splurged up into the cup. At the end there was over a hundred quid for the evening to continue. It did.

Spread a little happiness. In his lifetime Gordon Richards spread a lot. Arguably by his wondrous sterling efforts down the years he spread more than any jockey who ever lived. He is just the sort of man there should be memorials to.

Gordon Richards

30 March 1995

Size is a very different thing from stature. No one in sporting history better exemplified this than Gordon Richards. No tribute better spoke than the little ceremony at St Mary's Kintbury on Wednesday afternoon.

The village policeman was proudly doing traffic duty at the crossroads on the High Street. He was pulling on his raincoat against the drizzle. Some umbrellas were up among the throng of villagers outside the church gate. Inside there was a line of schoolchildren with baby Union Jacks. The Queen was coming. From Capetown, South Africa to Kintbury, Berks; different royal duties, but don't doubt that Her Majesty's heart would be in this job.

It is nine years since Gordon Richards died just up the road from this his place of worship. But the memory you want goes back a lot further than that. Back to as happy a photograph as the reign has yet produced. The newly knighted Gordon Richards standing in the royal box at Epsom talking to the newly crowned Elizabeth II. He, a 49-year-old grandfather, at last, on Pinza, winning the Derby at his 28th attempt. She a 27-year-old racing fan happy to share the great man's triumph, although it was her horse Aureole who had been runner-up.

Now she was a small, bespectacled, dignified figure in a red tweed coat and skirt and matching boater-style hat looking around the packed congregation at many familiar faces from the racing world. The years have not always been kind to the royal fortunes, certainly not in the Derby, where no horse since Aureole has ever finished in the first three. But the Sovereign herself still stands for much. So, too, did Sir Gordon.

Treasure young Frankie Dettori as we must, but remember against what monument his achievements should be measured. 24-year-old Frankie starts this season with one magnificent championship beneath his hungry belt. At this stage Gordon Richards had already won two championships, despite missing a year in between with tuberculosis. There were no fewer 24 championships still to come, over 4,870 winners in all.

But there was much more than that. In a sinful world Gordon Richards espoused integrity like a second creed. With Gordon you always got a run.

With Gordon, too, you had a hero who was humble as well as proud. At 4 foot 10, and with that rolling circus walk, he cut a chunky, dwarfish figure but no one called him a clown. He was always polite and patient with his fans. 'I think,' he once said to our cameras in that famous musical voice of his, 'that if you have a public position it gives you responsibilities to the public.' Pass the message round, lads. It hasn't worn with age and it is just possible some of you haven't read it yet.

Neither will Wednesday's memorial age too quickly. For the Queen had come to bless a bell that will toll down the centuries. A great bronze beauty standing with its pair on a table at the edge of the choir stalls. They will go aloft to make up an eight-bell octave whose oldest chimer goes back to 1576. There was a Queen Elizabeth then too.

It was a gloriously English tribute. While we waited for the royal car from Windsor we sang 'The sacred bells of England, how gloriously they ring, from ancient tower and steeple, for cottager for king.'

As a matter of fact we sang rather a lot of hymns as the organizers had packed us into the church at 4.45 while HM was actually not due to do her 20-minute stint until 5.30. Time to look around.

Quite a lot has happened at Kintbury since someone called Wulfgar, Thane of Inkpen first mentioned it in a charter of 931.

All sorts of worthies and sea dogs, mostly called Craven or Dundas, are recorded on the church walls.

Fine servants of the crown, no doubt. One of them was Governor General of South Carolina, another Commander in Chief of the Black Sea Fleet. But they were pretty brutal too.

In 1830 agricultural workers rioted against new machinery and low wages. Lord Craven and Colonel Dundas headed the troops who marched on the Blue Ball in Kintbury. One William Winterbourne was hanged, the rest of the ringleaders shipped off to Australia. We reap what we sow!

But now the Queen was with us. The monarch of the realm and of the Commonwealth these past 43 years, and still untouched by panic security. Just one familiar raincoated figure beside her, one other tall usefully-built suit with restless eyes who stood quietly by the door.

How could either be needed when Her Majesty was being guided by Billee Chapman Pincher?

Mrs Chapman Pincher is the wife of the now-retired super-sleuth Harry Chapman Pincher, who lives in Church House by the gates. Billee's life was invented for this.

Not much more than a year ago Billee had set about raising the £30,000 needed (£500 still wanted please) for the casting, setting and hanging of the bell in the great jockey's memory. Her method was best summed up by the Kintbury lady rector's description of what the bell will do: 'summon the faithful, remind the forgetful, and challenge the ungodly.'

Sir Gordon would have been proud of her. You can't say fairer than that.

Places

The grass is often greener even when the racing is on sand. One of the privileges of the racing hack is to take in big events in other countries, and this inevitably invites comparison with the equivalent or lack of it back home. It can be a humbling process.

So it is with wide and frequently envious eyes that I have taken in the likes of Melbourne, Tokyo, Louisville and Hong Kong. In each, the great races are surrounded with a back-up circus which puts everything over here bar the Grand National to shame. There are two reasons. First, that it is only very recently that the racing authorities realized that it's good business as well as good manners to lay on facilities for visiting hacks. Second, that, by comparison, our racing is almost skint.

Everyone knows the reasons. All those other territories run an off-course Tote Monopoly and consequently siphon far more of the betting money into racing. Back in the fifties Britain had an opportunity to do the same but neither government nor racing authorities wanted to, and private bookmaking companies developed the most intense customer service in the world with 10,000 betting shops around the country. They also drew off great profits for themselves, much to the chagrin of the racing authorities, who claimed that in other countries it would have been 'their' money.

But the truth is we are never going to have a Tote Monopoly in Britain. No government is going to legislate for the compulsory purchase of all betting shops and so force mass sackings on a 100,000 workforce already under threat from the National Lottery. What we can do is to make the best of what we have got. And comparing our Tote with its rivals round the world makes you realize how much more lively this could become. That's where progress will be made.

For what have seemed old institutions can take their place in the modern world. Cheltenham was the first race meeting I ever went to. In some senses it used to be the epitome of English county stuffiness. But the Cheltenham Festival is an absolute runaway success story. It's wonderful. Before the 1992 Festival I went back to find out why.

History forged by Festival fire

8 March 1992

The anvil of dreams. Cheltenham's three days of challenge and celebration. It's an addictive form of madness. Feel the craving coming on.

Hooked from an early age. 1952, small boy at home with measles and our first television. The black and white magic box showing pictures of Sir Ken wearing down Noholme in the Champion Hurdle, of Mont Tremblant young and flashily brilliant in the Gold Cup. The images pinned hard to the wallpaper of the brain.

Churchill was in No. 10, King Farouk was in Cairo, the budget put the bank rate up to four per cent; Cheltenham is the survivor. An absurdity of course, millions all over the country betting a sizeable portion of the national debt on the results of 19 races in the Cotswolds. But glorious too, because at the heart is a tested truth and the ultimate arena in sport.

Cheltenham doesn't just have the events – this is where the jump season's championships get decided – it has the backdrop. Cleeve Hill, a green and wooded screen set 1,000ft against the horizon, the sweep of the course reaching away towards it.

If you haven't been, you should. No other racecourse, no other event so completely puts its stall out for scrutiny. Wembley, Parc des Princes and Barcelona may have bigger, more sculpted stadiums. St Andrews or Augusta may have as exciting a Hall of Fame. But none sets its test as clearly as Cheltenham. Even that child could understand.

Go there first without the people. On Tuesday there were just a couple of old Toyota maintenance trucks and an optimistic skylark. Climb out to the top of the hill. Look back across to the empty stands and the huge striped marquees moored downstream of them. Take a breath and the ghosts will thunder by.

1964, Arkle and Mill House in the Gold Cup. Ice cold, arctic clear sky, no duel ever more awaited. Clay had beaten Liston the month before. Ian Smith became Rhodesian premier in April. But Arkle–Mill House was the clash to decide everything. Afterwards there could be no argument.

Cheltenham is not too full of might have beens. No whinging from the Mill House camp. Their champion jumped round the old course like the spring-heeled heavyweight he was. For three miles he led the Irish pretender. But then at the final turn, the unthinkable. Arkle destroyed him.

No moans from this quarter either. Just lucky, a few years later, to have had a ride-on part. Take fortune as it comes. Black Justice, a 20–1 outsider in the 1968 Champion Hurdle, we were almost down at the first, struggled sore-footed all the way round and yet hit such an enormous stride up the hill that we eventually finished third to Persian War and Chorus.

The course beat us too. The Cathcart in 1970; sweeping through to join the leaders at the downhill fence only for birch and gravity to play the double whammy. Three of us lying groaning on the grass, the race spinning away towards the beckoning crescendo of the stands. No bones, no legs broken. Not all have it too easy.

Cheltenham may be a temple but it demands its sacrifice. Think of Desert

Cheltenham in its toughest mode. Bobby Beasley and Roddy Owen
after the 1959 Gold Cup

Orchid's unforgettable slog through the mud in '89, but remember too the crippled Ten Plus waiting miserably for the executioner's bullet as Dessie worshippers ran amok in the unsaddling enclosure.

It is this very harshness, this heightened sense of risk, which lifts these three days of race-going from the Bacchanalian binge which they also are. It's a festival all right. Seventy-two hours dedicated to the perils and pleasures of playing the galloping jigsaw puzzle of the betting game. And added to that, an Anglo-Irish hooley.

This year they have a runner in every race. There will be shamrocks on bridles as well as buttonholes. One horse even rejoices in the name Rust Never Sleeps. If any of them win, the roar will have the strength and possessiveness of a home-team try at Lansdowne Road.

With them comes 'the crack', such a beautiful word now hijacked by drugland. 'Crack' as in conversation and stories more improbable than Behan. It was an Irishman who went into a Cheltenham betting shop in 1976 and said 'I want £10,000 on Brown Lad in the Gold Cup. Don't I have the money in this bag beside me?'

Brown Lad, like most selections, was a loser, and the tale is always told with the sympathy of shared disaster. Chancellor Lamont will announce his Budget on Tuesday and make all kinds of high-sounding pledges of a better world. Togetherness sometimes comes from having it worse. Cheltenham's attitude to its Emerald Isle guests has come a long way from the Regency jingle 'the churchyard's so small and the Irish so many, they ought to be pickled and sent to Kilkenny'.

Zany history is part of the charm. Cheltenham town is built on the eccentricities of the English; why should the racecourse be different? In 1849 the lake in front of the Pumproom where those instantly effective spa waters were drunk, was enlivened by a joker in an upturned tub towed by four geese at full paddle. 'Veritably,' said the advert, 'a car of Neptune.'

This week's tens of thousands will arrive by rather faster means. The ritziest of them helicopter in over the lip of the Cotswold plateau, the racecourse laid out in the bowl below them ready for the theatre to begin.

Some guests are there already. At the very top of Cleeve Hill Common, the windswept gorse-bushed grasslands where the first races were held to loud nonconformist disapproval in 1826, stands a little, lonely twisted beech tree. On Tuesday it was occupied.

Of all spots in the kingdom, a crow had picked these highest branches to make his nest. What's more he had made some fluffy, black-feathered attempts at comfort. Must be a hell of a view of the racing.

Going up high always gives you a chance of perspective. To do it on horseback adds both elevation and the shared effort with those legs beneath. Britain may not be a mountainous country in the Alpine sense, but its hilly regions are still some of the most beautiful places on earth. Travel the world and you will be hard pushed to beat the Lake District. List the racing privileges and they don't come any better than riding up there with the Grand National in sight.

Hopes and fears take flight over the Fells

29 March 1992

Up here you can understand. Looking across the Cumbrian Fells to where Saddleback rises high on the route to Derwent Water, you can feel the rawness of it all. Up here you can see why the Grand National doesn't daunt Twin Oaks and Gordon Richards.

For most of next Saturday's 10-million television audience the thought of risking your favourite horse around Aintree's awesome fences would spread the shakes from ears to toes. Up on the fells, fear is a town dweller's luxury. Challenge is what confronts you, and for Richards the National is merely the highest peak for a horse to climb.

He knows the exultation at the mountain top. Twice before, with Lucius in 1979 and Hello Dandy in 1984, his team have led back a National winner. But they also know the darkest hour. In 1987 Dark Ivy broke his neck at Becher's. All they brought home to Greystoke was an empty bridle.

That brave and brilliant grey was the best horse Gordon Richards had saddled for Liverpool's 30-fence, four and a half mile marathon. Now in Twin Oaks he sends out a runner talented enough to be allotted top weight on Saturday, and one who is such a kindred spirit that the sixty-one-year-old trainer loves nothing better than to ride him himself of a morning.

'He's such a lovely old 'orrse,' Gordon had said as he sipped his tea across the kitchen table first thing on Tuesday. Despite 40 years in Cumbria he retains the cidery West Country lilt of his childhood, and suddenly adds haspirate 'aitches' for emphasis. 'Twin Oaks is made for H'Aintree,' adds Gordon with relish. 'He's got the size and shape, great jumper, bags of class, great big feet on him.'

Richards lost a kidney in a serious operation two years ago. There is a touch of frailty in the voice as he puffs on his inhaler, but as we leave the stone slabs of the Old Vicarage entrance the coltish energy comes bubbling through. Three sheep have got on to the lawn. Gordon scuttles down to shoo them off, the tightly clad blue-jodhpured legs looking strangely youthful beneath the square-set old farmer's face.

That mix is part of the secret. All of sport has an element of grown men playing boys' games, and as Gordon indicates all the animals and sweeping, white-railed acres that are now his own, the memory goes back to early apprentice days on four shillings a week.

'I h'always remember going home for Christmas,' he says for no reason in particular. 'I had a lovely little pin-striped suit the boss had given us, a white £5 note and a chicken. When I got off at Bath station I could hear people saying, 'That Richards is back'. I felt like a bloody millionaire.'

He's probably not far short of that now. He and his wife Joanie have just had a break at their seaside house in Anguilla. But the money is hard-earned.

Twenty-eight years with a training licence has meant harnessing fierce practical ambition to the initial childish enthusiasm and, his jockeys will tell you, to the odd stormy tantrum of the dog that's lost his bone.

It has meant facing the harsh attrition of the jumping game. Up at his main training yard set in the old Cumbrian stone coaching stables of Greystoke Castle itself, a dark horse shifts gingerly in his box. It is Rinus, third in the 1990 National and much fancied again this year. His leg was cut through at Bangor last week. The vets will need all their skill to save him.

But central to Richards's training success has been the daily renewal of a morning. It is very obvious now. Twin Oaks comes out of his box. A great big solid brown citizen of a chaser. Gordon is legged up into the saddle. All around other partnerships get together, and a few minutes later our 20-strong posse winds out the drive and up towards the Fells.

For most of us this is trekking country, and compared with the manicured regulation of such centres as Newmarket and Lambourn, 'trekking' is the best description of normal Greystoke exercise. Through the farmyard, over the stream, up beside the winter wheat, along the path below the fir plantation and then to the foot of the crags.

Huge slabs of rock lour above us. The drizzle scuds in from the west. Gordon swivels in the saddle. Checks that we are still together and heads straight up the climb.

It's so steep that we ought to be roped together. Riding a racehorse at exercise it's usually brakes that are the problem. Up here it's just forward balance to try and keep the impulsion. The breath comes short as the horses' hindquarters heave us higher. At halfway we pause, re-group and set off again to the top. At last the ground levels off at the peak. Twin Oaks snorts defiantly as we walk towards the gate. A Tibetan mule train would be proud of us.

But that's only the warm-up. We hack on another mile or so across the top to reach a big grassy field reaching over to another fir plantation. In groups of two or three we blaze briefly up the side of the wall. After a couple of repetitions Gordon Richards takes Twin Oaks to the top just to watch us. His hard work was yesterday. The athlete is peaking.

'The old 'orrse is coming back to himself,' says Gordon (a virus had laid the stable low in February). 'He's 12 years old but by next Saturday he could be in his best shape ever.'

The view over towards Skiddaw is timeless, like looking over the very roof of the kingdom. But we are here with the clock counting down to Aintree. Neale Doughty will be aboard Twin Oaks as they pitch for history. Now he is on the talented chestnut Pat's Jester with one more wallside spin to do. 'At the start of the season,' he says with a deep Welsh chuckle, 'the old man said, "What about this interval training?" I told him we had been doing it for years without knowing it.'

Our horses buckle down against the collar, the squelching turf spinning by beneath us. Doughty tilts easily behind the ears with the sureness of a rider whose 20th-fence fall on Rinus last year represented his first failure to complete in eight Grand National attempts which included that '84 triumph on Hello Dandy.

As we pull up, Doughty's face is lean and hard beneath the helmet, but at 34 his tone is a lot mellower than it was during the fiery years which at one stage saw him split with Richards. 'The fortnight before Aintree I start running four miles a night and doing some weights,' he says. 'The horse is as fit as he can be and I certainly am.'

The enormity of what awaits us suddenly comes flooding in, yet Doughty's voice is steady. 'It's the most difficult thing to do as a rider, and I have to condition myself upstairs as well as physically, have to programme myself to do the business. You don't even think about failure. If you fall it's just tough luck.'

The mind goes forward to that scene in the Aintree paddock next Saturday. 'The last thing the old man does before I go out,' adds Neale, 'is to come across and grab me by the leg and say, "Make a job of him son." I like that. It shows he's screwed up too.'

Down in the valley the little village of Greystoke lies aslumber. The church, and at the castle gates the low-beamed pub, the Boot and Shoe, where Lucius banged his head when he was led in for a celebratory drink in 1979. The task awaits. Fear and be slain.

Old Twin Oaks couldn't see out that Grand National trip but what a wonderful raw morning it was above Greystoke.

Another morning and another set of hills; another very different kingdom. To Manton on the Marlborough Downs, high summer and the Derby beckoning. And this time we got the predictions at least half right.

The greengrocer's son bears fruit

31 May 1992

Fresh legs on an old grassland. The Manton gallops are counting down towards the Derby again. All sorts of wheels could be coming full circle by Wednesday.

It should have been far too bright a morning for the ghosts to surface, but watching Rodrigo De Triano and Dr Devious limbering up on Tuesday was to imagine whole hordes of shades and coincidences emerging from the distant Stone Age monuments to press their case for inclusion.

Let's start with Rodrigo. He's the youngest horse, Wednesday was his third birthday. He's ridden not just by the oldest pilot, Lester Piggott at 56, but by one who won the first of his record nine Derbys back in 1954 and who four years ago watched the race from inside Highpoint Prison. The odds that day of him looking through the favourite's ears next week must have been even greater than that of a horse named after Columbus's lookout winning the Derby on the 500th anniversary of that New World discovery.

Dr Devious isn't much better. He's teasingly named after the vet who originally bought him. His sire was a sprinter yet he's expected to stay better than

Peter Chapple-Hyam and Derby winner Dr Devious

the stamina-suspect Rodrigo (whom Piggott, *in victor veritas* immediately after the 2,000 Guineas, said wouldn't stay) and he attempts the unique feat of Epsom triumph following an unhappy sand-choked trip to the Kentucky Derby.

But above all else we come back to the place, to the man who bought it eight years ago as the crowning jewel in his racing empire, and to the unlikely young hustler who is now fulfilling the dream. We talk of Manton, Robert Sangster and of Peter Chapple-Hyam, his trainer with the double-barrelled name but single-line effectiveness.

Manton is the most completely-crafted individual training centre in the country. It is set on the Wiltshire Downs high above the Kennet Valley, three miles to the west of Marlborough. It was started by grim-faced Alec Taylor 120 years ago and developed by his brilliant son – 'Young Alec' – into a workbench on which the winners of four Derbys and 30 English Classics were fashioned.

But Taylor junior, aka 'The Wizard of Manton', left the place in 1927. Horses continued to be trained there, but the great days seemed in the past until Sangster stepped up in 1984. Robert Sangster had been the spearhead of the runaway bloodstock boom of the late Seventies. Manton was to be his new bastion against the rise of the Arab owners. All too soon it looked to be his Canary Wharf.

The plan had seemed convincingly simple. Unable any longer to buy the best, Sangster would stay ahead by breeding from the champions he already had and then by using the new wonder weapon of Michael Dickinson at Manton.

It was 1984, Michael Dickinson was the puritanical workaholic who had just broken every record in the National Hunt game. He was young, driven and ambitious. He seemed just the man to put Manton back on the map. He cut his ties with jump racing, went on a world tour to study the latest in training technology, came back and drew up a master plan.

That year Sangster won the 2,000 Guineas with the most brilliant of all the horses trained for him by Vincent O'Brien. The Derby looked to be a cakewalk, but tactics went wrong and stamina ran out. It was the turning point, but eight comparatively lean years on, deep in the shadow of the massive middle-eastern investors, the horse has repaid Sangster his debt. El Gran Senor is the sire of Rodrigo De Triano, who has now to be valued at upwards of £6m. 'That should see us through this season and next,' says Sangster happily.

Just one generation, but in racing terms it seems an age ago. Rodrigo De Triano came by on Tuesday, cantering easily on the oval-shaped woodchip gallop, one of the countless and costly developments which Dickinson crafted on to the old Manton set-up.

There are 12 miles of magnificently renovated gallops on the 2,500-acre estate. There is an eyesore modern office block, state-of-the-art security, a swimming pool, solarium, every aid and comfort a thoroughbred could be foaled for. But there's no Dickinson. After two years he left for America, a classic victim of not adding the necessary quick booster of success to the expectation that followed his launch.

The winners came to Manton. Barry Hills moved there and began to log 100 victories a season. But for Sangster the place became an elephant of the whiter hue. Hills was a public not a private trainer. Sangster was paying full fees to have his horses trained on his own land. Tax exile kept him away from the place. The Arabs kept him out of the big time. Manton went on the market. The jury went out to convict another Eighties folly.

Early on Tuesday morning the sun was already high, the sky impossibly wide and the larksong so noisy that urban busybodies would start complaining. Thirty horses on first lot, including the two who will be centre stage at Epsom, file through from the artificial warm-up surface to the real turf of old. Cars and television cameras bob hungrily in their wake. This Eighties dream lives on.

The two men principally responsible walk across the carpeted old turf to where modern-day traffic cones indicate the route of the Derby gallop. They are both in their late twenties but are a sharply contrasting physical pair. Ben Sangster, tall, fair and elegant; Peter Chapple-Hyam, dark-haired, shorter and with an earthy bulk about him whose every movements means business. They have come a long way in the twelvemonth.

At that stage the received wisdom was that Sangster was into a familiarly desperate final ploy. Unable to find a buyer he had installed the family. The 27-year-old Ben was the younger of the two sons from his first marriage. The 29-year-old Chapple-Hyam was married to the step-daughter of Robert's second liaison. Blood was looking thicker than the wallet.

It didn't take long before the cynics began to feel the first pangs of discomfort. For all his stylish good manners Ben Sangster was clearly locking his father's bloodstock business closer into Manton than ever before, and a quick inspection of Chapple-Hyam's pedigree revealed anything but a 'Hyphenated Harry.'

Dr Devious is to be the first to work. His Derby rider John Reid has just been legged up for the gallop. Now in his late thirties, John looks a senior figure among the boyish lads and trainer. But his blue helmet dips intently as he listens to his instructions. Winners, not years, are what command attention.

The first one came last spring, and at the first time of asking, a filly called Noble Flutter in a little race at Warwick. 'Oh yes, we had her well wound up,' says Peter Chapple-Hyam with relish, 'she just had to win.'

He may have been only 28, but Peter had been 12 years in the game, a dozen seasons thinking of what he would do if he got a set of trainer's cards together. The hand he was given was mostly the odds and sods from the Sangster pack. At first glance there would be no trumps among them.

Rodrigo De Triano walks past with two stable-mates as cannon fodder for his gallop. The sun now gleams from what used to be a pretty miserable chestnut coat. 'Physically he's improved a lot,' says Peter, 'He was an ugly looking brute as a yearling, shallow-sided with a very small, plain head. He wouldn't have made much at the sales, that's why he came to me.'

Dr Devious didn't have much better starting credentials. Another smallish, unscopey chestnut who was bought back as a yearling for only 4,000 Guineas more than he had been sold for as a foal. Neither horse looked to be big-time but it was big enough for the Leamington greengrocer's son whose main racing connection had been Saturday trips with his grandfather to jumping courses in the Midlands.

Whatever chemistry it is that attracts talent to its target worked now. Chapple-Hyam's only other ambition was to be a professional footballer. The former Coventry City manager John Sillett was a family friend but a trial proved fruitless. Peter focused on racing and began four years with the top jumping trainer Fred Rimell.

All stables have their quota of youthful hopefuls, most of them strung along by the thought of themselves in the saddle, their name on the jockeys' board. But Chapple-Hyam was different. He wanted to train, not ride. No doubt a natural bulk which belies his athleticism had a bit to do with it, but this was a man who was interested in what made his athletes tick.

He went to Barry Hills as full-time assistant in Lambourn and then at Manton. He began to spend his winters on working holidays in Australia. He took up with the politician Andrew Peacock's bright and racing-wise daughter Jane and was planning to start up in Melbourne when the Sangster call came.

Time won't stand still for reflections when Derby gallops are on their way. Three specks swing into view on the already shimmering green and gold horizon. As they grow in the eye you focus on the royal blue of John Reid's helmet on Dr Devious. A furlong from us he pulls his little partner to the left of his leaders and asks the Epsom question.

Dr Devious is compactly made, but at 455 kilos he is only four kilos heavier than the leaner-looking Rodrigo. However it's packaged, this muscle machine can punch. As Reid squeezes for effort, Dr Devious stretches low, neck set like a greyhound, and in 100 yards has destroyed his companions.

John Reid has had the leg-up on some top horses down the years but there is no mistaking the buzz which he gives off afterwards. 'What a lovely little horse,' he says to Peter Chapple-Hyam with the sort of conviction that makes you itch in your betting pocket. 'He has got all the right things about him for Epsom. He's very relaxed and he's got such a beautiful action that you could go flat out round a sixpence on him.'

Not bad for a salvage job. Having progressed magnificently through a busy first season to end up winning the Dewhurst Stakes, Dr Devious changed ownership for a third time. Sangster has always been ready to trade and was happy to get $400,000 from the Italian Luciano Gaucci in mid-season. It didn't look quite such value when Gaucci cashed his stock for more than two million in January. And with it came complications.

As part of the deal Dr Devious had to be prepared for the Kentucky Derby on 2 May. No easy deal in an English winter, even less so in March when the little chestnut first came up with a bruise like a melon and then compounded things by stringing himself up in his rug straps all night.

Despite this Dr Devious ran a fine race on his comeback only to go to America and lose himself on the unfamiliar dirt surface at Churchill Downs. 'He swallowed so much sand he coughed for a quarter of an hour afterwards,' said Peter on Tuesday. 'It gave him a throat infection and he had some blood in his left lung. But he's tough. Look at him this morning.'

Not much time for that either, as Rodrigo is on his way. He is to cover the same 10 furlongs Dr Devious travelled but less seriously as this is only 10 days after he had doubled his English 2,000 Guineas triumph with the Irish equivalent at the Curragh. 'I am just trying to keep him fresh,' says Peter. Successfully, too, if last week's show was an example. His work rider, Rory O'Dowd, only moved Rodrigo out to challenge his two sparring partners as they winged towards us but there was a deadliness about the way he closed up to them which reminded you that speed is already his essence.

It's a quality that Chapple-Hyam prizes above all other. 'The Australians put great emphasis on speed,' he says, 'and so do I. Even with long distance horses I like to let them do short bursts of speed to believe in themselves. The question about Rodrigo is whether that speed will still be there at the end of a mile-and-a-half.'

Which brings us to the man who will be on top this Wednesday. The first Derby Chapple-Hyam can remember is Lester Piggott's famous blitzing victory on The Minstrel (coincidentally in the same green and blue Sangster silks he will again wear on Rodrigo) in 1977. Lester had already been there seven times before.

The trainer-jockey relationship is a strange mixture of hero-worship and pragmatism. Chapple-Hyam is given to blunt little asides like 'it's my Derby too, you know' and firm assertions of the 'orders' he will give Piggott when Rodrigo and Dr Devious have a preparatory Tattenham Corner try-out on Tuesday morning. Yet he, like everyone else in racing, soon reverts to the marvel of it all.

He and Ben Sangster tell of Piggott so withdrawn and old-looking on the plane over to the Irish Guineas, of him champagne-sparkling and garrulous on the victorious return leg. John Reid recounts an absurd cameo of the great man losing his chips and conveniently helping himself to John's on a casino night in Macau last winter. Above all they talk of Piggott and the Derby.

'The crowd are going to give him such a welcome,' Robert Sangster said on Friday. 'I remember what it was like when Lester rode The Minstrel and other good horses of mine. This time it will be exceptional. Thank heaven Rodrigo is so laid back. All I have to do now is to keep the trainer together.' Sangster is entitled to be well pleased with his protégé. Including Rodrigo's Irish Guineas win, his horses have already won more than £300,000 this season and he is for the first time in years within hailing distance of Sheikh Mohammed in the owners' table. 'My operation is only a fraction of his size,' says Sangster, revelling in this unlikely role of the 'little man', 'but it's great to be back in with a shout in the Derby. This horse isn't bred to stay, but I think he could be a freak. I just hope Lester doesn't give us all a heart attack by leaving it very late.'

Robert should look out a respirator. When Peter Chapple-Hyam broached the matter of Derby tactics with Piggott last week the maestro pondered a minute and then said, 'I will send you a tape of what I did on Sir Ivor.'

Back in 1968 Sir Ivor had also come from winning the 2,000 Guineas with a lightning final sprint. In the Derby Lester left it later, quite impossibly later, before cutting down Connaught to win by a length.

When the field straighten for home on Wednesday don't expect too much early action from the coiled sphinx above Rodrigo's saddle. Just prepare, like history, to hold your breath.

As it happened, Piggott and Rodrigo de Triano never fired at all at Epsom and were distant trailers by the time the Derby field took Tattenham Corner. But Dr Devious wasn't. Dr Devious was the business. And our TV crew were on to a man. Indeed, so impressed was our producer with the little chestnut's gallop and with John Reid's subsequent glowing report, that he wanted to stop filming then and there to get to a phone and lump on at the bookies.

Manton on a sunny morning, the good times on the roll. But in racing and in wider life the trapdoor to disaster will always be only a step, a ride away. That's why you should come with me to another place. And a rather different feel.

Stoke Mandeville

14 December 1992

Everyone should visit at least once a year. For centuries it was just a little village in Buckinghamshire. Now its very name can enrich the spirit: Stoke Mandeville.

No other hospital, not even the superb Royal Marsden, so directly conjures up the image of triumph over adversity. Say Stoke Mandeville and you immediately see figures in wheelchairs setting out to prove that nothing in life counts as much as facing it. Down the years it has been a haven for all sorts of racing figures. Dick Hern was in for four months after his hunting accident in 1984. Ivan Newton Edwards has been around a bit longer.

It's now 19 winters since that Saturday night. Ivan was a 20-year-old apprentice engineer with everything to look forward to. The car crash limited his horizons but not as drastically as it did his movement. As a tetraplegic he can move nothing below his neck. But he was looking forward on Monday. Looking forward to checking his bets on the way home.

When Jimmy Savile set off on his astonishing Stoke Mandeville crusade in the early '80s, one of the fund-raising events was a 'celebrity' showjumping day at Ascot in July '81. The indefatigable and not-to-be-denied John Dunlop hooked in every would-be equestrian from Lester Piggott to the Prince of Wales. J. Savile co-opted every broadcasting unit this side of Kathmandu. A target of £100,000 was set. By the end, racing's contribution had topped half a million.

But something more than money was mustered. Ivan Edwards was one of the Stoke Mandeville party at Ascot. 'We had a great time,' he said in his flushed and enthusiastic way on Monday. 'Peter Walwyn and Barry Hills were in terrific form, Willie Carson too. To be honest they had had a lot to drink but they have never forgotten us. Peter Walwyn has had us round his stables twice a year ever since. We have got the Ascot programme up on the walls somewhere. I'll show you.'

That said, Ivan buzzed us off round the purposeful corridors in pursuit of the missing programme. It took a circuit and a half to find it. Time to take in the enormity of Sir Jimmy's achievement (was a title ever better bestowed?) Time to wonder at the distant view of the swimming pool and the gym. To peer in at wards where relatives sat round newly-stricken patients. Above all, time to reflect on what Ivan can do.

It had not seemed too obvious just how he would propel himself around. But in seconds a contraption had been strapped across his chest consisting of a wide webbing belt and an upright, handle-like joystick ending in a small leather-clad controller ball with which Ivan's chin commanded his wheelchair as effortlessly as any shepherd with his dog.

At last the programme was found, taking pride of place at a passage corner. It featured a lively cartoon of a paraplegic horse rocketing along a racecourse leaving large bore holes in the fences behind him. The drawing was ringed with signatures ranging from Prince Charles' clear and flowing fountain pen script to the strange Incan hieroglyphic that passes as the Piggott mark.

'It's that name at the top which always upset me,' said Ivan. 'It is Brian Taylor and he was to be killed next year in Hong Kong.' We could not linger on the sadness because Ivan was off back to the foyer where Joe, his helper, was ready to ship him back to his Aylesbury bungalow. There had been a possessiveness about his Brian Taylor concern. It was there again when he talked of 'my horses', the bets that had to be checked against the results when he got home.

It was real. Racing may be a game of sheikhs and monarchs, but it also belongs to Ivan and all the other fans.

Lord Wigg put it best. Before his own conspiratorial temperament and the interminable squabbles of racing politics embittered him beyond recall, George Wigg swept in as the biggest gust of fresh air since Hercules re-routed a river into the Augean stables so many myths ago. George was head of the Levy Board and after laughing at the Jockey Club's idea that he was raising money for them to spend, used to love to expound his own philosophy of the racing game.

'It offers freedom,' he would say in his great bloodhound voice, 'freedom to make a choice. More and more of life is constrained by regulation and machine. But every day of every week you can pick up the paper and you can make your own choice, have your own bet. In that way racing belongs to us all.'

It may be a long chain that binds George Wigg to Lester Piggott to Jimmy Savile to Ivan Edwards to Stoke Mandeville. But its hoops are of the strongest steel.

The human spirit, it's the most precious thing. Over the centuries young men have used the racecourse as one place to test their courage. In former Czechoslovakia they had one of the biggest tests of all. But that was on the racetrack. It was off it that their spirit has faced a challenge they can't escape.

Pardubice and the Czech dilemma

18 October 1992

It's a dreadful fence they have to face. So daunting that only the brave will try. So deep its ditch that even a decent attempt may still prove fatal. The Taxis? No, that's just a steeplechase jump. The real impossibility is to see how Czech racing can stay upright in the spiralling economic chaos of the post-Communist state.

The Taxis is the symbol. At five feet high, eight feet wide and with a 12-foot drop, it's the mightiest fence in world racing. But it's been jumped in the Grand Pardubice for 102 years. What was different last Sunday was that it faced politics on the loose. An animal rights protest that was eventually cleared, but the other obstacles loom ahead which make British racing's problems seem like squabbles in the hen-house.

The ironies are acute. Only three years after the triumph of the 'Velvet Revolution', Czechoslovakia's most famous race was all but ruined by a group of student activists who wouldn't have been allowed to squeak in the bad old days. What's worse, the whole Keystone Cops tragi-comedy was acted out in front of some Martell bigwigs who had just followed their sponsorship of our Grand National with support of this much needier Czech equivalent.

Sympathy swung first one way and then the other. Initial annoyance at the rag-tag intrusion turned to fear as the baton-wielding, boot-kicking police battered away in defence of The Taxis right ahead of us. But that switched to horror when the race got under way and met a line of demonstrators within the first half-mile.

With logic unseated long ago, this last act now doubled the very danger the protest was about. 'It was awful,' said Marcus Armytage, who rode the fancied Czech horse Cortez. 'We lost all momentum, and this isn't the sort of fence to go at without conviction.' Cortez, along with the local star Zeleznik, was one of five horses to turn over at the Taxis.

At the end of the day there was an almost 'after rugby match' feel. A tall, long-haired youth came by. He thought his gang had started their move too soon but that this had still been much more successful than his last outing, an anti-beefburger picket on the new McDonald's in Prague.

The Taxis loomed huge and daunting against the darkening Bohemian sky. It's not an obstacle a British public would accept, but in truth the Grand Pardubice needs a jumper first and a racer second. Hence Chris Collins' 1973 success on the hunter-chaser Stephen's Society, and Sunday's fourth place by Boreen Prince, ridden by Bob Crosby.

We were walking with a senior local trainer Frankie Vitek, a national hero when he ended years of red-silked, wolf-pack, Russian domination by winning the Pardubice in 1965. His son Roman is also a trainer and one of the deep thinkers in the game. 'I think the first protest was just protest,' he said, 'but the second protest was crime. Yet,' he added accenting his English 'the most biggest thing for Czech racing has nothing to do with the Grand Pardubice.' Next morning at Chuchle racecourse, just five miles south of Prague, with the wind coming raw off the Vltava river, Roman Vitek sketched out the black hole of financial abyss to which his business is headed.

He was watching his horses limber up before work. 'The figures don't really add up at all,' he said, echoing the words of many an English trainer at Newmarket last week but this time from the very bottom rung of the ladder.

The about-to-be-privatized (but who would want to buy it) State Racing Board is in the unholiest mess imaginable. Last year's pledge of 23 million crowns (£500,000) prize money for the 1,700 Czech horses in training has to square with betting revenue running at just 10 million crowns, and (wait for it) a debt on Chuchle's big new grandstand of another 250 million.

While we digest these statistics, two bulky, bossy, quite expensively-dressed men walk up. They are German agents. They want to buy Roman's best horse. Like a condemned man requesting a cigarette, he asks if he could finish watching his two-year-old gallop. That done, he leads them off, another victim to the mighty deutschmark.

It should be all gloom. Good stable lads can earn five times as much in Germany. Chuchle's impressive track has been disfigured by a banked, grey-sand arena plonked in the middle as part of a misguided, and some say corrupt, attempt to import trotting to Prague. And when you look at what other things Czechoslovakia has faced, and when you talk to Roman's principal owner, the remarkable Dr Fidelis Schlee, you can still believe that anything is possible.

Dr Schlee is quite a player. Imprisoned for three years by what he quite implacably calls 'The Bolsheviks' he is now close to Prime Minister Vaclav Klaus, owns Prague's evening newspaper, and drives the only Rolls Royce in the city.

'We have had 40 years of darkness,' he says, looking out of his newspaper office on to the busy railway station far below. 'There are still bad things here if you look and listen and [with a dramatic gesture of finger to nose] if you smell. But people and government are prepared to change. Racing has too much to offer to die.'

There are a million and a quarter people in Prague. There is an enormous untapped betting market to be wrested away from illegal bookmakers. There is a great tradition of racing and breeding which has survived the century. Somehow, with new investors, new concessions, a deal has to be put together.

Outside the trams still run beside the river but they too are under threat. With a 100 per cent increase in costs since the revolution, and no money for improvements, the whole system could foul up within the year. Under the Communists, however cowed, however drab, the trams, like the races, ran on time. In the brave new world there is no such thing as a free ride, let alone a lunch.

If Dr Schlee and Roman Vitek crack this one we shouldn't just give them a medal. We should send them a ticket. We could do with them here.

Things have remained very difficult for Czech racing but, as with wider life in Prague, the momentum is gathering. One day they may be able to pull off racing's essential modern-day trick of harnessing old interests to new money. One day they might earn a visit from the greatest globetrotter of our day. John Dunlop's stable sends horses all over the continent every weekend and has campaigned as far afield as Turkey, Australia and Japan.

For us hacks the only snag is that he has all but banned pre-big-race pictures of his classic hopes for fear of putting the jinx on them. Not to mention wasting his unbelievably well-organized time. Somehow we slipped in under the radar before Epsom in '94 . Arundel is another place again. Rolling Sussex hills as you approach it out of Pulborough, just a quick glimpse of the sea by Littlehampton as you crest the ridge. Then a quick flip left up to the old town and left again to the flint and brick walls of Castle Stables. To one of the best minds working in one of the most beautiful places, but still finding no easy answers.

Dunlop holds the aces in the biggest game in town

29 May 1994

Nobody knows. That's the mystery, the fun, the fabulous fortune of it all. Not even John Dunlop knows, and he trains the favourites for both the Derby and the Oaks.

'Of course not,' he says with one of those wonderfully brusque, self-mocking answers, 'no one has a clue really. You just have to use your common sense and try and get your horse to the race as right as possible.' He sucks on the permanent cigarette, looks across the parkland of Arundel Castle where some 70 head of horses are thundering past in line astern and adds wryly: 'It doesn't mean you don't have to try.'

They have been trying all over the country this week.

Everyday the racing pages have carried boggle-eyed reports of the latest Derby gallops complete with 'he's never been better' quotes from their hopeful trainers. From Newmarket, from Middleham, from Lambourn and Manton, even from the 'Fiver' and 'Bigwig' magic of Ian Balding's Watership Down, came the stories of new workouts for the horses who will strut into the Epsom spotlight on Wednesday. All these were supposedly full-scale big-race rehearsals, so how did the favourite, Erhaab, measure up at Arundel?

Well, it's all a bit disappointing. Dunlop doesn't join in this Derby game. Doesn't search out some specially undulating strip of turf to see if Erhaab can handle the Epsom gradients. Doesn't dispatch the little black colt something close to the Derby's 12 furlongs to assess his as yet unproven stamina. No, on Tuesday morning Erhaab, and Lester Piggott's ride Khamaseen, went the same, serpentine, uphill six and a half furlongs on the all-weather track they always do.

Does this Dunlop know what he is doing? Just because he won the Derby with Shirley Heights back in 1978 and since then six more English Classics, as well as endless big races overseas, from as far away as Istanbul, does this equip him to tear up some of our most cherished assumptions of the Derby build-up?

John Dunlop: a man with winners in every class

And the man calls himself a traditionalist?

That's his trick. From many angles John Leeper Dunlop, the son of a distinguished surgeon, seems the most conservative of countrymen. Tall, crisp, commanding, his pointed features too often likened to 'Prince Philip without the glare', he has show cobs and highland cattle and coursing greyhounds among his leisure pursuits, training racehorses within the walls of Arundel Castle as his long-time profession. Yet there is not a new idea he has not heard of. Not a good one he has not tried. It is perhaps the solidity and consistency of his foundations that has allowed him to be inventive. He has no truck with 'airy fairy' theorizing. 'Oh no, that's a lot of nonsense,' he will say urbanely. But he has endless time for input into the central mystery of what makes a thoroughbred tick.

'That's the thing about the guv'nor,' said one of the stable lads as we trotted up Arundel Park's driveway last week, 'he always wants your opinion. He will say, "That filly of yours is in at Haydock next week. Have a look at the race and see what you think".'

As you looked around that morning, horses stretched as far as the eye could see, some 70 of them trotting up away from the castle towards the oak plantation. From the saddle it seemed as if you had joined a cavalry squadron. And another 70 were back down in what was once the old coaching stables and where this lot had gathered as an ever-growing posse under Dunlop's watchful eye.

He was watching us now. A tall figure standing with an owner just out from their wagon. The stance and the voice are casual but the mind is not. 'Listening to John Dunlop go through his string,' said Marks and Spencer director David Sieff, 'is like watching an astonishing memory game. Every horse, its best run, its next objective, and not just in races here but all over Europe. How he keeps it all in his head I never know.'

One way is to clear himself of unnecessary decision-making. Unencumbered by any wish to 'do something different', he sets his horses through the same routine day after day. After 10 minutes we reach the top and the whole ride begins to circle a large sand ring set in the oak trees. 'That's the thing about this place,' said Heather Quorn who has worked in several major English yards as well as in Hong Kong and Macau, 'the horses here know what they are doing. There is no fuss, they all settle.'

As they circle, your eye begins to search out the horses who by next week may have taken their place in history.

Erhaab was walking serenely round, ridden by his lad Gary Hatfield. Erhaab is not very tall, but he is as chunkily muscle-packed as any scrum-half and his black coat has a shine on it like a polisher's dream.

Khamaseen is just behind him. He is a well-made horse with a keen and attractive head. Perry Docwra, the English lad with the Polish name, is in the saddle, not Piggott. Dunlop does not believe in having jockeys on the premises. This is the training ground, with training people.

Bulaxie, the tall, plain and powerful Oaks favourite, comes past, ridden by saddle lad Glen Osborne. It was Glen who first sounded the alert which found a minor infection before Bulaxie's intended tilt at the 1,000 Guineas.

The alert now is in John Dunlop's eyes. He is scanning his horses for changes, querying staff for any problems. There has been a little coughing in the stable. You can hear one or two give a splutter as they pass. Dunlop is not absolutely convinced Bulaxie was perfect the day before. The first canter will tell us more.

This entails winding our way down through the plantation almost back to the yard before walking 50 yards along a railed track and then off up a six-furlong woodshaving strip to where we had begun.

As you gallop up the incline the woodchip flips by like sleepers beneath a train. We reach the plantation in no time but hardly a puff is heard. These are fit horses.

But soon they will be fitter. The Dunlop concentration is total now. He is pairing off the 40 horses who will be put through a proper workout on the wider woodchip gallop the other side of the avenue. Obviously there has been plenty of thought beforehand, but there are no notes.

The horses start off almost back down by the castle three-quarters of a mile away. They begin single file as the track climbs to the left, right and left again. Three furlongs from the watching trainer they move 'upsides' and work in full action against the collar.

Erhaab and Bulaxie come past now. Erhaab has a rather short, scratchy stride in his slower paces but when he is asked by Hatfield you can remember the sizzling sprint which won him the Dante and which could well cut down the frontrunners on Wednesday.

The pairs comes by at 10-second intervals. Bulaxie is the most impressive sight with a great raking stride which devours the ground. You can detect well-being, but can you spot anything about this week's pressing questions of stamina and adaptability for the Epsom track?

'You and I can't,' said Robert Allpress, who has run the Arundel veterinary practice.

'On the face of it John has a very rigid system he applies to sprinters and stayers alike. But he has got it to a very fine tuning.

'He has an extremely knowledgeable staff right through from assistants to stable lads and he retains this extraordinary curiosity, always asking questions wherever he goes. Mind you,' added Robert with a laugh, 'he's a bit of a poker player. I think he often keeps a little bit to himself.'

The 'poker player' is now walking among his horses, quizzing his team on how the work went, standing back and putting an imprint of an individual into that extraordinarily active mind.

It is a scene which has been repeated literally thousands of times since Shirley Heights went out from this company to win at Epsom in 1978. How many training improvements have been made in the interval?

'Not a lot really,' said Dunlop with that shrugging laugh again. 'We've done a bit about raising the energy content of the food. We've changed the work slightly. Last year we started working them three times rather than twice a week in the early spring and I think they became a little fitter. The vets are better at diagnosis [shortly Robert Allpress would endoscope Bulaxie's wind passage and pronounce her clear] but for the overall balance you just have to use your head and listen to people.'

He was listening now. Hatfield was saying how Erhaab had 'grown up' since last year. Docwra and the rest of the yard were hoping Khamaseen would run a 'big race' for Lester. But the payoff came from Osborne as he stood beside the tall, somewhat Amazonian, figure of Bulaxie.

'Well, when it came,' said Glen of the filly who by next Sunday might well be acknowledged as the best three-year-old of either sex, 'it looked so common you would have thought it had a cart behind it. Then when it ran [beaten in a photo at 33–1, Bulaxie's only defeat] we got hold of this Irish girl and said, "Why didn't we know about that?". She turns to us, and remember she has been riding it and all. And she says, "Well, I didn't know neither".'

Long may the mystery remain.

The knowledge we thought we had gleaned that morning was that the lads were more bullish about Bulaxie than about Erhaab. At Epsom Bulaxie blew it and Erhaab pulled off the Derby with one of the most spectacular late charges ever seen. Ah well, at least we'd gone to the right place.

Now a trip up north to a dazzlingly beautiful spot and to a man who has looked at the tide of racing defeatism and relentlessly forced it back. If there was ever a parable of what a young mind can do with an apparently old and weary institution, it is what Mark Johnston is doing at Middleham. If you haven't been, you should treat yourself.

Miracle-maker in Middleham
24 July 1994

Stand with Mark Johnston on the High Moor at Middleham and share the best view in the kingdom. To the past and to the future. Anything is possible. You can feel the excitement running through you.

So too can the horses. In the last two weeks, his Kingsley House stables have been beehive busy. From these rows of modern boxes, somehow packed tight on the bank below the 13th-century chimes of St Alkelda's, the Johnston workers have sent out 55 runners and won with 16 of them. It's the best strike-rate in the country. It's a buzz that is reaching to the most coveted blooms in the land. On Wednesday, it's Goodwood's Sussex Stakes with Mister Baileys.

Win or lose this week (and Mister Baileys is joint favourite in most books), the white-nosed three-year-old whose victory in the 2,000 Guineas in May gave Middleham its first Classic for half a century, is already symbolic of his trainer's astonishing progress up the ladder of success.

In July 1987, Johnston was an unknown, unconnected Scottish vet who at 27 had just trained his first winner from an unlikely set of stables next to a bomber practice range on a beach just south of Grimsby. Today he trains not eight horses but 80, and from that solitary winner seven years ago he has increased his score

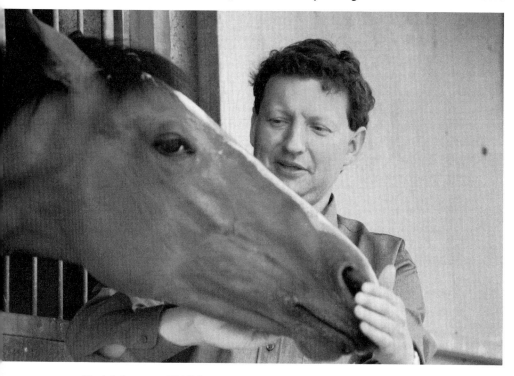

Mark Johnston at Middleham

every season and on Tuesday saddled his 79th winner this term which, with over £600,000 in prize money, puts him sixth in the table.

Every indicator suggests we have seen nothing yet. Last week, Mark and his business partner, Brian Palmer, completed the purchase of the adjoining Warwick House stables (the yard where Neville Crump trained the Grand National winners Sheila's Cottage, Teal and Merryman between 1948 and 1960) to bring his operation up to a 120-horse capacity. Last Monday, Mark travelled north to saddle a still scatterbrained two-year-old called Caerphilly to win a minor race at Ayr. But this little fish was sweet. It was owned by Sheikh Mohammed.

Yes, the world's most powerful racehorse owner, like many others, has beaten a path to Johnston's ever-open door. The big maroon helicopter has not actually scattered the sheep and landed next to the great ruin of Richard III's castle, but five of the sheikh's two-year-olds have this year been taking a Middleham education and you can bet that many others will follow.

For Johnston's challenge is a lot more than a new face on the block. His is already a mature and different system of training racehorses. At the same stage, the record-breaking Martin Pipe had yet to achieve 20 winners a season in the less competitive jump-racing game, and yet here is a young man already tearing up the record books as well as some of the most accepted tenets of the day.

In an age when most trainers, especially Pipe, won't let a horse walk out of the yard without checking some laboratory print-out, Johnston never takes a blood test unless an animal is obviously sick. In a heat wave, when many people say training is impossible without an all-weather gallop, Johnston keeps his horses on the sun-baked grass, saying: 'They have got to run on it, they might as well get used to it.'

At a time when many bemoan the fragility of the thoroughbred, he runs his horses more frequently than any of his rivals. Witness the victory of the stayer Star Rage at Beverley last Tuesday, the four-year-old's second success in a week and his seventh from 17 runs in the last three months, coinciding with an improvement of more than two stones in the official ratings.

When a trainer starts to turn over accepted norms so completely it's usually in one speciality – sprinters for Jack Berry, hurdlers for Martin Pipe. But Johnston's results refuse to be categorized. His first big success came with the sprinter Croft Express in the Portland Handicap. His breakthrough money-spinner with the Ebor-winning stayer Quick Ransom. His first Royal Ascot success with the two-year-old filly Marina Park. His first Classic winner last April with Mister Baileys, a miler who had not seen public action since the previous September.

Something's happening, so tongues will wag. Jealousy has long been racing's besetting sin and when anyone, especially a vet, rises from obscurity as fast as Johnston, the cry goes up: 'He must be giving them something.' It is therefore with provocative delight that I can confirm that the young Scotsman is indeed giving his horses something different.

Stand by for secrets. He is giving them food and exercise way beyond the norm. The Johnston horses are given four pounds of feed four times of day, at 4am, at noon, at 6pm and at 9pm. On a normal day, even the two-year-olds will make the eight-mile return trek up through the medieval market town and all the way to the high moor with its spectacular views of Swaledale, Wensleydale and Bolton Abbey. The theory and the practice is that the Johnston horses have more tiger in their tanks.

Mister Baileys is the most beautiful example both in himself and in his connection with the trainer's team. On Tuesday, he was a gleaming picture of fitness as the vet checked him over for his impending sale to the National Stud, a very different colt from the shattered athlete after his trail-blazing fourth in the Derby, the best advert yet for Baileys Horse Feeds, the company run by Paul Venner who has been with Johnston from the beginning.

The vet and the horse-feed man: it now seems so obvious. And if you talk to Baileys' chief nutritionist, Liz Bulbrook, she will baffle you with science but make clear that the racehorse mix established these past two years (and now used by other progressive trainers such as Mick Channon and Sue Bramall) has a different principle to normal feeds. It is especially high in the animal fats which are burnt as energy by the working racehorse, leaving extra glucose in the muscles for that final effort.

But training is not done on food alone and as Mark talked on the High Moor with the old spires of Middleham away in the distance, you realized how solid a base he put together from the very beginning.

Even in those earliest days the three vital people were already there: Venner as owner and feed consultant; Johnston's wife Deirdre, then doubling as a teacher in Grimsby to keep the boat afloat but now a full and brilliantly effective partner in every side of the operation; and Brian Palmer, whose previous company owned Hinari Video, that modest but crucial first winner at Carlisle on 1 July 1987.

It is the testimony of Palmer that is perhaps most interesting. Other successful stables have super-bright trainers and marvellous staff. Johnston's was soon allied to the canny skills of the veteran rider Bobby Elliott and more recently has taken on young Andrew Murphy as a dynamic head lad and dashing Jason Weaver as stable jockey. But few, if any, have a business system as sound.

'I recognized something special in Mark,' said Palmer. 'But when we formed Mark Johnston Racing Ltd and moved to Middleham in 1988 (the investment was some £500,000, the bank loans horrendous) I was determined to apply business practice. We budget very carefully, we have detailed monthly accounts, and we never have shocks.'

On the Moor, the trainer recognizes the partnership. 'I have been very lucky,' he said. True, but you make your own luck. Up at Middleham, Johnston is a manufacturer for the millennium.

The great thing about Mark Johnston is that he is positive. With his attitude everything is possible. Even competing with the new phenomenon in the classic picture, the hand-picked, sun-reared runners who have spent their winters in Dubai. Johnston after all won the Two Thousand Guineas first time out with Mister Baileys, who had spent his Christmas at Middleham and afterwards endured some of the worst weather even Yorkshire could throw at him.

None the less, what is happening in Dubai is the most remarkable challenge to the training scene this century. The results in '95 of Sheikh Mohammed's Godolphin operation are scarcely believable. The Derby, the Oaks, the St Leger, the Eclipse, the King George VI at Ascot and heaven knows what else. But when we went there in January the future, to coin a phrase, was written in the sand...

Desert sands set to yield rich and noble harvest

21 January 1995

Hope is an early bird in the desert. At 6.45 on Thursday morning the darkness was just draining away to reveal the sand and skyscraper spectacular that is the horizon in Dubai. Down at Al Quoz stables horses had already been on the move for an hour. So, too, had the black bearded figure in the watching Range Rover. Sheikh Mohammed was on the prowl.

He does this often. In Britain we have become used to him and his brothers as those slightly aloof and distant figures in the paddock and winner's enclosure, flanked by a dozen or so of their retinue and greeting yet another success from the most staggering investment – over a thousand horses in training – that racing has ever seen. In Dubai, where Sheikh Maktoum is now the Ruler, Sheikh Hamdan the Minister of Finance and Sheikh Mohammed the Minister of Defence and Crown Prince, there is plenty of formality too.

Thursday's *Gulf News* had its obligatory front page picture of Sheikh Mohammed hosting the royal visit of the Crown Prince and Princess of Japan, but if you dug about inside you could find witness to the most extraordinary hands-on sporting involvement of any royal anywhere.

Wednesday's excitement had been a horse race with a difference. Not one of those silk-clad, sculpted-turf affairs that we know from Ascot, Longchamp and Leopardstown and where last year Sheikh Mohammed set new records by being leading owner in all three countries, his horses winning 230 races and almost £5 million in prize money. No, this was racing back where it began. This was 27km across the desert. It is something which if you hadn't seen it, you wouldn't believe. I can hardly believe it now.

We were somewhere to the east of the Emirate on the border with Abu Dhabi. Forty horses, transport wagons, support vehicles and a few bemused visitors gathered some way off the road staring at where the wind tugged route flags stretched into the distance. On the way we had passed the sprinkled greens and white-domed club house of the mind-boggling Emirates Golf Course where on Sunday the Sheikh would have been handing over a huge trophy and vast cheque to Fred Couples as winner of the Desert Classic, now established as the first event in the PGA Tour. That had been a world media number.

This now had a white-smocked TV man interviewing anything that moved, photographers snapping away like monkeys, even a circling helicopter. But it was strictly a local event. It had a gymkhana, participant-centred feel. But a gymkhana from another world.

It was as good an example as you would find of the strange mix of medieval customs, petro-dollar billions and new millennium technology which is at the heart of life in the Gulf. This wasn't done for Western eyes and tastes, like the golf, the snooker and the powerboat racing which have been used to put Dubai on the sporting and tourist map.

Horses jig-jogged, riders swathed their faces against the dust, we watchers
jostled to get a decent view of the start and someone in charge tried to tell
competitors to get behind the line as cross and hopelessly as they have always
done.

*Sheikh Mohammed competing in one of Dubai's endurance races
in the desert*

The animals themselves may be predominantly pure or partly arab bred but
they have been head-hunted from Europe, America, Australia and beyond. The
race is off now and we are in pursuit. A hundred Range Rovers in the hunting
pack bumping and grinding along the sand and scrub of the desert floor.

The 37km (24 miles) is like galloping from London to Windsor without a
stop. At the back of the field Sheikh Mohammed's racing managers Anthony
Stroud and Simon Crisford were proceeding at a prudent canter, up front no such
caution reigned.

The winner was the latest star from the Abu Dhabi royal stable. His origins are as a stock horse on a cattle station in Australia. He is a mud-coloured brown and must be as lean and tough as any Oz who ever looked through a bridle. Get alongside him, check the speedometer and he was doing 25mph.

But he only won by 16 seconds. At 20km there was a brief dismounted chicane which the horses had to be walked through for veterinary inspection, otherwise he thundered along in front of his Dubai-trained pursuers on what has to be the longest finishing straight in the world. It was built last year to accommodate a horse-versus-camel endurance race. It is railed on both sides, is about a quarter of a mile across and, wait for it, is no less than 16km long.

As the winner crossed the line to a triumphant cacophany of honking car horns there were just 60 minutes and 40 seconds on the clock; 37 km in the hour and you run up to the horse and he is still quite together in himself. One or two of the others were understandably weary but not so the riders.

Five or six have finished and a great cry goes up as a grey horse comes careering through the dust. His tiny rider is just a bit wobbly in the saddle but has his face set in determination. As he passes the post a huge swirl of white smocks descend upon him and Sheikh Mohammed himself lifts him out of the saddle and gives him the kiss and the bear hug that tells of a delighted dad anywhere. Little Hamdan al Maktoum is just 10 years old.

That scene deep in the desert on Wednesday does much to explain the mystery which continues to follow the Maktoum involvement in our European racing scene. To the Western eye, the scale of their investment since Sheikh Mohammed bought his first horse, Hatta, as recently as 1977, is utterly incomprehensible.

His operation alone has some 700 horses in training and with major studs in both England and Ireland, has some 2,000 head of thoroughbreds in all. There may have been those £5 million of gross winnings but the cost would outrun them by a distance. The Western eye will blink in wonder as it struggles to put some business logic to the deal. They should come to Dubai and blink a lot more.

For what you learn, and I happily declare the interest of visiting Dubai on Sheikh Mohammed's business for 12 years now, is that if you apply British values to the money spent, you get too flabbergasted to think at all.

Since the oil came on flow these have been riches quite literally, beyond the dreams of avarice. With them have come the trappings of commercial and tourist development which have transformed a tiny 4,000-square kilometre trucial statedom into a major modern business centre in the Middle East. Who knows what is going to happen when the oil revenue, still a third of the GDP, runs out in 20 years or more? Who can tell how the local politics and personalities will mature? But what you can say is that the new Dubai has put itself firmly on the map.

It has done it with very personal input from the ruling family and so it is appropriate that its biggest impact of all is in the world of the horse. That long-standing physical affinity which was so clear as he held his son aloft on

Wednesday is very obvious in everything that has been done in putting Dubai's own racing operation into being over the last three years.

Of course it doesn't quite fit our perceptions, no betting and no entrance money, but the horses are well cared for, the facilities are superb, an international TV jockeys' event has already happened, a world-class race is being discussed and, best of all, it is in Dubai that some of the best thoroughbreds in the world are spending their winter training.

Last year Sheikh Mohammed upped the ante by creating the Dubai-based Godolphin stable from which he sent Balanchine over to become Europe's champion three-year-old with those Oaks and Irish Derby triumphs before succumbing to a life-threatening colic attack. Balanchine was out early on Thursday morning, much bigger and better looking than last year. She will be back for all the big prizes and she will not be alone.

Among the 30 horses out that morning there were Cezanne and Shepton Mallet from the older generation, 13 Classically engaged three-year-olds, and, for the first time, seven speed-bred two-year-olds who will return to Britain with a major sunshine advantage on their peers. It's very early days in the racing year, but listening to Sheikh Mohammed and his Godolphin manager Simon Crisford there was no mistaking ambition's beat. At this stage it's the filly Moonshell who seems to be making the greatest vibrations and she may even have an Epsom entry to at last win the Derby, the one great race to have escaped those colours in maroon and white.

But once more you can't put any limit to the story. The Godolphin aims are not only at European targets. Major forays to Hong Kong, Australia and Japan are being lined up in the next few months from this new heart of the game. Hope again is on the wing. The desert harvest will be coming in.

And what a harvest it proved to be. Impressive though it all was during that trip in January, even Sheikh Mohammed's wildest dreams (and that would be an interesting category to access!) could not reach what this Godolphin team would have accomplished by the end of September. Not just that string of classics and big races in Britain, but major events in Europe, Hong Kong, America and Japan. In every sense Godolphin has brought a new dimension.

Yes, things are a-changing but that is as much in revitalizing old places as setting up the new. Nothing epitomizes this better than what has happened to a valley, a village, a few hills and a lot of horses. On the British racing map, there came a whole new image to Lambourn.

Horse power

12 March 1995

You have to listen early for the village voice. Before the church clock struck seven on Monday, two horses stepped out into the lane. It was a clear and bell-like morning with birdsong at last proclaiming spring. But the sound you wanted was the firm and even note of thoroughbred on tarmac. That's the voice which counts at Lambourn.

From the outside it's easy to get over-lyrical. John Betjeman knew the church. 'The stained Carrara headstone,' goes his poem, 'where in nineteen twenty three, he who trained a hundred winners, paid the final entrance fee.' But you can bet the old boy was writing wistfully in the comfy afternoon. On Monday morning what you noted was the big swinging walk of the chestnut and the shorter, stumpy stride of the dark bay beside him. These were Master Oats and Alderbrook, favourite and second favourite for the Gold Cup and the Champion Hurdle. Many gravestones will come nearer if these two don't collect at Cheltenham.

Put not your trust in horses. The 11th commandment becomes the most sinned against as the sporting world closes on those three days in the Cotswolds when Prestbury Park becomes the centre of the firmament. Nowhere is the sin more frequently committed (along with a few of the others) than in the Berkshire valley of Lambourn and its surrounding villages, no more than 4,000 people, almost 1,500 horses, the most intense two to four-legged ratio in the country. There is a lot more than Master Oats and Alderbrook for the notebook.

Four hundred yards from their Old Manor stable in Upper Lambourn is the Oliver Sherwood yard which houses one of the Champion Hurdle favourites, Large Action. A quarter of a mile the other way is where Jenny Pitman trains Garrison Savannah, a Cheltenham runner again four years after he became the most recent of Lambourn's seven post-war Gold Cup successes. Over the other side of Mandown is the Seven Barrows stable of Nicky Henderson, whose 15 Cheltenham winners, including See You Then's Champion Hurdle hat-trick, heads the local list for the last decade.

In all there will be more than 50 runners sent out from these and surrounding stables next week to compete for the 20 races which constitute the climax of the jumping season. The Cheltenham Festival now holds a place unique in British sport. For while the National Hunt game operates for 12 months of the year, to win at the Festival remains the abiding ambition for everyone involved. It is the 'die happy' epitaph every competitor seeks. It is the explanatory label tagged to landmarks everywhere.

Master Oats and Alderbrook move off along a newly-railed streamside path called Fulke Walwyn Way in honour of the trainer whose Saxon House yard was a legend in his lifetime: two Champion Hurdles, four Gold Cups, horses like

Mandarin, Mill House and The Dikler and always a party in the Malt Shovel afterwards. The little pub is on the right as the horses push on towards their daily destination, Charlie Brooks's new sand-and-rubber Eurotrack gallop on the bank by his Uplands stable where the great Fred Winter trained Cheltenham

Lambourn . . . Old Downs with a new message

heroes like Bula, Lanzarote and Midnight Court.

But it is the future that counts and, despite the apparent timelessness of the country morning, there is a revolution abroad in attitude, in business application, even in the rhythm of the training routine. In Walwyn and Winter's day the workouts used the full sweep of the downland gallops on which Lambourn trainers have sent horses for a full century now. Today Brooks, Sherwood and in particular Master Oats and Alderbrook's handler Kim Bailey are now using versions of the short, sharp interval training system so sensationally pioneered by the once maligned Martin Pipe in Somerset.

It is an interesting turn of the worm. For come to Lambourn five years ago and much of the talk at the breakfast tables would have portrayed Pipe as some sort of blood-sucking vampire full of doping and dodgy deals. It was part ignorance, part fear, part blatant snobbery towards the little, limping book-maker's son from Nicholashayne, who projects a very different style to the Eton and Radley ethos of the Lambourn fellowship.

'Things have changed a lot,' said Bailey tall and cheerfully last week. 'Five years ago I would never have believed I'd be doing this. But the system seems to suit the horses beautifully. They know exactly where they're going and what they're doing which means they're more relaxed. And because they're having short, sharp repetitions, they're definitely fitter too.'

For his Cheltenham pair Bailey has adjusted his system even further. Having done their three spins up the bank in the morning Master Oats and Alderbrook forswear the rest afforded all other horses and repeat the exercise in the afternoon. 'You've got to treat individual needs,' says Bailey. 'Master Oats has to go out twice a day because we daren't go fast with him after he broke a blood vessel last year. Alderbrook doubles up because on Champion Hurdle day it will still be only eight weeks since he joined us from his winter holiday in Newmarket. The first time he went up the bank, he could hardly make it to the top.'

Bailey's energy and enthusiasm has paid off to the score of 47 winners, top of the Lambourn rankings this season. He has been ably assisted by stable jockey Norman Williamson, who with 86 winners already has only Maguire and Dunwoody ahead of him. What's even more important in these word-hanging pre-Cheltenham days, he has the sort of measured Irish tones that give you the serious impression that he knows what he is talking about.

Williamson is much taken with Master Oats's victories this term but admits that the big, ground-banging gelding will need the soft conditions that had seemed guaranteed until a strange object called the sun put in a belated appearance above us on Friday. About Alderbrook, top class on the Flat and striking winner of his first hurdle race in two years a fortnight ago, the cool-headed young pilot can't hide his enthusiasm.

'For a horse with so little experience, his jumping was exceptional,' said Williamson of the runner he nominates as the most talented he has ever ridden. 'He's a six-year-old colt and though he had schooled brilliantly [so brilliantly that some sharp eyes got themselves 50–1 about the Champion Hurdle] I thought he just might back off a bit in a race. But he was marvellous. He could be travelling very easily on Tuesday.'

Such conversations in the countdown to Cheltenham tend to create a fidget in your betting pocket. The trouble at Lambourn is that you are spoilt for choice. Within five minutes of seeing Alderbrook you are on the very skytop of the downs watching his rival, Large Action, cruising up another bank with the rest of the powerful Oliver Sherwood team. Third in the Champion Hurdle last year, beaten only once this season, Large Action glides impressively past us with the great iron-age panorama from Sincom Hill to Uffington Castle laid out behind him. Naturally, his stable say he is in 'terrific nick'.

So too the much-touted Sherwood novices, Berude Not To and Callisoe Bay. The more you listen about these and the other runners in your eyeline the more dangerous the conviction that Lambourn might give Cheltenham something like the eight-winner pasting achieved in 1992 (or even the record 11 winners logged in the Fred Winter heyday of the 1970s). They talk of Rouyan from Jenny Pitman's, give Nick Henderson's Travado another chance, the Charlie Brooks stable are sweet on Sound Reveille. The message is that Lambourn is the place to put your money. And on Monday there was more than betting to it.

For, as the Sherwood team cantered past two by two in the sunshine, they were watched by a small gaggle of spectators with that keen but slightly baffled look that betokens a new experience. They were part of the British Horseracing Board's drive to attract new owners. Of course, it remains to be seen just how many of Monday's visitors actually graduate from the heady delights of lark-serenaded morning sizzling manor house breakfast to the cooler business of producing the cheque book, but there's no doubt that at this stage Lambourn has attracted more horses and more investment than ever in its history.

We are in the throes of Cheltenham but look down into the hollow and see where Barry Hills is completing a brand new hi-tech Flat training yard at the foot of the Faringdon Road. Remember the four-legged traffic jam down in Upper Lambourn as you waited for a long string of two-year-olds to pass bearing the banner of 73-winners-last-season Mick Channon. Channon didn't go to Eton or to Radley but years on the great soccer pitches of Europe and plenty of postgraduate work in the university of life have equipped him as a major player in the valley scene.

This new investment is part due to the VAT concession two years ago which put racehorse ownership in Britain back on a level playing field with France and Ireland, and part something much more interesting, a form of collective spirit for which neither racehorse trainers (nor anybody else for that matter) are much noted for these days.

For all its odd mixture of the rah-rah and the rustic, Lambourn has a clear and proud identity. Its Open Day on 14 April will again draw thousands to the village and raise five-figure sums for charity and the local community. Its trainers have a well-organized 30-strong association under the inspirational leadership of Peter Walwyn, handler of Grundy, the area's first post-war Derby winner in 1975. They even now have a sponsor.

Among the little band watching Sherwood's team was a figure whose smart overcoat and black city shoes spoke of an appointment with the London train. Martin St Quinton was watching his Cheltenham runner Coulton come up at the head of the string but his overseeing eye also had a business look. For it is St Quinton's office equipment firm, Danka UK, which that day was to announce a three-year, quarter of a million pound deal to sponsor every runner from the Lambourn area.

'No one should think that just because I have a horse in training here this is some sort of sweetheart deal,' he says crisply. 'Now the rules have been changed to allow the logos on the front of the jockey's silks as on a soccer shirt, it means our company, which is the second biggest but still largely unknown office equipment outfit in the country, will get plenty of the public exposure it needs. Especially if we have winners at Cheltenham and the other big meetings. It's the first deal of its kind and I believe it could be such a success that when we come to renegotiate we may not be able to afford it.'

St Quinton has to rush to the station, we make slower progress back down the lanes to the village. Up until the last war these downs were sheep-graze all the way west to Avebury and beyond.

Beside us Eddie Fisher, 40 years a tireless tender of the Lambourn gallops, shakes his head at the wettest ground in memory. He remembers hardly 300 horses here in his early days. You wonder how such an old-fashioned scene should draw quite so much present-day cash.

The lane is temporarily blocked as a vast muck wagon manoeuvres in our path. Many of the mushrooms on the menu will have been grown thanks to the 400 tons of horse dung shipped out of Lambourn each week. Such manurey thoughts make you search for old heads to put the new boom into perspective.

Darkie Deacon should be into pipe and carpet slippers, not yet more soaking mornings and luggers on the rein. But Darkie has the most famous hands on the hill. In the glory years with Fulke Walwyn they were the hands that held The Dikler, just about the most renowned puller in history. Instead of pension time, Darkie has hitched himself to the new trainer Charlie Mann and in two years they have seen their horse strength grow from two to 20 times that number.

Darkie is impressed with the fresh investment – 'there seems plenty of money around' – but not so much with the new training methods – 'a monkey could do it, it's taking the art out of the job'. These reservations and a few more besides are shared by Brian Delaney, head lad to Charlie Brooks and to Fred Winter before that, and as such just about the most respected stable figure in the whole of the valley.

'We may be getting horses fitter,' says Delaney, 'but we're having to do things in more of a hurry with horses, and with workers also.' Delaney has seen them come and go. He even had the formative experience of trying to control John Francome as a stable lad. But his concern is for the staff of the future. 'Pay may be better,' he says (although £170 a week is not exactly Cedric Brown-type wages) 'but the demands are greater. At least three to four horses to look after and I can show you places twice that. And whilst there is now a sports ground and an indoor centre, we could do with a club like they have at Newmarket. Sponsorship must work at the bottom too.'

One more visit before the open road. Jack Dowdeswell first came to Lambourn in 1931 as a two-shilling-a-week apprentice. A long career in the saddle took in winners at Cheltenham, a jump jockeys' championship in 1947 and the sobering statistic of 13 consecutive concussions in the days when helmets were little slips of cork and proof of fitness was the ability to stand upright unsupported.

No fortunes have been made but Jack now sits in his house with his wife and his memories and a rare form of contentment. 'You know what I say?' he asks, looking around the room with its photos of family and of horses. 'I say that I have never had a bad day.'

Betty Dowdeswell is a great reader. One of her books is *Gulliver's Travels*. People remember Lilliput but they often forget the fourth part where Jonathan Swift introduces us to the Houyhnhnms, the land where horses rule. Two hundred and sixty-nine years since publication, it is at Lambourn where the tale is nearest true.

In the great annals of sponsorship deals Martin St Quinton's Danka number must be hard to match. Within a fortnight of his signing up, Alderbrook and Master Oats had won the Champion Hurdle and The Gold Cup, and Norman Williamson had been pictured in every paper with Danka emblazoned across his chest. And of course the joke now is that some at Lambourn will think that instead of a godsend they have sold their sponsorship cheap. Many beautiful qualities though these racing places have, absolute contentment is unlikely to be amongst their number.

For the laws of the game, the attrition rate amongst the equine athletes means that failure will always dog even the most successful stride. To that end the great trainers are often not easy men. They have to be driven by an endless quest to avoid the inevitable, to minimize risks and to maximize potential. André Fabre is famed for being one of the least easy of all.

But then as Europe's most successful trainer he has the most to show for it. Anyway, if we go closer we might understand.

Headmaster plots glittering career for his equine charges

4 June 1995

For ten minutes the sandy ring they call the Rond Trempolino had been filling up with thoroughbreds in the Chantilly Forest on Thursday morning. Finally, André Fabre rode in to survey this, the strongest team in the whole world of racing. It was 8.21am, exactly on time. But it was nothing to shout about.

Why should it be? The late Phil Bull may have dubbed racing an 'inexact science', but study Fabre's ever-burgeoning training career and you begin to wonder. At 48, the diplomat's son who forsook the law for the turf has now topped the French money list for the last eight years and in the same time has won with 22 of the 83 runners he has sent across the Channel – a 25 per cent strike rate, a £2.3 million prize money haul. When Fabre aims, the arrows usually hit. Pennekamp goes for the Epsom bullseye next Saturday and this afternoon at Chantilly his stable fields no fewer than four runners against Celtic Swing and company in the French Derby, the Prix du Jockey-Club.

Even in the great days of François Mathet and Etienne Pollet, France has never threatened a European dominance of this magnitude. Over 200 horses, well over 100 staff; the Fabre stable has become the largest and most select four-legged boarding school on offer. Pennekamp's owner, Sheikh Mohammed is but one of a company of big names who include Khalid Abdullah, the Saudi prince; Daniel Wildenstein, the art dealer; and Jean-Luc Largardère, the electronics tycoon newly entrusted with the leadership of French racing. The big names come because they think Fabre is the best. In Britain, the trainers championship is still wide open; pick Stoute or Gosden, Dunlop or Cecil and it still might be the wrong answer. In France there would be no betting. The Paris figures show André Fabre, 64 winners; next, Robert Collet with 28.

The statistics are clear and the reasons for them not unfathomable. Fabre is at the top because his assessments, his strategy and his organization are more instinctively accurate, more directly arrived at, and more meticulously effected than those of any of his rivals. But some central energy has to create and drive this. The mystery lies in the man.

He's with us now, a neat, still youthful, leather-chapped figure as easy in the saddle as you would expect from someone who took the French Grand National in his days as a jockey. He rides an Argentinian polo pony but this is no feckless, noisy gaucho. This is a headmaster in a quiet cocoon of his own concentration. Success has only been achieved by taking each move, each decision seriously. Rather too seriously for some.

For the little headmaster is a proud man. If he has taken the trouble to give an answer, he finds it hard to forgive sloppy or snide distortions in a report. When the Paris Turf printed an article insinuating that his early dominance of the jumping game (he trained four consecutive French National winners between 1980 and 1983) might have been by some sort of doping, he severed all relations with the paper. To this day the aftermath of a major Fabre victory in France produces the bizarre spectacle of the trainer haughtily boycotting local media attention. With us British hacks he is much more approachable, although some of his looks in those jostling unsaddling enclosure press conferences suggest he supports George Bernard Shaw's advice not to 'waste time on people who don't know what they think'.

Fabre's whole dynamism is about eliminating the unnecessary. There was a time when he was happy to submit to long profiles and to expound wide-ranging views on the weaknesses of French racing and much else besides. Nowadays, his success has to do the talking. Looking at the 90-odd horses gathered in that forest glade on Thursday was to know that much was likely to be said before close down in December.

But now Pennekamp must pose for his photograph. Other trainers often shout and semaphore. With Fabre the orders are almost reticently low key but the response is immediate, the control very apparent. Monsieur Fabre's class pay attention as if it were exam time tomorrow. Pennekamp and exercise rider Thierry Deschaud come over to the side of the clearing bidden by little more than the crook of a finger.

In his ordinary, un-preened working strip, medium-sized and almost moochingly relaxed, the Derby favourite hardly takes the eye more than any other horse. It was ironic to think of Peter Savill, back in London, screwing up his mind to decide that Celtic Swing should duck the rematch with Pennekamp at Epsom, while back here in Chantilly the French horse was not exactly strutting his stuff.

Those who have panicked about Celtic Swing's slightly crooked forelegs should think about the opposition. 'This horse is not perfect either,' says Fabre, pointing to how the bay colt turns his off-forefoot slightly out at the walk. 'And while all last year I was convinced he was a Derby horse,' adds the trainer, 'that stamina would be no question. Now he is showing so much speed that I am not so sure.'

Such candour might suggest that Savill has made the rick of a lifetime, but Pennekamp's supporters should still treasure the tributes of the man who trained the French colt's half-brother to become a winner over one and three quarter miles. 'He was always a lovely yearling,' says Fabre looking across at what is now already a fortune on the hoof but which Sheikh Mohammed's racing manager Anthony Stroud secured for a bargain $40,000 (£25,000) at Keeneland in September 1993. 'He could use himself, and by last June I was thinking that he could be the one.'

Those who carp at Fabre's slightly stiff formality – unlike most small men he does not bustle, but walks with the measured exactness with which he weighs his words – should remember the animation on his face during a television interview immediately after the Dewhurst Stakes last October. 'This is my first real Derby horse,' he said of Pennekamp, as we fought to keep cameras and microphones and foothold in the crush. 'All winter I can be thinking of that.'

Thinking, too, of the history stacked against him. It was 1976 when a French horse last won the Derby. That was the Maurice Zilber-handled Empery, but he was ridden by Lester Piggott. You have to go right back to Yves Saint-Martin's victory on the François Mathet-trained Relko in 1963 to find a French pilot who has mastered the unique horseshoe-shaped helter-skelter of the Epsom track.

The lack of success is not entirely coincidental and the reasons for it weigh against Pennekamp and Thierry Jarnet, just like all the others before. Firstly, the rhythm of the race demands an immediate and intensive effort to keep a good position in the first uphill half-mile. This is quite different to the much slower opening stages in France and will put an extra premium on Pennekamp's unproven stamina. Secondly, the inclines and cambers are a test French jockeys never face at home. Jarnet's memory is already scarred with two deeply unhappy rides in the Coronation Cup over the full Derby course and Pennekamp's late-finishing style will require the nerve of Lester Piggott on Sir Ivor.

But Jarnet is a winner too. He is already three-times French champion, looked positively Piggott-like winning last year's Coronation Cup on Apple Tree and adopts the same focused self-possession which has served his mentor so well. If France is to break the hoodoo against raiders, this is the team to do it, even if Jarnet is having his first Derby experience and Fabre's five runners to date have never done better than ninth. It is a stage perfectly set. 'André is just a bit of an actor,' said one not critical Chantilly admirer on Thursday, 'but this is a man of challenge. He wants to make his mark.'

With Pennekamp and with many others. The horses are filing out now, along with Fabre's wife, Elizabeth, a brilliant rider and very much a lynchpin of the operation. There are stars and potential stars in such abundance that the unbriefed observer is in danger of confusion. Carnegie, last year's Arc winner, Dernier Empereur, who took the Champion Stakes, Valley of Gold, winner of last month's Italian Oaks, Diamond Mix, the stable's first choice for today's French Derby and Bobinski the highly-rated favourite for today's Prix Jean Prat.

What is clear is that with Fabre, regardless of their owners, each one will get the attention it needs. 'I think,' he says carefully, 'that you should respect racehorses, not pet them.' Once again it is a slightly formal but very clear remark. The headmaster must have no favourites. That privilege is likely to be confined to the wise-looking, hog-maned chestnut beneath him who, in another life, would no doubt be playing 'high goal' at Deauville.

André Fabre puts a hand on his polo pony's well-groomed neck and gives a rare but revealing smile. 'You have no idea,' he says, 'what fun it is to ride one of these.' Time is getting on. He shakes the reins, leans forward and rockets out of the clearing to pursue his business. Much has been made of Fabre's stony-faced ambition. He deserves some sweetness in savouring it.

Fabre's sober assessment of Epsom's difficulties proved more accurate than the headlong national gamble which saw Pennekamp start favourite before cracking a bone on Tattenham Corner and trailing in an also ran.

Hopes rise, hopes are dashed. It will be ever thus. But there is one abiding, redeeming feature which all racing places tend to share. New every morning the hopes are there.

Personal

It's a good life even if often a silly one. If racing in Phil Bull's memorable phrase is the great triviality, those who earn their living merely by following it cannot have great claims to any very serious station in life. That said, we have our moments. We deal with people and animals locked into high endeavour. For them each day matters. For us that happens too. And if you are reporting, one day matters more than all the rest. Even if some say our life is a doddle now. Here's that big day, at Aintree.

Aintree deadlines

9 April 1992

Yes, it's going soft. It's no longer quite the dry mouth, wake-up-screaming ordeal when men were men, fences were fences and modern technology was a telephone with a dial-face. Not riding in the National, writing about it.

Ah, for those hairy days when Lord Oaksey was a lad. Or rather when he was ace amateur Mr John Lawrence, who would scuttle out from the weighing room to ad-lib the finest Grand National reports ever printed. To be a hack then was far from Wordsworth's 'very heaven', it was the absolute pits; the big story you didn't see, couldn't check and whose transmission hardly stretched to a flying pigeon.

But by god it was exciting. As, still panting, you got through to the Sunday paper and the tapes went up on your thousand-word journey, the mind had to be shuttered down just as tight as any jockey heading off to Becher's.

It would be 4 o'clock for the first edition. The race, which you had watched from the Press stand and had therefore only seen the start and finish of, would have ended but half an hour ago. In those intervening 30 minutes you would have to try and get some order from the notes of fallers, snatch a gasping 'quote' from winning connections and beaten favourites, and then get the hell out of the track.

This was the ultimate obstacle, the writers' version of Aintree's 494-yard run-in, except that you had to traverse it before filing the story. The Press facilities were so Crimean War – no room, no telephones, no result sheets – that your only chance was to leg it off the course to a 'safe house' in nearby Ormskirk Avenue where a nice lady called Denise would bring coffee and biscuits whilst you sat on her bed shouting the copy down the line to London.

It was a team game, dependent not just on Denise but on a fleet-footed, fact-hungry colleague who would come crashing up the stairs before the report took the field out on the second circuit. This was a crucial moment. Honeyed words to put the copytaker on 'hold' whilst your mate unloaded something much closer to what actually happened, what people had really said.

Now was the time to make a move, get the race into shape. Horses you had incorrectly eliminated had to be re-injected into the story, false leaders faded without trace. On and on went the paragraphs, faster and faster ran the fleeting minutes towards the deadline. You would think you had got there, ask 'how many words is it?' only to find we were still 150 short. Denise's whisky was always needed before nightfall.

There were some dreadful cock-ups. One year we got to Becher's second time round before the copytaker realized that Andy Pandy was a horse. Another, we had the poor old Duque de Alburquerque jokingly unscathed in the early part of the story but practically in the arms of the Grim Reaper when the late wire came through. There was the terror of invention.

But now there are no excuses. Sure, the National isn't off until 4 o'clock but to offset this and to drag racing towards the twentieth century, Aintree has installed Press facilities not that far short of the Open Golf or Wimbledon.

In an admittedly fairly cramped marquee at the back of the weighing room any conscious hack is bombarded with information from the incomparable BBC coverage, from the closed circuit TV interviews and from the ubiquitous Mark Popham, whose greenjacketed squad feed us endless streams of printed results, figures, quotes, in fact all you could need to write a Grand National report.

Well, nearly all. For these obvious improvements also risk a change of Grand National character every bit as real and not necessarily as welcome as the claim that, with easier fences and fewer fallers, it's 'just another long-distance chase'. Here is the means to homogenize the National story into one seamless 'received wisdom' report.

The beauty, the sometimes ugly compulsion of Aintree, is that there are at least 40 different stories. The BBC captures this unbelievably well. But just retelling its perspective is reheating last night's casserole. There is nothing to match what your own eyes tell you.

This thought stems from an image of Docklands Express afterwards. Nicole Rossa had him cropping grass in the ring out by the stables. Party Politics came past and you saw how small and exhausted the little horse looked.

There was an ugly gash inside his off-side stifle. 'It's nothing bad,' said

Nicole. 'And although he was very tired, he's come back safe. That's the great thing.'

The race hasn't gone that soft. Is it the reporting that's got too comfortable?

Comfort is something we nowadays take far too much for granted. Imagine the whingeing if we had to put up with half the hassle of our colleagues overseas. It can take a visitor's tale to put you into perspective. It's not quite so simple being a racing hack in Southern Africa.

Tipping in the township
16 July 1992

We have all had the odd problem with the family but James Maphery's is a bit different. His brother runs a trading stall in Soweto.

It sells everything from local goods, to post cards, to 'I love Soweto' key rings. John Oaksey bought one of those when James took him on a visit last year. But John wasn't there last month when the man pulled the gun out.

The man was one of three who had come strolling round from the Workers Hostel and after looking at James's brother's stall said with casual menace: 'We want some money or there will be trouble.'

The bullet missed James's brother's left ear by about three inches. The gun had looked too small, too toy-like to send such a deadly message. The crime and the hopelessness of any identification was too minor to even make a statistic in the Soweto tragedy. But James's brother had to move on.

This little cameo from a distant land may seem a bit remote to the 'great triviality' of our own four-legged game. But James Maphery was in England last week. He is a racing presenter on BOP TV in South Africa. He used to have tea at the Mandelas' house on his way back from school. He is one of the most recognized people in Soweto.

You don't get too many James Mapherys at the July Meeting but he was there for punting not political statements. Michael Roberts had to be sought out, and Bruce Raymond, and even Lester Piggott who was down in Durban last winter. James went a bit coy when asked how much he put on Mr Brooks.

There was something comforting in the familiarity of the gestures. The tall black visitor pouring earnestly over his racecard whilst the dapper little riders point out this horse and that. It is the same the world over. Even, for all its wider dramas, in South Africa.

Which is what John Oaksey discovered when James took him into a betting shop on the way to visiting the neat-as-a-pin Maphery household in Soweto last summer. There was just one punter in the shop. He had a rather ancient looking jacket and trousers and for some reason carried an even more ancient umbrella.

He was having trouble with picking the Tote Treble for that afternoon's card in Capetown.

Now as you know, the Noble Lord is nothing if not a trier and there now ensued a touching scene which flies on that betting shop wall will tell their kids about for generations.

'Well, of course I would love to help,' you can hear the noble tones ringing across the township, 'I usually like Felix Coetzee myself.'

Busking it is the same under any sun and Channel 4 admirers will be pleased to know that Oaksey achieved an admirable summing up of the offending race in the Cape, shook his new friend confidently by the hand and then stepped out to drive to the Maphery house along the way.

'John was wonderful,' said James as he told the story last week, 'he was really enjoying himself. Then, when we went round the corner, there was a dead man in the street.'

Quite recently but not very controversially dead. Someone was throwing a coat over his face. The police were taking names from a small group of unexcited onlookers. They have had and will have to see much worse than this.

It's when James Maphery relates incidents like this that you realize how spoilt we all are. Many years ago I reached the giddy heights of being a judge in the Miss Thames TV contest. The fellow panellists included the splendid Jean Marsh at the height of her *Upstairs Downstairs* stardom and the then mega famous Pete Murray.

As we went through to the cameras one of the doormen asked for a tip. I did the usual thing of 'the best tip is to keep the money in your pocket,' and Pete said a touch languidly 'oh, you poor thing, always the same line'. In terms of hardship it rather pales before James Maphery.

'Oh yes, everybody comes up for tips in Soweto,' he said whilst discussing the volatility of a political situation which he believes will get worse before it gets better and which can only be improved in the short term by the closure of hostels like the one which caused his brother grief.

'But the trouble is,' he added, 'that not everybody really understands racing and so I always say "no I cannot give you a tip because I want you to be my friend. If it loses you will not be my friend. So tips are only on TV. Then if it wins we all win."'

And if it loses? Well that's racing wherever you are.

I went back to Soweto in the spring of '95. It is still an extraordinary landscape: long rows of shabby shacks and drifting smoke; long rows of people waiting for minibuses into Johannesburg, that is when the 'minibus wars' allow the vehicles to run.

But considering everything, there was still an extraordinary feeling of hope. A year earlier the street we walked had dead bodies on it. A year earlier many people predicted the election would have a bloodbath sequel. But now life, and racing with it, has another chance. Anyone who hasn't read Nelson Mandela's Long Walk to Freedom *should give themselves a present. Much remains to be done, but there has been something close to a miracle at work.*

That's a word I used in a smaller, more personal context in October '92. It will probably be judged as saddle-bound hyperbole, but take a read of this and see if you can forgive me for it.

The fates were kind
1 October 1992

How do you repay a miracle? Yes miracle, no other word will do. Out of a grey, leaden sky at Ascot last Friday the fates plucked a scenario straight from my most cobwebbed dreams. Twenty-one years after the last one, 29 years from the first, they landed me on a winner. Miracle is an understatement.

You should have heard Michael Roberts on Friday morning. He is Kitaab's usual jockey. He was trying to be helpful. But after imparting the unwelcome news that the horse would dislike the going, the distance and any form of struggle, the best advice he could impart was 'watch him in the stalls, he panics a bit.' Just like his rider.

So another humiliation was coming up. Off through the deluge with sinking heart. The Shadwell Stud Private Sweepstakes (aka the Old Jocks and Tossers Race) is Sheikh Hamdan's incredibly generous way of pledging $10,000 to both the Injured Jockeys Fund and to Ascot's Charity Day provided six of us old has-beens don jockeys' kit once more. It shouldn't be depressing but on Friday it was dire.

It took half a sodden hour to walk the course. Half an hour to contemplate Roberts' words 'I am afraid he hates it now'; and the cautionary 'he might pull a little going to the start.' Mockers looked like supping full.

In truth the whole thing had plenty of the unreal, 'exhibition match' feel, a sense not impeded by Bill Smith's production of two large bottles of Krug as 'jumping powder'. But it was still a race. Still every chance of fouling up.

Yet the saddle is a sustaining place. You are not on your own. You are the top end of the centaur so it's time to get the best out of your other half. Even out of Kitaab.

Too late to rubbish him now. Belief is the only hope. His lads had backed him when he won first time at Brighton. So what if he had dogged it at Haydock and Epsom? He cantered down like a prince. You couldn't ask for more than that.

Once at the stalls his worries began. He behaved himself but his chest tightened up and the sweat poured off him. He's only three. He had only run five times. Suddenly you felt sorry for him and not yourself.

The race then unravelled like some ridiculous galloping game exactly weighted to spin out in our favour. Greville Starkey set the pace complete with hand signals. The only ambition was to keep near him to avoid being swamped by the others and Kitaab packing up completely.

The little chap had the sweetest stride but his heart wasn't in it. With a bit

Kitaab and the miracle at Ascot

of coaxing and clicking we got to the turn still second, and as Starkey sailed off up the hill towards the post you felt the rest could swallow us now and honour would still be satisfied.

But the rest didn't come. And suddenly Starkey was in choppy water. The whole thing was grinding down like some movie reel on the blink. Kitaab didn't want to go either. One tap down the shoulder brought obvious, ears-back signs of resentment. In desperation I began to cross the reins and shout at him. We seemed to be going up and down in the same place.

Seventeen seconds it took to get from the two furlong post to the one furlong pole. It seemed like an age and the number board and the winning line still looked miles away.

Now we were in front but there was no wind in our sails and precious little breath left in my body. It had become an agonizing waking dream. Unfit, undeserved and totally unexpected, we could actually get this. At long and unbelievable last the winning post swam by. It had happened.

By any normal standards it was an event of no importance. But we are all only sparrows on the face of the earth and for this little life those moments at Ascot swept in like some almost religious experience.

I had forgotten how much it mattered. Just how sweet any sort of winning could be. As they led us back I thought not just of Bunkering at Ludlow in March of '71 but of Arcticeelagh at Lingfield way back in '63. He had been the first. He had paid 40–1 on the Tote and my old dad had almost fallen off the stand for shouting. Yes it had mattered so.

Only memories now but one more added on Friday even if not every punter was affected by all this mystical guff. As Kitaab carried his puffing pilot across the line one *Racing Post* colleague groaned at the amazement of it all. 'Nonsense,' said a voice from across the betting shop floor. 'He's stitched you up. He was like that 30 years ago.'

What could they mean?

I saw Kitaab again that winter. He was racing in Dubai but was back into his loser's mode. Perhaps they should call me back. No, perhaps not.

A month after Ascot I was back in the usual TV role, but this time there wasn't much normal about the place. Or about what happened.

The end seemed nigh

5 November 1992

It was the situation we have long dreaded. Ever since Lester Piggott's 1990 comeback and his bare-faced robbery of time, there has always been the fear that the old gunslinger would get involved in just one shootout too many. It seemed to have happened in the Breeders' Cup on Saturday.

It's impossible to exaggerate the impact of those first gasping moments when Lester was fired into the dirt by the stricken Mr Brooks at Gulfstream Park. British viewers only saw the edited version. Out there the seconds and minutes had the desperation of actuality – no limiting of the replays, no cushioning of the pictures, no hurrying through of the recovery news.

As the Florida sun beat pitilessly down we had to live with the shot of Mr Brooks' foreleg snapped and swinging at full gallop. With the instant realization that Lester was in the most critical trouble. With the overwhelming horror of the fall. We thought he was a goner.

American TV networks make few concessions for the squeamish. Their crews are trained to get in and put the camera where the suffering is. They have brought us Vietnam. They weren't going to hold back when the world's greatest jockey lay pinned and bloodied beneath his dying horse.

The protocol is clear. As long as the doctors have room to work, the cameras show it as it is. So while 50,000 locals cheered a horse called Thirty

Slews back to the winner's circle after that Breeders' Cup Sprint, our little contingent huddled aghast over the TV monitors as the paramedics did their bit.

To be fair, they were mighty impressive. An oxygen mask over Lester's face, a neck brace fitted, leg splints supplied, a stretcher slid beneath the unconscious form and then the whole party lifted towards the ambulance with the 'move it' American cry we know all to well from the movies.

Of course we were panicking, but what would you do?

Lester is 57 today. For all his legendary toughness and iron fibre nerve, the ground grabs them all in the end. His daughter Tracy rushed past us, eyes narrowed in anguish. We thought the same.

But then another professional factor bit. If Lester's condition was half as bad as it looked our TV programme would have to be drastically reshaped. It was already fiendishly complicated. The production team in London would have to somehow edit seven world championship races down into a 50-minute show which would start before the final event had begun. We had already recorded an upbeat opening. Would it be tasteless to leave it in?

Satellite communications may be marvellous but they don't half make life tricky sometimes. For while aides were scurrying round to the ambulance room for the news of Lester's safety, we got involved in a three-way talk between London, ourselves at the winning line, and our Gulfstream production scanner behind the grandstand. At the height of the debate the phone rang beside us. It was ITN from London. Could they have the Piggott update?

The runners for the next race were filing on to the track. We were way behind on the links which needed recording.

McCririck was on to his second sweat-soaked, tent-sized tee-shirt. We needed some help from above. It came in the short, self-possessed Scottish shape of Jimmy Miller. Jimmy is one of the lynchpins of the Clive Brittain stable.

They were running Love Of Silver in the Breeders' Cup Juvenile. Miller's tale came from their jockey Michael Roberts. He had seen Lester. The old wonder was conscious and upright. A cut head, a broken collarbone, broken ribs perhaps. He was on his way to hospital. But he would be all right.

In human terms it was the most massive relief. But in a technical and a racing sense it was only the beginning. Over the next three hours, six races came and went, each time another European dream broken. Marling, Arazi, Selkirk, Dr Devious – finally there was only Rodrigo de Triano left.

He came out to parade, his coat matted with dried sweat. He ran worst of all. The rout – too hot, too hard, too fast – was complete. The gloom was gathering as fast as the Miami night. There was nothing else to say but goodbye and start the long trek back to the British winter.

We had barely been home a day before the hate mail began. More frequent and more venomous than for any show I remember. All sorts of insults including one card from an Arazi supporter with the bluntly imprinted and maybe accurate assertion: 'Every one thinks you're an arsehole.'

Ah well, it had been a night of unremittingly bad news. If you take money as the messenger you are likely to get the bullet. At least Lester didn't.

Needless to say, the least-moved person in all that drama was L. Piggott himself. 'I had a fall,' he muttered. 'What's all the fuss about?' In September '95 he announced he was quitting the saddle altogether, but what these last few years have shown us is something that was often forgotten in his pomp. That he is one of the few sportsmen who truly deserves the phrase, both physically and mentally, 'as hard as nails'.

But we softer creatures can get involved with horses without riding them. Indeed, you can get preposterously parental even if you own only a leg of a horse. My son and I own whatever passes for a 170th – a fetlock joint, perhaps. Whatever it is, it was giving us a lot of pleasure leading up to Cheltenham in '93.

Fraction of a favourite equals fun

14 March 1993

She's the apple of our eye. She's our four-legged Mona Lisa. She's the cream in our coffee. And she's ours, all 170 of us, and she's the favourite for the big race on Thursday: Beauchamp Grace for the Triumph Hurdle.

Sorry, we'll pass the sick bag. Another person's glee is always revolting. But then, racing is so full of also-rans that when you come up with a winning system there's a terrible compulsion to shout it from the rooftops. Beauchamp Grace has won four out of four. The luck will never hold, but please let it last through Thursday.

The syndicate is the key. All the excitement, the absurd first-person possessiveness of ownership, at only a fraction of the price. My part of Beauchamp Grace cost just £1,000 last November but, and here you will need the sick bag again, she's not our only one. We also have another hurdler called Thinking Twice who runs at Lingfield on Friday (the trainer's very keen) and no fewer than five two-year-olds. There is going to be a parade of them at Newmarket in a fortnight, accompanied by much slurping of wine and ridiculous noises of optimism.

The two-year-olds are called names like Mint a Million and Million at Dawn, because the original game plan, three years ago, was to buy cheapish yearlings to pitch at the massively valuable Goffs Million that October, hence the syndicate name of Million in Mind. This scheme, whereby that £1,000 represents your total costs for the whole year, is the brainchild of David Minton, the Newmarket bloodstock agent, who believes that there is little point in being alive unless you are going to have some fun.

Those who are attracted to, but baffled by, the racing game, are well-advised to try this or the many other racing clubs and syndicates that offer direct involvement on a shared basis. You may not have your name in the paper, but you get newsletters, stable visits and wonderful phone calls full of first-name tributes: 'Richard is very sweet on the filly. He says she is absolutely winging.'

Richard, of course, is Richard Dunwoody, at present 20 winners clear of Peter Scudamore in his relentless quest for his first jockeys' title. He will be board Beauchamp Grace when she tries to break the jinx on fillies in the Triumph Hurdle on Thursday. He was down at David Nicholson's new Cotswold kingdom on Monday morning, but he had other of the trainer's horses to ride. Our star was in the hands of Jill Wormall, the 19-year-old stable girl to whose care she was entrusted when she arrived in October. Jill thinks 'she has been never better'.

There we go again, shared intimacies already. The hanging on every word, ready to embellish it ever more exaggeratedly in repetition. Jill understands horses: she was a champion in the show ring. She knows the risks: she has already needed hospital treatment for a perennially dislocating shoulder. She is in the big time: on Thursday, she will also lead up Another Coral in the Gold Cup and Viking Flagship in the Grand Annual. But she is really ours.

She says we shouldn't worry about the continuing dry spell which has given us just a quarter of an inch of rain since January, and last week forced Cheltenham to take the unprecedented step of watering.

And she won't be fazed by the stable's other Triumph runners, Clurican and Kadi. She won't even be worried by that whopping great lump on Beauchamp Grace's knee. It's as big as a pomegranate, and you don't see many of them at Cheltenham. She did it hitting the final flight of hurdles on her last run at Newbury. 'Richard says she was put off by the photographers,' Jill said. 'It's not very nice, but it isn't sore and it doesn't affect her action at all.'

In truth, the lady is not a fantastic looker. She never was, but then that's not what she is there for. Bred at Eric Penser's stud at Compton Beauchamp, near Swindon, she was too backward to run for John Dunlop, the trainer, as a two-year-old and, even when she did get going last spring, it was clear that she would need a long trip to overtake the others.

'But let's not run her down,' Dunlop said on Friday. 'She ran well enough at Sandown to make us plan for Royal Ascot and the Queen's Vase. But she had some niggling problems and, after she won her maiden at Carlisle, she had only one more race. She wasn't very quick, but being by Ardross she was likely to improve with age, and always had a great attitude to the job.'

That was clear last Monday. She may have weighed 480kg when she won first time at Cheltenham at 12–1, but she now strips lean and hard at 460kg (Waterloo Boy, Nicholson's star chaser, weighs 510kg, and last year's fallen hero, Carvill's Hill, pulled a good 40 kilos beyond that).

The training centre that Nicholson has developed with Colin Smith, his landlord and business manager, is all along the wide Cotswold bank that runs up the hill from the village of Ford, only 10 miles from the wondrous natural amphitheatre of Cheltenham itself. Even at the easiest of paces, no horse gets to the top of the gallop without knowing it. The tougher it is on Thursday, the better our filly will like it.

Looking around the other Nicholson horses on Monday was to revel in the company we keep. They have 20 runners at Cheltenham, a squad second in numbers only to the mighty Martin Pipe battalion, and bowing the knee to nobody for quality. The likes of Wonder Man, Hebridean, Barton Bank and Baydon Star will all have millions of pounds of punters' money with them this week. So will Beauchamp Grace: we are talking big business now.

But it is still a game. The Cheltenham Festival now represents three of the most popular and most successful days of the whole sporting calendar. Cheltenham is an enormous operation on the ground and across the nation via television, newspapers and betting shops. But at heart it comes back to the horses, and one of them is going for us. What on earth are we going to do afterwards?

It's no small question. We are a pretty disparate lot. We include barmen, peers of the realm, assorted Minton friends and relatives, Graham Goode, the television commentator, and even a touch of the Jockey Club to add respectability. We are having our own marquee. If she wins, we will be utterly insufferable.

But, win or lose, the genial Minton is going to face a diplomatic impasse. Under the terms of the syndicate. Beauchamp Grace is due to go to the Doncaster sales in May. She could fetch up to £100,000 as a 1994 Champion Hurdle prospect. The prudent thing is to take the cash for future fun. The passionate way is to try to buy her back – from ourselves. John Major may not have granted a referendum. Minton may need to. Meanwhile, we remember the sun easing the early shiver last Monday morning. Jill was taking our apple back to the orchard. On Thursday you can all have a bite.

It was all too good to last. The ground came up firm at Cheltenham. Beauchamp Grace made a mistake at the first hurdle and it was always a struggle thereafter. All the more incredible that next March the Million in Mind syndicate were to have a filly which went all the way: the spring-heeled little Mysilv who went unbeaten right through to Cheltenham and then ran the whole field ragged in the Triumph Hurdle. There wasn't much room, or much quiet, in the unsaddling enclosure.

Happy days, but if you deal with animals the sad ones will come soon enough. In June that year our family had to face what, with animals, will always be.

Alas, poor Buzzy

10 June 1993

The real sadness didn't come until Monday. It made those anguished headlines about Tenby's Derby flop seem like the moans of greedy whingers. For on Monday the old dog had to die.

It was a beautiful morning, the sun high, June in fullest bloom. Fourteen summers he had seen. He had been a little, bumbling, golden puppy when Troy won Willie Carson's first Derby in '79. He had become a big run-all-day Labrador by the time Tenby's sire Caerleon won the French Derby in '83. But now the fire was all but out. A stroke had reduced him to a stumbling, fuzzy wreck. It was time to do the kindest thing.

Sentimentality can be the curse of the English but sentiment has its place. At least we try to connect, even if when it comes to Derby talk there is something hilarious about the sheer promiscuity of our affections. 'Tenby!' the Racing Post front page had vowed on Wednesday morning. But 24 hours is a lifetime. 'Hail The Chief!' swore Thursday's headline. Two different colts, less than a dozen races between them, and our only link an image on the screen and a bulge or lack of it in the wallet. A dog is rather different. This one was for always.

Down the years he became a fixture, a certainty in an uncertain world, the one member of the family who never sulked or wrangled or answered back. He did fight a bit though. But that was Hector's fault.

Hector was an enormous reincarnation of the Hound of the Baskervilles who lived in the big house up the hill and for a few dreadful months terrorized everything short of full-grown cattle. One day he set on poor little Buzz (our dog) whilst we were walking with what were then two very small children in the woods. It was a horrible scene, the young labrador pinned by the throat. The kids recoiling in horror. Me desperately belabouring the attacker with a stick.

After that Buzz took to the understandable, but socially unacceptable, practice of getting his retaliation in first. Castration was the only cure. We could try it on the All Blacks but the Kiwis would be bound to squeak. We certainly should have done it to Hector, but he eventually disappeared. That last event probably not unconnected with a conversation I had in the pub with a dodgy but uncompromising detective, who got the picture, nodded darkly and muttered something about 'a car accident'.

Buzz used to come out with the horses. He would listen attentively whilst I recited mind-numbing TV links. The runaway brilliance of Shergar, the sensational defeat of Dancing Brave, the impossible victory of Secreto, the majesty of Nashwan; old Buzz had heard the clichés about the four of them and more. But by this year he was far too deaf to log rehearsals. And on the day after Commander In Chief atoned for his sire Dancing Brave at Epsom, a stroke brought death to the very next room.

The vet came with stimulants and tablets, but over the weekend there was no sign of improvement. He could just about totter to his feet, but if he got out into the garden he hardly knew where he was, let alone how to get back again. I flew to the French Derby with a heavy heart.

Chantilly and its chateau and those ridiculous chateau-style follies called Les Grandes Ecuries (The Big Stables) were more ravishing than ever. The temperatures were in the 80s. The Asmussen-Boutin hot streak continued in the Classics, but you couldn't expect the French to understand. Hell, they are so much more avarice than animal-orientated that Le Figaro had seven-eighths of a page on an 18-runner handicap because it was designated for their 1–2–3 Tierce bet, at the expense of just 500 words on the Derby contenders.

That sort of thinking would never understand someone getting soppy about a dog.

Back in Britain it had been a scorcher too. There had been no escape from the heat, now there was no hiding the truth. He had drunk some water and eaten a little chicken, but the old boy wasn't going anywhere. We had brought him in to this world. It was time to help him out.

Next morning dawned quite glorious once again. Our little girl walked across the field to see if the neighbour's cow had had its calf. As she came back the old dog pottered out from the kitchen on swaying legs. We clapped him and he looked rather proud of himself. But I was still going to call the vet once Tessa set off for school. Hugging him, you would have thought there would have been a Judas sense of betrayal. Oddly, it was quite different. He had had such a good innings. It was no fun any more. Now we could bring him peace.

Think of all those times when he had been the willing accomplice to any outdoor game. Think of that lean summer when we were training for the Guildford marathon and Buzz, surely at that stage the fittest dog in the south of England, guided a shattered Tim Richards and John Oaksey home after they got lost in the fog one morning.

There was one last fog to come. The vet's car had arrived. His strong leather shoes crunched on the gravel and soon he was kneeling beside Buzzy and me. There was a simple form to sign, and then a part of the front leg to press whilst the vet slid the injection into the vein. There wasn't even the semblance of a wince. The old head just hung drowsy for a second or two and then dipped deeper, deeper on to my arm. Another instant and it was over.

Derby defeats come and go. They didn't matter like Monday.

Sobering thoughts for a not always totally sober lifestyle. If you have ever travelled on a race train you will know that it's long odds against all its occupants passing a breath test. Sometimes this can lead to illuminating offers of help. One day coming back from Newbury I bought a drink for a 'face' from the

betting ring who in gratitude volunteered his services if anyone gave me any 'aggro'. He waved his glass airily and looked out over what seemed very law-abiding Berkshire. 'We could,' said the 'face', 'make it quite confidential.'
     One day it looked as if I was going to need his help.

Strangers on a train

25 November 1993

There were just four of them but they had trouble written from top to toe. Yes, as the Aintree platform filled up on Saturday evening for the train back to Liverpool, they looked like trouble with a capital T.

You heard them first. Unmistakable snatches of unmusical chant challenging the world to notice. It had been a long day at the races and not all of it on orange juice. You shuffle along the platform and hope the drink will soon die out of them. Goodness, it's cold enough, freezing fog is closing in and we stamp our feet and hunch our shoulders against the darkening night. That cosy armchair and Match of the Day seem a distant and unobtainable dream. Back here nightmare threatens.

Somehow you just know the trouble won't go away. We all try and be terribly British and middle class, ignoring the noise from further down the platform. What we need is allies. Here's a steady looking couple in their 50s, Mr and Mrs Nice Racegoer to the life. Both have good sensible overcoats, he still has his binoculars round his neck and is even reading the *Racing Post*. It's getting crowded but we could be a team.

As the train finally draws in, there is a surge forward and as always, the door just passes by and you have to scrabble back to the next coach. Miraculously there are three seats up to the right. We plump down with a sigh of satisfaction. But the sigh is a short one. There is a scuffle on the platform, our door reopens and 'The Lads' get in. A closer look is not a better one.

They are in their late teens, early-20s, and do not at first sight appear to be entries for this month's competition to find Mr Squeaky Clean of Birkdale. Clearly there has been a bit of bother during the course of the afternoon.

Lad No. 1's right eye is nearly closed. It is possible that this dated back to something nasty earlier in the week, but Lad No. 4's mouth was definitely today. It was still bleeding freely and the palms of his hand looked like Macbeth in the murder scene. Encourage the younger racegoer by all means, but what we really want now is to encourage these to get off.

You are recognizing the inherent hypocrisy of the TV performer. Someone like me is very happy to smirk at the lens and say 'Hello everybody'. Why should he start getting all snooty if one or two 'everybodys' want to say 'hello' back? Yes, of course you are right, but rattling through Walton and Orrell, we do rather hope they will leave us alone. Besides, there is a more pressing problem.

Deadlines wait for no man. Particularly not for Sunday hacks who are hurrying off to catch the last train from Lime Street. The *Sunday Times* must have a check call. Public place or not, there is no alternative but to get the portable out of the bag and furtively dial the number like a spy in a B movie. No, we were never going to get away with it.

The first attempt at sub-editors' desk discussion of such grammatical niceties as to whether there is an apostrophe in a horse called Ushers Island, is cut short by the train going through a tunnel. We have just been reconnected when Lad No. 1 suddenly lurches across and towers above me. He prods me the way people do when they discover TV figures in real life. 'Just look who we have got here,' he says triumphantly.

Many years ago at the height of his fame I asked Eric Morecambe (if you are going to drop names, drop them big) how he handled the sea of fans that looked like overwhelming him at some charity function. 'Just keep moving,' he said, lifting his spectacles up and down his nose, and smiling and signing as we pressed through the housewife throng. But this was no throng. This was Lad No. 1. 'Keeping moving' wasn't an option. And, thanks for not mentioning it, I am no Eric Morecambe.

So for a few seconds we had this ludicrous three-way conversation with me trying to sign off from the Sunday Times whilst also mouthing 'blokeish' pleasantries at Lad No. 1. Of course there was a degree of cowering fear of retribution for duff tips down the years. What actually happened was for a moment or two almost more frightening. It was friendliness.

Strong, loud, arm-shoving Scouser friendliness. Lad No. 1 peers again at this rabbit-like figure crouched over its laptop computer with the mobile to its ear. He calls the other Lads over and in one great crashing chorus we are suddenly the best of mates. They don't keep it secret either. All four of them start chanting my name to the old rabble-rousing beat of 'Here we go. Here we go. Here we go.' Macbeth's blood-soaked palms smack up the accompaniment. The other passengers gave me some funny looks but this wasn't trouble. This was living proof that at Liverpool as in other places, you shouldn't judge a book by its cover.

The Lads got out at Kirkdale. We're going to have a drink next time I'm up.

With all friends you miss them most when they are gone. And once you pass the fifty watershed you begin to find yourself attending more funerals than christenings. This is a fact of life, but it's easy to get mournful about it. If only we could take strength, not sadness, from the partings.

In an odd, totally unpremeditated way, that's exactly what happened on what was otherwise a very grey day in London town.

Two different lives – one sense of loss
24 February 1994

Always answer the letter. Cliff Temple did and so too John Hislop. Cliff died last month, John Hislop went on Tuesday. In athletics and in racing, the world is a lesser place.

Their passing was very different. Cliff's was an appalling and very public tragedy, found dead on his local railway line at just 47, a sweet, sensitive, ultratalented journalist and coach but a man unable to stand the personal and professional pressures which beset him, the alleged role of athletics's 'Mr Fixit' Andy Norman in the latter now a *cause célèbre*. John Hislop died of a heart attack at 82 – there is great sadness at his death but he had lived a full span as an outstanding rider, writer and as breeder of the peerless Brigadier Gerard.

What linked them was a passion for their own sport and a commitment to encourage others towards the fulfilment which only participation could give. At Cliff's memorial service on Monday, the address centred not on his award-winning writing in 24 years as *Sunday Times* athletics correspondent, nor even of the coaching triumph of Mike Gratton's victory in the 1983 London Marathon.

Much could have been told of all that; instead David Smyth chose to take us back to the grassroots, of Cliff at the smallest of athletics meets, of timing his runners between the lamp posts on Folkestone's promenade. David hit a perfect chord. That's what so many of us packed into the choir-filled sanctuary of St Brides, Fleet Street, last week remembered Cliff best for. As a helper.

It's a gift and it emanated from Cliff even at the worst of times. In December I had an article to write about Sally Gunnell. A starting point for all athletics stories was a call to Cliff. No matter his own troubles, he was as insightful and funny as ever. He knew every telephone number, updated you with all statistics, even signed off with a great story of Sally dragging drunken hacks on to the rostrum at the Athletics Writers Dinner to have a go at her latest video exerciser. A fortnight after he was at our Christmas party, smiling behind those shaded glasses. We thought the black clouds were lifting. We were wrong.

The tears as we sang 'Abide With Me' on Monday were for a life cut short, for the family (four children, the youngest but five years old), and for all the good Cliff could have done in the future. It was a marvellous service, the Rector held it together with great skill and humanity, the music of Bach and Mozart lifted you up towards the stained glass of the tallest windows. But it was all desperately hard to take. Here was a helper. And he was gone.

John Hislop has gone too and here the helpline goes back a long, long way. In any sport, indeed in any branch of the journo's craft, the aspiring writer takes as his intended saviour the man who makes the pictures sing. A letter is despatched high on self importance and wishful thinking. Many don't even bother to reply. John did. It changed my life.

He made no promises, bore no gifts, did not bother with flattery. But he encouraged. No typed missive with a 'p.p.' signature, but two pages in his own elegant hand. He was operating in the limited and often scornful confines of the racing parish. But he was a man of style. Excellence illuminates wherever it may be.

His own career had been exemplary. Thirteen times amateur champion on the Flat, probably the best gentleman jock on the level that ever was; and after writing for years about the theory of breeding, he put words into deeds, he bred the super-champion Brigadier Gerard, in a world of hype one of the few animals who would deserve discussion as 'Horse of the Century'.

But it was not those achievements that lit this scribbler's imagination. It was the way he described things in his articles and especially in his compellingly evocative volumes of autobiography. He was somebody who might help. Who bothered to write back with detailed suggestions ranging from the unprompted even to the unwelcome.

I still remember smarting with injured pride on receiving a Hislop letter two days after (by some amazing fluke) I rode a big-race photo-finish double at Newbury. John didn't waste time on back-patting praise, he pointed out (complete with diagrams) that if I was ever to improve as a jockey, the body position would have to get a lot lower in the finish.

He was right of course. Probably less so when he put my name forward to the *Observer* more than 25 years ago and an awed youth slipped into the Punch Tavern off Fleet Street to meet the legendary sports editor Clifford Makins.

I was back in the Punch on Monday thinking of another Clifford. After the first glass of wine somebody came up and offered me a place in the London Marathon. Maybe it's madness but we'll do it in Cliff's memory. We'll raise money for his cause. It's an answer that is deserved.

The Marathon was exactly seven weeks away that Sunday. The man in the pub took me on as a challenge and kept sending high-powered schedules of the mileage I should be doing on a daily basis. The plan was to beat four hours, which at least proves you ran all the way. The time-span made the preparation very dodgy. Try too hard in training and you would break down. Do too little and the London streets would find you out.

It was a rather fascinating challenge, particularly as Ladbrokes laid me 2–1 against breaking four hours, and I had £500 on my own bobbing, sweaty nose. The Sunday Times *were very supportive and readers clubbed round and raised some £30,000 for Cliff's family. It was a bit difficult fitting in the training and I remember one uncomfortable effort around Cheltenham racecourse during Festival week and one extremely hot plod across the desert in Dubai.*

But the project was so worthwhile that the motivation was easy. It was always going to be tight and coming round the final bend in the Mall I thought the finish was going away from me. But we did it. Did it with just 82 seconds to spare.

Afterwards I remember at first feeling triumphant and then suddenly very weary, and more than a little sad. Thinking both of Cliff, for whom I had done this, and secondly of all those whose health would never allow them to do it at all.

Good fortune can do this to you. It's only right that it should. That is why I would like to close with these thoughts from one of the luckiest breaks that we have had.

Grateful for the chance to face this challenge
24 November 1994

In the afternoon we were to have our first Channel 4 trials at the racetrack. In the morning I jogged out to my parents' grave to give thanks for it. Yes, doing Cheltenham really is as strong as that.

Through some amazing out-of-season deal, the Channel 4 team had been put up at the Lygon Arms in Broadway the night before. It is all oak beams and open fireplaces and likes to refer to itself as an Inn. Actually the Lygon, at this 'Gateway to the Cotswolds', is second only to Gleneagles on the rich Americans' British schedule. It has come a long way since we kids cleared the dance floor by scrunching open a stink bomb sachet at the Christmas holiday highlight they called 'The 8 to 80'.

Forty odd years have come and gone since those happy, silly days, but in the early morning you don't notice much that's different. With Broadway that is. It's prettified of course but then it always was. The Swan looks a bit smarter and the place opposite is now a restaurant called Sheikhs. Is there no limit to the Maktoums' munificence?

Going out of the village on the Snowshill road almost nothing seemed to have changed. This was as you remembered it when television was a snowy box in the corner of the room and Cheltenham races were the biggest event on the whole horizon. What a privilege it is to be broadcasting them next year. How golden, overlucky a childhood it must have been.

The doctor's house, with its great cedar trees standing sentry, still looks out across the cow meadow to Broadway Coppice on the hill. This was hunting country and in those pre anti-bloodsport times ours was a well-insured pursuit. The doctor was usually out in his top hat and scarlet. And if you were beyond his help, the old galloping rector could always help you out. The rector was quite a card. One day he sat down for tea and suddenly realized he had left his wife in Cheltenham.

When he finally passed over, his successor was such an oddball that the parish was ruined, the congregation was reduced to single figures, and so poor old Mum and Dad's last resting place was out here against the ivy clad graveyard wall of the ancient church of St Eadburga's. I hadn't been for a couple of years. There was a pang of guilt to see the leaves all unswept. A start of surprise to see a smart new sandy headstone set in right close beside them. Read close and bow in acknowledgement. It was the doctor's wife.

Even sadness can soon have a comic side. Scrabbling around clearing the leaves revealed a little vase begging some flowers as a filial tribute. A peep over the wall showed no blooms for the nicking but the memory jogged of fine floral arrangements in the Lygon bedrooms. Within minutes I was back beside the headstone with a bunch of carnations and tiger lilies good enough to impress the florist royal. How Ma and Pa would have smiled when told where the bouquet came from.

They were owed smiles enough. Because soon it was the drive to Cheltenham. This was a journey we had taken together so often. Straight across that flat Vale to Winchcombe with the Cotswolds, a curtain to the left of us. The heady excitements of the March Festival would only come after school days.

First came awestruck trips to the New Year's meeting and then the physical intoxication of getting hooked on the actual riding. That was on this road too. Up over Cleeve Hill and down the other side to where Frenchie Nicholson trained right beside the course at Prestbury. His son David was a heron-thin, super-fit, yet asthma-plagued jockey then. Bulkier but a top trainer now, he was to have another big winner in the afternoon.

Yes Cheltenham in the afternoon. It is no cliché, no exaggeration to say that this is a racing man's dream. Drive in to the car park and there suddenly you have it. The very temple of the steeplechasing game laid out in a giant horseshoe in front of you with Cleeve Hill as its skyline. In all racing, in all sport, there is no natural arena to match it.

Yesterday was quite modest and sober stuff compared to the demented Anglo-Irish howls of that special week in March. But it still had its moments. Drama when that second-last fence kept reaching up and toppling over the luckless David Bridgwater. Glory when tired horses tug aching limbs up to that most coveted winning post in the game.

We at Channel 4 were only fiddling about testing sound and camera angles. Some of John Francome's material was definitely not fit for public broadcast. But even he, who has touched Cheltenham's very heights as a jockey, was quickening at the challenge of bringing this place to our TV audience.

He's lucky that both his wonderful parents are still with us. For me yesterday was yet another reminder of how lucky I was to have had mine at all.